THE KINDRED CHRONICLES
Book I: Origins Unknown

To Lyssie

Love from

uncle James

First Published in Great Britain 2018 by Mirador Publishing

Copyright © 2018 by James Foard

First edition: 2018

Any reference to real names and places are purely fictional and are constructs of the author. Any offence the references produce is unintentional and in no way reflects the reality of any locations or people involved.

A copy of this work is available through the British Library.

ISBN: 978-1-912601-19-6

Mirador Publishing
10 Greenbrook Terrace
Taunton
Somerset
TA1 1UT
UK

THE KINDRED CHRONICLES
Book I: Origins Unknown

By

James Foard

For Gill, Tom and Max.

Thank you for your understanding, patience and belief during my total absorption in this novel.

It means more to me than I could ever convey verbally or in the written word. I couldn't have achieved this without your endless support.
I love you all very much.
Bring on book two!

Thank you to everyone else who has assisted me in any way. No matter how big or small, you have all helped in bringing this novel to fruition. There will be no claim on any royalties though ☺

Thank you to Mirador for taking a chance on my novel and on me as a debut author.
You have helped make this dream come true.

1. The Outcast

2. Connection

3. Any Tree in a Storm

4. A Brief History

5. Inhuman Travel

6. A Room without a View

7. Many Happy Returns

8. Derma-Morphs

9. Time for Change

10. Dogged Determination

11. Morphing and Entering

12. Watch where we're going

13. A Feeling in the Water

14. Tracking and Trepidation

15. The Borders of Malustera

16. A Vulgar Display of Power

17. Let Battle Commence

18. Three Heads are better than one

19. More Time than you thought

20. Indistinct Revelations

21. From the Freezer to the Fire

22. A Scintillating Idea

23. Incarceration or Liberation

24. Ignis Vallis

25. Enemy Territory

26. Into the Interria

27. The Aftermath

1.

The Outcast

Throughout his whole life, Alex had never felt like he belonged. He could never explain his overwhelming desire to avoid social situations or why he felt so much more comfortable in the company of animals, particularly his only real friend, Axis, his loyal pet dog. Axis had been with him for as long as he could remember. He felt that his dog understood him far more than anyone else ever had. His parents treated him quite well in so much as they fed him, clothed him and put a roof over his head, but there was never any real affection shown towards him. They never spent any time with him, engaged him in conversation, or challenged him in any way. In Alex's mind, they preferred it when he was out of their way, which he often was.

He spent countless hours roaming the nearby woodland with Axis. This was a place that he could escape to and not have to deal with another soul. On their walks, they always ended up stopping by the same huge tree that was located in the densest part of the forest. Alex always felt completely at ease there, so he would sit on the ground, lean against the monstrous trunk and daydream. Other than school, when he was by this tree was the only time Axis would leave his side. Alex always assumed that he was off chasing rabbits, as he was never gone for too long.

Axis was a huge, muscular dog of indeterminate breed, with a shaggy black coat. He was fiercely loyal to Alex and also seemed abnormally intelligent. When they were walking or running in the woods, he would keep in step, almost as if he were guarding him. When people saw them together they often had to double-take because at first glance it appeared that Alex was being flanked by a shaggy haired bear, such was Axis' size.

Alex would often confide in him, he felt quite silly sharing his innermost feelings with a dog, though he was convinced that he could see understanding in Axis' eyes. He found great comfort in this.

At five foot ten inches, Alex was tall for his twelve years. Despite his height, he wasn't gangly; he had a strong, athletic build that belied his young years. This had no doubt been honed during his daily ritual of walking and running for countless hours in the woods.

He was cripplingly shy which may have been one of the reasons that he wore his hair so long – a subconscious way of shielding himself from people. If you could see behind the mass of shoulder length black hair, you could see that there was a huge amount going on behind his dark blue eyes.

He had moved home many times in his short life. This probably contributed to his sense of detachment. If he had ever wanted to make friends, it would have proven difficult as he was never in one place long enough to get to know people or integrate properly. Initially, he would ask his mum why they had to move. She would brush over it and say that it was to do with his dad's job. Alex never really believed this and as time moved on he stopped asking about the impending move, as it had now gotten to the stage that another home and another school were inevitable, so why bother putting up a fight?

School never really had any major appeal to Alex, he wasn't a disruptive influence but he just found the whole process uninteresting. Despite this, he did still manage to achieve at an above average level without ever really exerting himself. This was enough to keep his teachers satisfied. He was neither a slacker nor an academic, so they never really felt the need to either discipline or encourage him. This suited Alex just fine. The only teacher that did show any kind of encouragement towards him was Mr. Beauchamp, his P.E. teacher. Alex was a natural athlete and excelled at most sports. He loved to run, and run he could. No other student at the school stood a chance in a race that he was involved in, they weren't even in his league. Mr. Beauchamp tried to push him towards competing nationally, but the thought of being around so many people and having large crowds watching, filled him with dread. For someone who wanted to fly under the radar of life, this was a veritable nightmare. Every time Mr. Beauchamp would mention it, Alex would politely decline and usually used his parents as an excuse not to compete.

"My parents wouldn't want that, they don't believe in forcing children into competition," would be his stock excuse.

"Let me talk to them, Alex, I am sure that I could convince them otherwise. You have too much talent to let it go to waste," would be Mr. Beauchamp's reply.

"Thank you. But I'd really rather you didn't. They are easily offended."

Mr. Beauchamp would let it lie at this point, but always brought it up at every P.E. lesson.

One thing that would bring Alex out of his shell was bullies; he hated to see people being picked on. He would come to the aid of anyone who found themselves in this predicament, even if the perpetrator was much older than him. Even if there was more than one, it didn't matter to him, he would stand his ground and a combination of his size and appearance would usually see the bully or bullies turn tail and run off.

His time at school only served to intensify his need to avoid people. Other pupils would point and snicker at him as well as making derogatory comments about his height or the length of his hair. He would generally fix the perpetrators with the sort of stare that said so much more than words ever could. The mocking would cease immediately and they would move on. A few of the pupils had taken to referring to him as The Outcast. All of the other teasing, he could cope with but being called this name particularly struck a nerve with him, as an outcast was precisely what he felt like.

Alex was intelligent enough to realise that the signals that he was sending out to people contributed to the teasing and name calling and the fact that he didn't have any friends. Although he couldn't help this, he could accept it for the most part, but as much as he wanted to avoid people, he also wanted more than anything to be liked by them. He really longed to make that one special friend, someone who understood him and liked him for who he was. It was quite the paradoxical situation.

Most school days were quite uneventful; he would keep his head down, do the work assigned to him and then disappear as soon as the bell rang to signify the end of another mundane school day.

But one Monday morning, something very different happened.

2.

Connection

It was the eve of Alex's thirteenth birthday as he filed into classroom 8M on Monday morning preparing for his tutor and also his head of year, Mrs. Danksworth to go through her dreary registration process. Doris Danksworth was a bitter woman with a voice like a blocked vacuum cleaner. You could tell straight away that she didn't really like children. Alex often wondered why she actually chose this profession. He thought that a purveyor of ancient torture devices would have suited her far better.

"Settle down, everyone and take your seats," came her nasal drone.

"Karen West?"

"Here."

"James Foote?"

"Here."

Alex felt himself drifting off, in part due to Mrs. Danksworth's monotone drawl and also due to his lack of sleep of late. For the last week he had been having extremely vivid dreams. These dreams were always in the same setting, a seemingly far off land with rolling woodland and fields, leading onto a huge lake that led up to a walled city that was shrouded from behind by a mountain range whose peaks were obscured by cloud cover. The focal point was a huge fortress that was elevated on an outcropping that overlooked the entire city.

"Emma Wilkinson?" Mrs. Danksworth droned on.

In his dreams, he would always be moving at speed towards the city from the first person perspective. Sometimes he would be approaching from the air and sometimes on land, either over a mountain pass or the lake embankment. Every time he drew near to the city's entrance he would wake up in a cold sweat.

"Alex Masterson…? Alex Masterson!"

Alex jerked back to reality. "H-here."

"Just barely," quipped Mrs. Danksworth. A sneer broke across her face as she glared at him. She was visibly pleased with her attempted witticism.

The sneer that she had generated was still present as her eyes scanned to the next name on the register.

"Eliza Anderson?"

"Here," came a slightly timid voice.

Alex spun round when hearing this new name being read out.

"Everyone. Eliza is new to the school, so I expect you all to help make her transition a smooth one." Mrs. Danksworth forced a smile at this point, which actually looked like it was causing her a good deal of pain. Whether she meant it or not, the effect was quite menacing.

"Bradley Jones...?"

Alex tuned out everything else in the class, something that he was very practised at and looked at Eliza. He was trying not to stare but he seemed to be drawn to her, it was almost as if he had known her his whole life.

Throughout the rest of the morning, he was completely oblivious to his schoolwork. He was far too intrigued by Eliza. He couldn't quantify in his own mind why he felt this way, but kept feeling his gaze drawn to her. He had to keep wrenching his eyes away as he didn't want her to think he was staring, but on more than one occasion he caught her staring back, only for her to realise and quickly avert her eyes.

Like Alex, at five foot seven inches, Eliza was tall for her age. She had a runner's build, long blonde hair that almost stretched the entire length of her back and piercing blue eyes. She was very pretty, with a very expressive face. But as pretty as she was, there was far more to what Alex was feeling than pure adolescent attraction.

The last lesson of the day was English. Alex arrived late to the class, a fact that didn't go unnoticed by his teacher Mr. Chancell. "Nice of you to join us, Mr. Masterson, hurry up and take a seat."

Alex apologised and then scanned the room for a free chair (ideally a free table); he spotted one at the back of the class. He made a beeline for this, sat down and took out his books. Just as Mr. Chancell had managed to settle everyone down, the classroom door opened and Eliza tentatively entered the room. Hushed chatter started to break out on a few of the desks. Mr. Chancell looked slightly miffed that he was going to have to go through the process of settling the class down again, but managed to compose himself. He looked at his register. "You must be Miss Anderson?" Eliza gave a shy smile and nodded. "Welcome. I'm Mr. Chancell. Please take a seat." She scanned the room much like Alex had just done. He saw her look in his direction and slowly, she started to draw closer. Alex felt a sharp, sudden pain in his forearm. He grimaced as he looked down at it. The pain's centre seemed to be within a mole cluster that he had on the underside of his right forearm.

Eliza took her seat next to him and despite the pain he smiled and said, "Hi."

Eliza smiled and returned his greeting. As she took out her books and drew up her chair, Alex couldn't help but notice that she flinched slightly and favoured her arm.

Throughout the lesson the pain that Alex was suffering from seemed to intensify. He needed some fresh air so he asked Mr. Chancell if he could be excused in order to go to the toilet. Mr. Chancell was reading through some emails on his tablet and without looking up, gave Alex his permission. Alex made his way to the boys' bathrooms still rubbing his forearm as he walked. He got into the bathroom and immediately went to one of the mirrors; he looked quite pale. He studied his forearm around the source of the pain, but there was no obvious indication of what was actually causing it. With that, he splashed some water over his face, took a few deep breaths and then decided that he should probably head back to class.

He had his head down as he exited the bathroom. He bumped into someone. "Sorry," he said and as he looked up he saw that it was Eliza.

"No problem," she said and gave him a bashful smile. "Are you okay?" she enquired. "You ran out of class in quite a hurry."

"Oh yeah; I was just in a bit of discomfort," he said as casually as he could.

Eliza noticed that he was favouring his forearm and as she looked closer, she spotted the mole cluster. She stared at him for what felt like an hour.

"This is really freaky," she said and showed Alex her forearm. She had the exact same mole cluster, in the exact same position. "I have been suffering from a pain in my arm too!"

Alex, looking startled asked, "When did yours start?"

"When I first came into English," she replied.

"Mine too," he said, trying not to sound too shocked.

They stared in silence for another few moments, before Alex said, "This isn't meant as a line or anything, but I really feel like I know you, have we met before?"

Eliza thought about this for a moment and then said, "This is so weird! I have been thinking the same thing since I saw you this morning. I feel like I know you, but just cannot place you."

Again they stared in silence, both having so many questions but unsure of how to broach them. The silence was interrupted by a ringing bell, signifying the end of the school day.

"We really should be heading back to class to collect our bags," stated Alex. "Can I walk home with you? We can talk some more."

Eliza smiled, "Sure."

He couldn't explain it, but he felt an immediate connection to her. He just felt so comfortable in her presence. All his life, he had struggled to talk to people and was always concerned that his shyness came across as arrogance or hostility. But with Eliza just now, his words came out with consummate ease.

As they wandered in the opposite direction to the majority of the pupils, some of which were pointing and smirking at them both, they spotted Mrs. Danksworth. She was approximately twenty-five foot ahead of them in the corridor and she was not alone. They could only see the back of them, but they could tell that she was being flanked by a hulking man who must have been at least seven foot tall. Not wanting to be questioned by Mrs. Danksworth, they both hung back. But they were curious as to who the man was, so they kept them in sight.

After a few moments, Mrs. Danksworth and her guest slowed and turned left off of the main corridor. Alex and Eliza looked at each other and without exchanging any words they decided to continue to follow. This route would take them past their English classroom, but their bags could wait, they were intrigued. To their surprise, Mrs. Danksworth and her large companion stopped outside Mr. Chancell's classroom.

Mrs. Danksworth knocked and opened the door. Both her and her guest disappeared through the door and they heard it slam firmly shut behind them. Alex and Eliza picked up pace now so that they could get to the classroom as soon as possible and try to find out what was being said. As they approached the half glazed classroom door, they ducked so that they were hidden from view by the wooden panel that adorned its lower half. They both strained their ears to try to hear what was being said, but to their surprise, they could both hear every word with comparative ease. They heard Mrs. Danksworth's familiar drone. "I'm terribly sorry to bother you, Andrew. This is Mr. Canly.

He is from Social Services and has requested this opportunity to have a conversation with Alex Masterson."

Andrew Chancell seemed a little sceptical about this request. "This seems a little unorthodox; shouldn't Alex's parents be present for something like this, Doris?"

Alex and Eliza then heard a voice that was so guttural they were sure that the glass in the door that they were pressed up against shook. "There is a suggestion that there has been some abuse in the home. I wanted to speak to Alex independently so that he could speak freely without the pressure of his parents being present."

The sound of Mr. Canly's voice was so intimidating that they could both hear fear in Mr. Chancell's voice when he replied. "Oh, I-I see, this sounds like a very serious allegation. Well you are in luck, Alex left to use the toilet a short while ago, so he should be back to collect his belongings very soon."

Alex was extremely confused and taken aback by what he had just heard. His parents weren't the most attentive, but they had never so much as laid a hand on him. He wondered where Social Services had received this information from.

He regathered his thoughts and turned towards Eliza who looked just as confused as he was. They both had an ill feeling. Alex looked at Eliza and in a hushed voice said, "Forget our bags we can get them later. Let's get out of here!"

Just as they had started to creep away from the door, it creaked open and they heard Mrs. Danksworth's dreary voice, "Ah, Mr. Masterson and Ms. Anderson. We have a gentleman here who would like a conversation with you, Alex. Ms. Anderson, you can collect your belongings and go."

As he turned to face her, he got his first look at Mr. Canly; he was the scariest looking person that Alex had ever seen. His face appeared to be frozen with an expression of pure, gleeful rage. But there was something else, Alex was convinced that for the briefest moment, he saw the man's eyes flash red and show an outline on his face of some kind of creature. He looked across at Eliza who, judging by the look of horror on her face had seen the same thing.

"Run!" Alex shouted and they both bolted at top speed down the now clear school corridor.

"Stop! Get back here!" they both heard Mrs. Danksworth yell.

Alex looked back almost apologetically only to see Mrs. Danksworth being thrown clear across the school corridor and crashing through the closed door of the classroom opposite. In her place was Mr. Canly still wearing that same expression. "You may as well come quietly as you cannot escape," he bellowed. "You would be most unwise to make me have to chase you."

This seemed to propel them both on. Alex was a natural athlete, by far the fastest runner in his year, if not the entire school, but he was amazed to see that Eliza had overtaken him. As he caught up to her he raised his eyebrows, partly in admiration and partly in exasperation. But there was no time to dwell on this. One longer corridor, followed by a left hand turn would see them at the school exit. From here, they could run across the playground and onto the school field. The woodland that Alex loved to explore so much backed onto the school field, so he was confident that if they could reach it, he and Eliza could lose Mr. Canly in the countless acres of trees. Alex could hear a noise behind him. He turned expecting to see Mr. Canly giving chase, but to his horror it seemed they were being chased by some sort of huge beast. Was that a wolf? Surely not!

Alex, who had always had an overactive imagination, thought that the stress of the situation was causing his mind to play tricks on him. He kept running. He looked across at Eliza who looked completely freaked out.

"Was that a wolf?" she screamed.

"No, of course not," said Alex, but he was not totally convinced by his own response. As they approached the sharp left hand turn that would take them towards the exit, they heard an explosive crash coming from behind them that caused them to both look back. Lockers had been scattered everywhere and in amongst the twisted, crumpled wreckage, they could see a huge shape start to emerge. Alex decided that Canly must have lost his footing.

That should slow him down a little, he thought to himself.

They had both reached the exit at this point and Alex looked back once again expecting to see a dazed Mr. Canly. His worst fears were confirmed. Emerging from the wreckage was a huge wolf! It did look slightly disorientated though. Alex and Eliza took this opportunity to tear across the playground at full speed. They reached the edge of the school field.

Alex shouted to Eliza, "Get to the fence at the bottom of the field; we'll lose him in the forest!"

Eliza nodded and like a gazelle, made for the trees. They heard the crash of the exit door explode against the wall behind them. They didn't dare look back and continued to sprint towards the fence line.

As they ran, it seemed like the trees were pulling further away from them. They could hear the heavy paws of the huge beast thundering on the ground not far behind them. Alex didn't dare look back, but at this point, he knew that he wasn't going to be able to outrun the wolf. He could, however, save Eliza. Suddenly, he broke off to the left, and this sharp change of direction caused the wolf to lose its footing and go careering along the ground to the right. Eliza who was a few foot from the fence line stopped and shouted,

"Alex, what are you doing?"

"Run, Eliza! Get yourself to safety!"

She stared back, "I'm not leaving you!"

The wolf had now regained its footing and was bearing down on Alex. All of a sudden there was a thud and the wolf let out a huge yelp. It turned to see what had hit it; Eliza was standing there, stones in her hand. She had reached the fence line and had searched for any sort of weapon that could be used against their pursuer. The wolf started to make for her.

"Eliza, get away!" Alex yelled. But she seemed frozen in time. Realising this, he started to yell at the wolf in an effort to get its attention. He looked around for a weapon and found the large stone that Eliza had hit it with moments earlier. He scooped it up, took aim and hit the wolf on the side of the neck. The wolf yelped and wheeled around on him. The speed of this took him by surprise and he slipped and fell over, the back of his head impacting onto the grass. As he tried to regather himself, he could see that his shot with the rock had drawn blood on the beast. The wolf prepared to pounce. Alex was prone and could not defend himself – was this the end?

In slow motion and out of nowhere, Alex saw a huge black shape crash into the side of the wolf, sending it sprawling. As his eyes came into focus he saw Axis staring back at him. But then he heard something that he didn't expect, "Get to the forest, Alex and make for our tree, I'll meet you there!"

"What the…" Alex started to retort. Had he heard Axis speak to him? He must have hit his head harder than he had thought when he fell. The wolf was starting to stir.

"Get to our tree, Alex and take Eliza with you – now!" Alex got to his feet and stared at Axis in disbelief. Eliza was quite far ahead of him, but even at that distance, the shock on her face was evident. The wolf was now back on its feet circling Axis. "Go now!" barked Axis, "I'll hold him off!"

Alex stared in shock as he staggered his way into a run and caught up to Eliza. He took one look back at Axis, who was preventing the wolf in its efforts to give chase and with that, he and Eliza disappeared into the trees.

3.

Any Tree in a Storm

"What on Earth just happened?" Eliza asked.

That was the first time either of them had spoken since they entered the forest.

Alex was still trying to compute everything. Mr. Canly, the wolf, Axis...

"I don't know," said Alex. "What I do know though is that wolf would have killed us had it not been for Axis."

"You know that... dog?" asked Eliza incredulously.

"He's my pet and my best friend," said Alex with a mixture of pride and sorrow, as he was sure that the wolf would have killed Axis.

"Well I think that it is safe to say that he is much more than just a dog," said Eliza. "I can't believe *it*, sorry, *he,* spoke."

Neither could Alex. "You heard it too?"

Eliza nodded. "I heard it as clearly as I am hearing you now. How is that even possible?"

Alex did not know how to respond to this as he had no idea. His mind was spinning as they continued to wend their way deeper into the forest.

After what seemed like hours, they arrived at a small clearing, the focal point of which was a gigantic tree that seemed to rise far above and beyond the canopy of the forest. The tree was huge, so much bigger than any of the other trees in and around it. It looked ancient, with its huge, knotted trunk and twisted, gnarled branches that stretched ever upward.

Despite everything that had just happened, Alex felt a small sense of relief as he moved into the shadow of the familiar tree. As he stepped towards it, he felt warmth wash over him. Exhausted, he sat down and leant against the trunk. He invited Eliza to do likewise. They both felt somehow protected under its huge branches and unwittingly, they fell into a deep sleep.

Alex awoke with a start to a cracking sound; somebody or something was heading in their direction. He gave Eliza a gentle shake in order to wake her, she too woke with a start and was about to say something when Alex put his hand lightly over her mouth and indicated that she should remain quiet. He silently pointed behind him and she understood straight away. He then motioned that they should move around the other side of the tree and climb.

They managed to get about twelve foot off the ground when a black shadow appeared in the clearing. It was dark now and only a few intermittent shards of moonlight were able to permeate through the thick tree covering. But despite this, Alex could make out that whatever it was, it was limping.

Is it the wolf? Has Axis injured it whilst trying to protect us?

The black shape didn't approach the tree but instead disappeared behind the huge trunk of a fallen tree some fifty yards from where they were hidden. They heard rustling and cracking noises and all of a sudden, the ground began to shake. They both clung extra tightly to the thick branches from fear of falling, or was the greater fear being spotted by the dark shape?

The shaking stopped and after some time they heard the rustling of the leaves that littered the forest floor and the cracking of twigs. The dark shape was about to re-emerge! Out it came from behind the huge tree trunk. This time it was fixed on heading towards the tree that was hiding Alex and Eliza. They both stared wide-eyed at one another not even daring to breathe as the shape approached. Then something strange happened, as it drew closer, there was a blinding flash of blue light that completely engulfed the creature. Once the light had cleared, they could still see a dark shape, but it was somehow different. From a crouched position, it drew up to its full height. Alex strained his eyes and realised he was now looking at a man! A tall, heavily built man with a face almost completely obscured by a thick black beard. He also had long black hair that along with the beard, served to almost completely hide his facial features.

The man looked all around him and then shouted, "Alex!" As he said this, he flinched and favoured the upper part of his right arm. "Alex! Are you here?" The man had a voice that immediately commanded respect. Alex didn't know what to do, who was this strange man and how did he know his name? "Alex, show yourself. You are not in any danger – it's Axis."

"Axis," Alex mouthed silently to Eliza. He looked completely bewildered.

Axis scanned the tree and then called again.

"Alex, I see you and Eliza in the tree. Please come down, we need to talk."

A thousand thoughts raced through Alex's mind. Most were what terrible things might happen to he and Eliza should they descend from the comparative safety of the tree. But in spite of this, he began to make his way down. He looked up at Eliza who too, had started her descent.

Alex's feet hit the ground and he was now face to face with the man (it was actually more like face to chest). He heard Eliza's feet hit the ground just behind him. Axis was a giant of a man. He was at least six foot eight inches tall and was solid muscle. He had an intimidating air about him. What could be seen of his face was focused and stern. But despite this, Alex saw kindness and a familiar look of understanding in his dark eyes. Alex noticed that he was still favouring his arm and saw the crimson of blood trickling through his fingers.

The three of them stood in silence for a few moments until Axis said, "Alex, Eliza, it is so good to see you again, through these eyes." He then proceeded to hug them both. It was how one would imagine an anaconda would hug.

They were both taken aback by this and by the time Alex had regained his breath he asked, "What do you mean, 'these eyes'? What is going on?"

"There is so much I need to tell you both," said Axis. "I just need a bit of help with this first." He removed his hand from his arm; he had a huge wound in the shape of a bite mark. "Canly took a chunk out of me and then made off into the woods."

Alex started to look around frantically.

"Don't worry, Alex," smiled Axis. "He can't find us here. You remember the blue flash of light that you just saw?" They both nodded. "That is called a Ring of Protection. It is designed to let only certain people in and once you enter it, you see a person in their true form."

Alex didn't speak. He took off his school jumper and tore off one of the arms. He then proceeded to tie this around the wound on Axis' arm. Axis thanked him and put on a long black coat that he had obviously retrieved when he was behind the felled tree.

"What do you mean 'true form'?" Alex inquired.

Axis smiled a tired smile. "Where do I begin?"

4.

A Brief History

The three of them were now seated on the ground, by the tree. Both Alex and Eliza were listening intently to Axis. "I have so much to tell you, some of it will sound ridiculous and some will be hard to accept. I know that you will have about a million questions, I don't have all of the answers but I will give you all that I know."

Axis addressed Alex directly.

"I am not going to beat around the bush. That wolf was a hunter sent to kill you."

Alex looked stunned.

"Kill me! Why would anyone want to kill me, I haven't done anything wrong – I am no one of importance?"

"You may be many things, Alex, but you are not unimportant. In fact, you and Eliza may well be the only hope for the salvation of our entire world."

Both Alex and Eliza looked extremely confused.

Axis continued.

"Alex, you know how you would tell me on a regular basis, how you didn't feel like you belonged here?" Alex looked away feeling slightly embarrassed. "Well that is because you don't – neither of you do." They both had confusion etched on their faces.

"What do you mean 'don't belong'?" asked Eliza.

"I mean that you are not from this place – this world."

Eliza accidentally let out a slightly sarcastic laugh. "Of course I am from here, my parents, my home."

"They are not your parents and this isn't your home. These were just necessary illusions created for your protection." Eliza was about to retort when Axis said, "Did you ever wonder why your adoptive parents never paid any real attention to either of you and left you to your own devices, or why you have moved home so many times in your young lives?"

They went silent as this comment resonated with them both.

"As I was saying, you were both put here for your protection. After your parents were killed, your real home was no longer safe for you."

"Killed!

"How? Why?" they both asked.

"Patience. I will get to this."

Axis continued.

"We all come from a place called Ignius Novus. It is affectionately referred to as Igni. In some ways it is similar to Earth in terms of the atmosphere and landscapes. But in many ways, it is very different.

"We are Derma-morphs. Our true form is human but due to a slightly different sequence in the structure of our genetic makeup, we have the ability to transform into creatures that are representative of our personalities."

Both Alex and Eliza laughed at this.

"This is no laughing matter!" Axis snapped. "I am providing you with details of your true history and identities."

They both looked on apologetically, before Eliza spoke.

"If we are Derma… whatevers, and can turn into creatures, then surely we should be able to transform? I don't know about Alex, but I have never changed." She had a slightly self-satisfied look on her face.

"You can, but not until your thirteenth birthday. A restriction was put in place by the Elders of our world, many years ago. They believed that anyone younger than thirteen wasn't deemed responsible enough to possess this ability."

Axis looked at them both. "Show me your right arms," he said.

"What, why?" asked Alex.

"Just do as I say."

Reluctantly, they both stretched their right arms out for Axis to see.

"You see this?" said Axis pointing to the mole clusters on the underside of each of their forearms. They both nodded. "It is called a Hindrex. This will basically restrict your ability to morph for a given period of time." Eliza and Alex looked on silently.

"Have either of you been feeling any sort of pain or stinging in and around the Hindrex?"

They both nodded but both had a look of, 'how could you possibly know this?' on their faces.

"This pain indicates that you are almost of age and that the power of the Hindrex is starting to wane.

"Alex, your parents – Cordium and Amara are, were, king and queen of Arcamedia.

"Arcamedia is the largest city on Ignius Novus. Under their rule, we had enjoyed our most prosperous times for almost a millennium. But as is the case when things are going well, there are those who wish to derail it." He paused, seemingly for effect. "Eliza, your parents were the rulers of Kessler, a neighbouring realm. During our times of prosperity Arcamedia held a strong alliance with Kessler. So strong was the alliance, it was decided that both realms would be merged, so your parents entered into a pact that would see the first born male and female from each family promised to one another. You feel a connection to each other do you not?" They both looked surprised at his knowledge of this, but nodded. "This is because once this promise has been made it creates an unbreakable bond between the two of you. A bond that will intensify over the years. You also spent a good deal of time together as each of your parents became firm friends. This only served to solidify the bond."

They looked at one another, even though they had only really known each other for a few hours, there was an undeniably strong connection between the two of them.

Axis continued, "Both of your mothers would travel together and it was during one of these excursions that tragically, their carriage broke free and fell off the side of a cliff into the freezing cold waters of Lake Ancora." Both Alex and Eliza let out audible gasps at this point. Axis let this sink in for a moment and then continued. "I am afraid that the sad news doesn't end here. Stricken with grief, Eliza, your father took his own life, orphaning you in the process. You were then taken into care by your Guardian."

"Guardian?" said Eliza.

"Yes," said Axis, somewhat impatiently. "I am Alex's Guardian, your Guardian was Aroura."

"Our dog?" said Eliza.

"The very same. She passed away last week did she not?" Eliza nodded solemnly. "That is why you were moved here under my temporary Guardianship until a replacement could be sent. The truth be told, Aroura was killed protecting you, Eliza. As is the case with Alex, a hunter was sent to kill you and Aroura performed her duty. She was a good soldier and a good friend." Axis paused looking solemn; he then composed himself and continued. "It was pure bad luck that the hunter found you as you do not become visible to them until your thirteenth year. To him, you would have been just a normal human child. He must have recognised Aurora in some way.

"Kessler grieved the loss of both of your parents. But without their respected leaders at the helm, the city soon fell into disarray. It is currently under the stewardship of Aldar Molia. He is a corrupt man who only cares about his own interests; he is ignorant to the suffering of the people of Kessler. Besides, ultimately he answers to one person."

"Who?" Alex and Eliza asked in unison.

"This would bring us to your stepmother, Alex."

"Stepmother?" Alex repeated.

"Yes. After your mother passed, your father was distraught beyond measure. He would shut himself away from everyone, leaving others to oversee his duties. I was the head of your father's guard, his confidant and closest friend; it pained me to see what he had become."

His voice trailed off.

"This was when somebody who I believe has always craved power saw the opportunity to swoop in and take advantage.

"Magissa Veil." The disgust in his voice was evident.

"Magissa was a prominent member of your mother's entourage, Alex. She played the role of loyal subject almost to perfection. But I started to notice a few things that alerted me to her and as a result, I decided to watch her more closely from then on. I started to follow her more and more and I came to suspect that she may have been involved in both of your mothers' deaths somehow, though I couldn't provide any proof."

Axis continued.

"Soon after the accident, I tried to talk to your father about this, Alex, but he would not hear of it and banished me from Arcamedia. By this point, your father was totally disconnected from you; it was almost as if he wasn't even aware of your existence.

"During my monitoring of Magissa, I came to find that she is practitioner of witchcraft and not the good kind. I also noticed that she had moved in on Cordium very soon after the accident – too soon. His behaviour seemed to change immediately. Initially we thought that this behavioural change was due to grief, but it soon became clear to those that were closest to him that he was under some kind of spell. We tried to reach out to him, but it was too late, she had a total hold over his thoughts and actions.

"Fearing for your safety, I made preparations for you to be evacuated from Arcamedia. I sensed that Eliza would also be targeted by Magissa, so I contacted Aurora and made her aware of the evacuation plan."

"Why would we be unsafe?" asked Alex. "It seems to me that we swapped one set of negligent parents for another." This was a harsh comment that he regretted immediately.

"There is far more to it than that, Alex!" said Axis with a raised voice. He then calmed himself. "As I pointed out earlier, you and Eliza were bonded at birth. Through your parentage and this bond, you would become the eventual rulers of Arcamedia and the surrounding realms. Should you *no longer be in the picture,* Magissa would have an uncontested rule over all the realms."

The reality of the situation sunk in with them both.

"So she was the one that sent the hunters after us?" said Eliza.

"That is correct," said Axis.

"Magissa also has full control over what happens in Kessler. Aldar Molia is completely devoted to her and ensures that her commands are carried out to the letter. I believe that he sees himself ruling by her side – the misguided fool!" he spat.

An uncomfortable silence then set in before Alex asked, "Are there likely to be more hunters coming?"

"Undoubtedly. It is likely that they are already here and have been alerted to your whereabouts by Canly," said Axis.

"So we cannot stay here then?" said Alex.

"No, we cannot."

"Well where can we go?" asked Eliza.

"We have to go back to Ignius Novus," said Axis.

Alex and Eliza looked horrified.

"Surely we are more likely to be caught or killed if we go there?" they protested.

"We still have a few allies there, something that we do not have here. You both share a birthday, so you will both be thirteen in a matter of hours. I need to get you to a friend – Maven Cowlark. He can help increase the protection for you both. Aside from this, there is another pressing reason to get back to Igni, but I will let Maven explain."

"How exactly are we supposed to get there?" asked Alex.

"A very good point, follow me."

5.

Inhuman Travel

"Follow me, come on," Axis called to them both.

Alex's mind was spinning, this was so much to take in and was all so bizarre, yet something in his head told him that Axis was speaking the complete truth. He had only known Axis the man for a few hours, yet he already felt a strong sense of trust growing towards him. He sensed that he should be feeling sadder to hear the news that his real mother had died and that his father was under the control of an evil witch, but felt slightly numb to it. How can you feel deep sorrow for people that you have no memory of?

He then thought of the two people who he thought were his parents. Although they left him to his own devices most of the time, they would be concerned if he didn't get home soon. Then it dawned on him, what if Canly and the other hunters trace him back to his home?

"We need to go back to my home first," Alex stated.

"No, Alex. There is no time, we must leave for Igni," Axis replied.

"But what about my parents? They will be worried about me if I don't return soon. And worse still, what if the hunters track me back to them?"

Alex's words had obviously twigged the same realisation in Eliza as she echoed his concerns.

"I have already told you, they are not your parents. You have said yourself that they were negligent," came Axis' infuriated response.

"They may not be our real parents, but they are the only ones that we have ever known. You cannot be with people for that length of time and not care for them," Alex retorted.

Axis nodded. "You are right. I did not mean to make light of your feelings for them. But you don't need to worry, before I came here, I relieved them of their duties."

Both Alex and Eliza gasped.

Axis suddenly realised what he had just said. "No, no, not in that way, my friends. I mean that they no longer have the burden of looking after you. I have taken them back to the point in their lives before either of you were a part of it."

"What do you mean?" Alex asked.

"They have moved back to their first homes and they have no memory of either of you ever having been a part of their lives."

"How is that even possible?" asked Eliza.

"All you need to know is that I used something that Maven had created for this eventuality. The important thing is they are safe and the fact that each of your adoptive parents no longer has any memory or knowledge of you makes them even safer."

Eliza didn't look totally convinced, but accepted what she had been told with a nod and a slightly forced smile.

Alex on the other hand knew that what Axis had told them was true and although he was relieved that his adoptive parents were safe, there was a part of him that felt sad that they would not remember him in any way, shape or form.

They made their way over to the felled tree that Axis the dog had emerged from a few hours earlier. Axis stopped and said, "On Igni we have learned to harness the power of gemstones in different ways." He reached into the inside pocket of the long coat that he was wearing and withdrew a gem. Alex and Eliza watched as he rotated the crystal in one of his shovel-like hands and stared as it started to glow. It was the most striking blue colour that either of them had ever seen.

"Now I must warn you both, this will not be particularly pleasant. When I release the gem, we must all join hands and we will then be teleported to Igni."

"Teleported? That's impossible," said Eliza.

"Everything else that you have experienced so far today would fall into that category, wouldn't you agree?" Axis responded with a knowing glint in his dark eyes.

Neither of them had a response to this, so they stood quietly, awaiting further instruction.

"So on three, we all join hands. Brace yourselves, this will be over soon.

"Ready?" They nodded nervously.

"One…Two…Thr… Oh, one more thing, whatever you do, do not let go of my hands."

"You are not filling us with confidence," said Alex. "Can we start agai..."

"Three!" shouted Axis.

Both Eliza and Alex felt Axis grab their hands and then the whole forest seemed to glow blue. There was an eerie calm and then all of sudden Alex was gripped by a force so strong he felt like his bones were being pulled out of his body. He let out a scream of pain. He could hear Eliza screaming too. He tried to open his eyes to check that she was okay, but the force or whatever it was, was preventing this from happening.

After what felt like an age, the crushing pain that he was feeling subsided. It now felt like he was just floating in space. "Are you both okay?" he heard Axis call.

"I... I think so," said Eliza.

"Good – Alex?"

"Um Y...yes."

"Excellent. We are almost there, remember, don't let go – hold on!"

Out of nowhere, Alex started to spin uncontrollably like he was being sucked into a giant whirlpool. Again he heard Eliza scream, this time it was strangely comforting as it indicated that she was still with them. The spinning then increased to the point where he felt like he was going to explode, then just when he didn't think he could stand it anymore, it stopped. He was floating again. Moments later, he felt himself touch down onto something solid.

"Okay, open your eyes, slowly," said Axis.

Alex obeyed. His first thought was for Eliza, he tried to focus but everything was so blurry. *Are those trees?*

"Here, drink this."

Alex groped about in the air and felt a strong grip take hold of his wrist, followed by the feeling of something being pushed into his hand and then, against his will, his hand was moving towards his face. As the liquid touched his lips, everything seemed to normalize immediately. Moments earlier, he felt like he had been put through a blender and now it was as if nothing had happened. He looked ahead, everything was in perfect focus. He saw Eliza, she looked totally disorientated but as Axis helped her drink, he could immediately see that she too was feeling the healing effects of the anonymous liquid.

"What did you just give us?" Alex asked as he pointed at the silver hipflask.

"It's called Leirix," said Axis. "As you can probably tell, it has healing properties. If you needed further proof that you are not entirely human, a human would not have been able to survive what you just went through." He trailed off. "Thank goodness. We wouldn't want them to do to Igni what they have done to Earth."

Alex and Eliza looked at him, expecting him to qualify his last comment. Nothing was forthcoming. Axis continued, "Without the Leirix, you would have been extremely ill and disorientated for days, but your life would not have been under threat. You do get used to it." He smiled, "But only as an adult will it not affect you."

Alex looked around, he *had* seen trees. They were in a forest – right next to a familiar looking, gigantic tree.

"Have we actually gone anywhere? This all looks the same," he said as he pointed to the tree.

"We are on Igni," said Axis. "The reason why you felt so comfortable by the tree was because it was from your home."

"How could it be?" Alex asked.

"That's... impossible?" smiled Axis.

"Once you passed through the Ring of Protection, you were home, well... in a way. The small area around the tree was a projected illusion that was intended to give you the impression that you were home. It not only kept you safe but also helped to maintain your connection to Igni."

Axis looked skyward, it was getting dark. "We must get you both to Maven."

"Normally I would make camp for the night, but it is imperative that he applies the protection to you before midnight."

"Why?" asked Alex.

"It is best that Maven explains; he is the Mystic after all. Come on. We must move. Magissa is certain to have patrols in the area. We must take a longer path to Maven; we are less likely to be spotted on this route."

Axis pointed to the left. "This is our road. Walk where I walk, keep up and be silent."

They set off.

It was a clear dark night and there was a full moon in the sky. Considering Axis' huge frame, he barely made a sound as they proceeded deeper into the forest. As Axis had requested, they moved without uttering a word. It was very dark now and Alex was amazed at how well he could see. He assumed that Axis was holding a torch of some kind just in front of them. He peered ahead only to realise that Axis had his arms down by his sides and there wasn't any light glowing in front of him. How could he see so well? He looked over at Eliza, she must have felt his eyes on her and she turned to look at him. Alex double-took and Eliza lurched back. Her beautiful blue eyes were glowing much like the crystal that had brought them here. Judging by the way that she was staring at him, he guessed that his eyes must have had a similar glow. He pointed at her eyes and then at his own, Eliza nodded very slowly, still seemingly trying to take in what she was seeing.

At some point during this silent exchange they must have stopped walking. Some distance ahead they could clearly see the huge man that was Axis. As he turned, Alex could see that his eyes were glowing a burnt orange colour. He motioned to them to catch up. Quickly and quietly, they caught up to him. Without a word and through a series of hand gestures, he made it clear to them that they needed to move on and stay in step with him.

It seemed like hours had passed since they had set off on their silent march through the forest. The tree cover was becoming thicker which would only allow the moonlight through intermittently. Alex was aware that he couldn't see quite as clearly as he had earlier. He looked over at Eliza who met his gaze and he noticed that the glow in her blue eyes had dimmed slightly. All of a sudden Axis froze and raised his hand, indicating that they should stop. Both Alex and Eliza froze on the spot. They watched as Axis slowly scanned the area. His deliberate movements made him look like some sort of huge cyborg. They heard a rustle some way off to the left. Axis' head immediately spun in the direction of the noise. As he attempted to locate its source, there was another rustle, but this one was much closer.

Axis motioned to both Eliza and Alex to get down and hide behind a nearby tree stump. He then spun around and silently made off in the direction of the disturbance.

Eliza and Alex looked at each other wide-eyed and scared, neither of them dared to move a muscle. Another rustle, this one was close – too close. They both peered around the side of the tree stump in the direction of the noise and to their horror, they could now make out the clear outline of a person and he or she was making their way to exactly where they were hiding. They both pressed up against the tree stump and tucked themselves into the foetal position, hoping not to be spotted. The figure was getting closer. They had been spotted! Then a noise that sounded like a person clearing their throat emanated from the figure's direction. "Hel... arghh!" came the sound and the figure rose into the air. It was being held up by another huge figure that they recognised as Axis.

"Maven! What the devil are you doing?" roared Axis.

"Axis – Axis my old friend, put me down," croaked Maven.

Axis lowered him gently to the ground.

"What are you doing out here? I could've killed you."

Maven coughed, "I got your message. I was getting concerned that you had not arrived so decided to come out to look for you. I didn't announce myself straight away as I thought that you might have been one of Magissa's patrols. For the last two weeks they have been venturing deeper and deeper into the forest. I'm not sure why, I can only assume that Magissa must have sensed something."

He turned around, "Ah, you must be Eliza and Alex! My name is Maven Cowlark and I am at your service." He removed his hat and bowed so low that his beard brushed the forest floor.

Both Eliza and Alex looked somewhat taken aback by this. They both smiled. Eliza said hello and Alex raised his hand in welcome.

Maven Cowlark was eccentric looking. He was tall and thin with long brown hair that was flecked with grey and a long brown-grey beard that started thick and wide at the point of his chin. Its width decreased until it ended abruptly in a sharp point just past his sternum. He wore clothing and a hat which both appeared to be made out of some sort of plant leaves, as well as a silken scarf and he carried a staff that was covered from top to bottom in intricate carvings. They noticed that his eyes had a faint orangey-brown glow to them.

"Right, I must get you all to my home and quickly," said Maven. "There is much to do."

6.

A Room without a View

Silently they all followed Maven. After a short while, they came into a clearing. This gave them an unobscured view of the moon. It was so huge and low in the sky that Alex thought that if he were to climb a nearby tree, he could almost touch it. It had a red hue to it which bathed the entire clearing in a beautiful silvery-pinkish light.

"We have arrived," pronounced Maven.

Eliza and Alex both looked all around them but saw nothing that would remotely resemble a house. Maven must have noticed the confused look on their faces as he said, "My home is cloaked by a Ring of Protection. Only I know its location and others can only enter if I allow it. Which reminds me," he walked up to Axis and lifted his arm. He held his wrist between his thumb and index finger and muttered some indistinguishable words under his breath. He then walked up to Eliza and repeated the process. Finally, he walked up to Alex. "No need to look so worried, my boy," he said with a soothing smile. "This procedure will allow you to enter my home." He took Alex's arm and as he had done with both Axis and Eliza, held his wrist and muttered the same words. Alex strained to hear what Maven was saying but it was a strange language the likes of which he had never heard.

"Right, you are all primed to enter. Follow me."

Maven walked a few more yards and stopped just in front of a very large, very old, gnarled looking tree that wasn't dissimilar to the tree that Alex used to daydream against. "We must pass through the Ring of Protection individually," he said. "There was an incident recently where several of Magissa's men must have spotted me pass through. The ring is slightly vulnerable when it is scanning an entrant. The three of them decided to charge at the same time. Fortunately, I spotted them and was ready as they came crashing through."

"What happened?" asked Alex intrigued.

"The three of them will have had the mother of all headaches and will have no idea what happened at all that day, they won't even remember what they had for breakfast." Maven smiled and there was a mischievous glint in his eye. "Suffice to say, had they caught me unawares, things could have been very different. I have now put measures in place that only allow one person through at a time. Should multiple persons or a person that hasn't been 'granted access', try to enter, they will be ported to a random location and will have no memory of how they got there or of any of the last twenty-four hours. I have dubbed it the 'Amnesiacs Day Trip'." Maven chuckled, clearly amused and pleased with his play on words. He looked at each of them in turn, hoping for a positive reaction to his wit. Alex and Eliza both smiled but it was more out of politeness. Finally he looked at Axis who stared back at him stone faced. Feeling a bit awkward, Maven turned around, muttered something about no sense of humour and disappeared into a blue flash of light. "Okay, come on through, one at a time though," came his extremely muffled voice.

Axis looked at them both, smiled and said, "See you on the other side," before being swallowed by the blue flash.

Eliza and Alex looked at each other. "Ladies first?" said Alex awkwardly.

Eliza rolled her eyes at him, then smiled and stepped forward delicately. She was drawn in by the blue flash, and then she was gone.

Even though they were only a few foot in front of him, Alex felt completely alone. The world – wherever he was, felt totally still and quiet. He prepared to step forward but seemed rooted to the spot. Then he heard Eliza's muffled voice, "Don't worry, Alex, it's just like stepping into a sauna."

He felt fortified by this and stepped forward. The whole world turned blue and he felt soothing warmth expand across his entire body. Then he saw all three of them and smiled in relief. Eliza smiled and fleetingly held his hand. Alex smiled; her touch was more warming and soothing than passing through the Ring of Protection.

The sound of Maven's voice brought him back to the present. "Right, here we are, in we go." He was pointing at a huge opening in the trunk of the tree.

Alex surveyed the tree. As large as it was, there was no way that they could all fit inside. "How on Earth are we all supposed to fit in there?" he asked.

"Firstly, you will find that appearances can be deceiving and secondly, you should choose another term, because you are no longer on Earth." Maven winked at Alex and smiled. Then without saying another word, he stepped into the opening and was lost from view. Axis gestured for Eliza to go next, she duly obliged. Then he turned and spoke to Alex. "Don't worry; Maven is a good man and a good friend. You can trust him; he has much to tell you."

Alex stepped into the darkness with Axis following close behind.

Alex was expecting all four of them to be crushed inside the trunk of the tree but to his surprise, there was ample room for both he and Axis and just in front were Maven and Eliza.

"Right, everyone, this way please." Maven swept his hand dramatically indicating that they all go ahead of him. Alex manoeuvred past Maven and was now standing alongside Eliza. They were both standing at the top of a staircase that spiralled downward into the darkness. "Down you go," Maven called from behind them. "Don't worry about the darkness, lanterns will light your way as you descend."

"Shouldn't we be able to see in here as clearly as we could see outside?" asked Alex.

"You are referring to the heightened sense of sight that you experienced whilst walking here?" asked Maven.

Alex nodded.

"You need to absorb a certain amount of natural light in order for this to happen. The moon provided this at points whilst you were in the forest, but as there isn't any natural light in here, your sight will be normal, hence the lanterns," he explained.

Alex, feeling slightly embarrassed that he had sent Eliza in through the Ring of Protection ahead of him, decided to redeem himself by taking the lead on the stairs. Cautiously, he stepped onto the first stair and then onto the second. Just as Maven had promised, lanterns that seemed to be floating in midair flickered to life as he drew close to them. His shadow danced around the walls as he continued his descent. Every time a new torch flickered into life, it magnified his silhouette on the walls that shrouded the auger-like staircase – the whole effect was very eerie.

Finally, he reached the foot of the stairs. The view ahead was obscured by complete darkness. He stepped slightly to the left and looked behind to see Eliza disembark the final step. There was a huge bear-like shadow expanding across the wall that almost swallowed the feeble light that the lanterns cast, then Axis came into view, closely followed by Maven who was muttering incoherently to himself, it seemed like he was lost in thought. As soon as he stepped off of the final stair, his mind sprung back to the present.

"Ah, a little light is in order methinks." With that, he stretched his hands high above his head, rubbed them together and then, bringing them down in front of his chest he clasped his hands tightly and then flung his arms out in front. Once they were at their full extension, he unclasped his hands. All of a sudden, the area that they were standing in was bathed in a tremendous light. Maven looked at Eliza and Alex and smiled, their faces were agog. He certainly seemed to have a flair for the dramatic.

They were standing in a huge circular room. Alex noticed straight away that the whole perimeter of the room had elaborate looking bookcases that were stocked floor to ceiling with books. Each bookcase was partitioned by intricately carved figures. On the left of each bookcase there was a carving of what appeared to be a human and on the right, there was a carving of an animal of some description. This pattern seemed to repeat itself around the entire room. Alex looked on in awe, how such an incredible room could be located underneath the gnarled tree that they had entered not twenty minutes earlier, boggled his mind. There was more; instead of the dirt floor that he had expected, he noticed that it was covered in huge tiles that appeared to be some kind of marble-like material. They were a very deep crimson colour and the lustre on them, coupled with the light, made it look like a red mist was swirling around under their very feet.

"I welcome you all to my humble home," said Maven. "Please take a seat." Alex was pleased to hear this offer because, as fantastic as the floor looked, it was very disorientating.

He and Eliza both sunk into an extremely comfortable sofa. Axis sat on Alex's right in a huge high-backed chair and Maven pulled a chair across and sat so that he was opposite them all. He stared intently at Alex and Eliza, stroking his beard, and then he said, "Okay, what has Axis told you? How much do you know?" Alex and Eliza turned and looked at each other; neither seemed sure what to say. There was silence. Maven drummed his fingers on the arms of his chair and then took out a pocket watch; he flipped the lid open and stared absent-mindedly at it for a few seconds. "By Ignius! Look at the time! You are both about to enter into your thirteenth year. First things first, I need to apply the protective mark to you both."

"What do you mean?" asked Alex.

"I assume that Axis explained that you would be easier to track once you turned thirteen and that he needed to get you to me before this happened?" Alex nodded. "When a child of Ignius Novus turns thirteen, there is an energy, an aura that starts to emanate from them. This aura is indicative of their ability to morph. You may have felt some early onset effects of this, a tingling or stinging sensation in the arms, especially around this area." Maven pointed to the mole clusters or as Axis had explained earlier, the Hindrex that they both had on their forearms. Eliza and Alex, thinking back to their experience in their English class earlier in the day, both looked knowingly at one another. Maven continued, "A hunter can sense this aura from one hundred yards. The protection that I am about to apply will all but stifle this, though if a hunter is very close by, he or she will still be able to sense it.

"I have so much to tell you both, but first I must apply the mark. This will also fully remove the Hindrex, thus giving you the ability to morph."

Maven turned around and started to rummage inside a huge trunk. He turned back to Eliza and was holding a small, clear pot with a red powder inside. He smiled and said, "Right, my dear, please can you roll up your sleeve?"

Eliza looked very uneasy; she looked in turn at Alex and then Axis. "No need to look so concerned," said Axis calmly. "Maven and I are your sworn protectors. Your safety is paramount to us."

This seemed to calm her somewhat and she turned back to Maven who was still smiling. She rolled up the sleeve on her right arm and held it out in front of her. Maven took the lid off of the powder and dipped his finger inside. With his other hand he held Eliza's wrist and gently turned her arm over. Then with his powder-coated finger, he drew an elaborate symbol on her forearm that surrounded the mole cluster. "This will sting a little," he said. "You might want to close your eyes and grit your teeth." She did as instructed.

Still holding Eliza's forearm, Maven wiggled the fingers rapidly on his other hand and then proceeded to make a closed fist and then open his hand. Alex looked on and noted that Maven repeated this process exactly thirteen times, slowly at first, until he reached ten. The last three hand movements were so rapid, it was almost a blur. On the thirteenth fist clench, Maven drew his hand up. Alex could see that Maven's entire palm was glowing a bright orange colour. He then placed his open palm on the mark that he had made with the red powder on Eliza's forearm. Eliza immediately flinched and she had a pained grimace on her face. Maven started to chant incoherent words and as he spoke, he appeared to press down harder on the mark. Eliza strained against the pain that she was feeling.

Alex, seeing that she was in pain shouted, "That's enough! You're hurting her!" Maven seemed not to hear, and continued with the ritual. Eliza started to cry out. "Stop!" Alex roared. He lunged to try and remove Maven's hand but felt himself being pulled back down. Axis was restraining him.

"Don't worry, it will be over in a moment," he assured Alex. "It is imperative that Maven complete this and that he is not interrupted. If you break his concentration, it could cause a lasting negative effect on her."

Alex was still uncertain but he sat back down and looked on nervously. Maven continued to chant for a few moments longer and then opened his eyes and removed his hand from Eliza's forearm. She still had her eyes closed and was biting her bottom lip. "It's over, Eliza, you can open your eyes."

Eliza's eyelids fluttered slightly and then she opened her eyes. She looked at her forearm and saw a bright orange glow slowly fade away. After a few seconds, all she could see was the faint outline of the strange mark that Maven had made – the mole cluster or Hindrex, was gone.

"Here, take a sip of this," Maven was holding out a small silver flask. "It's Leirix."

Eliza took the flask and drank as instructed. The liquid took effect immediately. She smiled and handed the flask back to Maven.

"Right, Alex. Your turn."

Reluctantly, Alex held out his forearm and Maven repeated the ritual.

7.

Many Happy Returns

Alex watched the glowing mark fade as he handed the silver flask back to Maven.

"Now let me take a look at that wound," said Maven as he shuffled his way between Eliza and Alex to get to Axis. So much had happened in the last few hours that Alex had completely forgotten that Axis had a nasty bite that he had bound with the sleeve of his school jumper.

Maven started to remove the bandage.

"Arrgh! That's a nasty looking wound." He looked Axis in the eye. "Canly?" Axis nodded. "From a nasty character," mused Maven. "I have some Derma Regen around here somewhere." He wandered off towards a large piece of furniture that seemed to have hundreds of drawers all over it. "Now let me see," his finger scanned across a number of drawers. "Ah yes, this is the one." There was a clinking of glass as he opened one of the drawers. He was holding a glass jar as he made his way back over to Axis. It seemed to have a substance inside it that closely resembled honey. Maven surveyed the wound once more, unscrewed the lid, put his hand inside and scooped out a full handful of the 'honey', which he then proceeded to apply to the wound. Axis didn't even flinch as Maven worked this vigorously into the affected area, but judging by how close to the bone the wound was, the pain must have been almost unbearable. Maven then wrapped a bandage around the wound. "I think we'll leave that to work for a few hours," he surmised.

He then flicked open his pocket watch once more.

"Many happy returns! You are now both officially thirteen years old."

"Happy birthday to you both," said Axis. Eliza and Alex thanked them.

"Ah, that reminds me, I have something for you both," said Maven. He wandered back over to the large trunk that had held the red powder and started to rummage around. After a few minutes he returned. "Here we are, Eliza, this belonged to your mother." He held out a beautiful necklace with a locket attached. Eliza took it and thanked him. She opened the locket and saw a picture of a man and a woman smiling with a young child, who was maybe three years old, sat between them. They all looked so happy.

"That is your mother and father and I'm sure you can guess who the young girl is?"

"Me," said Eliza.

"Correct," said Maven. "I believe that this picture was taken about a month before the acci…" Maven stopped himself. "Oh, I assume that Axis explained what happened?" Eliza nodded, looking as if she were about to cry. "Your parents loved you beyond measure, my dear, they would have been so very proud of the fine young woman that you have grown into." She forced a smile and continued to stare at the picture inside the locket.

Maven continued, "Your Guardian, Aurora Astell managed to collect that from your mother's belongings before Kessler fell to ruin and she gave it to me for safekeeping." Eliza continued to stare at the picture, completely lost in thought.

Maven then turned his attention to Alex. "This belonged to your father." He held out a silver pocket watch. Alex took it from him and began to examine it. There was an engraving on the outer casing of a falcon with its wings spread and it seemed to be clutching the top of a huge crystal in its talons. By one of its wings and facing inwards there was what appeared to be a lion and by the other wing, again facing inwards was a horse. They were also clutching the huge crystal from either side.

"That is your family crest, Alex," confirmed Maven as he pointed at the engraving. Alex gave an impressed nod and then proceeded to open the lid. The dial was nothing short of astounding. The watch face was pearlescent, with four beautifully crafted silver hands. There were also gems in place of some of the numbers. Where the twelve should have been on a traditional watch was a yellow gem, instead of a three, there was a green gem, instead of the six, there was a blue gem and instead of the nine, was an orange gem. Finishing the watch off in the centre was a larger red coloured gem. The light hitting the centre seemed to create a myriad of different colours. This truly was one of the most impressive looking things that Alex had ever seen.

Alex continued to look the watch over and noticed a picture on the inside of the lid. There was a man and a woman with a small boy sat on their laps. They all looked very happy. Even in the picture, the man exuded a sense of importance. The woman was truly beautiful, her smile radiated from the picture and her deep blue eyes were comparable to the blue gemstone that sat some four inches south of the picture. The child looked very content. "That is obviously you and your family, Alex," said Maven.

Alex continued to stare at the picture, before he said, "If this belongs to my father, why have you given it to me? He isn't dead. He should still have it."

Maven let out a deep sigh. "His mind is gone. Everything and everyone that he ever knew has been eradicated from his memories. The hold that Magissa has over him is so great that he does not even recognise himself! Axis recognised that your father's mind was failing and was able to secure this before he was banished from the city. We could not let it fall into Magissa's hands.

"It is a beautiful piece isn't it?" said Maven. Alex nodded. "It is so much more than just a simple watch though."

Alex stared at Maven with a furrowed brow. "What do you mean?"

"It is key to helping to banish Magissa and to breaking the hold that she has over your father."

Alex pondered this a moment and then asked, "It does look very impressive, but how can something like this hope to help us achieve either one of those things?"

"It is a tracking device," said Maven.

"For tracking what?" asked Alex.

"This will take some time to explain. Before I begin, let me get you both something to eat and drink."

With this, Maven wandered off deeper into the circular room and disappeared from view. When he returned, he was holding a tray that contained four goblets and a jug. "Join me over here please." Eliza, Alex and Axis stood up and walked over towards Maven. He was setting the tray onto a large table that was already set for four people and in the centre of the table, almost stretching the entire width there was a variety of different foods: bread, meat, fish, fruit and cakes.

"Please, sit down."

They all did as instructed and Maven then encouraged them all to tuck into the feast that lay before them. They all loaded up their plates and began to eat.

"Now where was I?" said Maven. He stroked his beard and looked all around the vast, windowless room almost as if he were looking for the lost thought. "Ah yes, you wanted to know what we need to track."

Eliza and Alex both nodded.

"You are familiar with the four elements of Fire, Water, Air and Earth?"

They both nodded once again.

"On Ignius Novus, the significance of these elements take on a much greater importance. In the explosion from which our world was born, a gemstone for each of the elements was created. We refer to these as the Origin Stones. The Origin Stones were imbued with the power of the element that each represent. Thousands of years ago, it was decided by the Elders of Ignius Novus that the Origin Stones would need to be housed in something that could hold their vast power in check. So the most powerful Mystics in the land were tasked with creating such a device. What they came up with was a talisman. The creator of the talisman wanted to name it after himself, but the Elders overruled this, much to the chagrin of the creator. It was decreed that it would be called the Muleta. The Muleta was fashioned in such a way so that it could contain and withstand the power of the stones. It was also decided, that to stop the power of the stones from falling into the wrong hands, the Muleta would be inextricably linked to all of our future kings and queens. The Origin Stones are the lifeblood of our world; they serve to keep everything in perfect balance. The Muleta can only be handled by the king or queen or by any of their line, any attempt by another to do so would cause the Origin Stones to break away from the Muleta and be scattered to the four corners of Igni."

Maven paused. Alex and Eliza seemed to be on the edge of their seats. Recognising this, Maven continued.

"Magissa knew of the power that the Origin Stones hold, but what she didn't know was, she couldn't touch the Muleta that houses them. Once she had a total hold over Alex's father, she attempted to take the Muleta from him. So, as a result of this we know that the stones are somewhere on Igni. This is where the watch comes in. As I said, it is a tracking device and it will aid us in locating the stones. Unfortunately, the watch doesn't tell us exactly where they are, but the secondary hands," Maven pointed at the slightly shorter hands, "will point us in the direction that we need to go and the corresponding gemstone will light up on the watch face once we are close.

"We know that Magissa is searching high and low for the stones, so far without any success. She found out the hard way that she cannot handle the Muleta, but I feel that she will use your father to carry out whatever plan she has for them. We must find them before her, or the consequences for all of Igni could be dire." Maven paused at this point and looked intently at both Alex and Eliza. "So by now you should both be starting to see your importance."

They both stared blankly, then Eliza asked, "You say that the stones have been scattered to the four corners of this world?" Maven nodded. "Then surely Magissa will have an army looking for them. How can we possibly hope to cover the ground and find these four Origin Stones before her?"

"Whoops, I should have said, it is actually five stones that we need to find," said Maven almost absent-mindedly.

"What do you mean five?" said Eliza and Alex together.

"We also need to find the Panastone. This stone sits in the centre of the Muleta. It links all of the stones together and also creates the link to your family's blood line. The Panastone is the Master Stone – the crown jewel, that can quite literally give life, and in the wrong hands, death and destruction."

"This is getting better by the moment," said Eliza.

"Is there anything else?" Alex chimed in sarcastically.

"As a matter of fact, yes there is," said Maven. "We need the Muleta; the stones are no good to us without this and vice versa."

Alex rolled his eyes.

"Where is the Muleta?" he asked, already half-expecting the response.

"I believe that it is in the king's fortress, probably locked away and under guard protection."

Alex and Eliza slumped back in their seats.

Maven lowered his voice for effect, "I appreciate that this must be very hard for you, as you have both been through so much already. I really don't want to put more pressure on you but we need your help, because without it, I fear that life as we know it will end."

8.

Derma-Morphs

"How exactly do we get into the fortress and take the Muleta?" asked Alex.

"A mixture of stealth, deception and no small amount of luck," said Maven. "But firstly we must help you to control your newly acquired abilities." In light of all of the other revelations and impossible situations that Alex had experienced in the last twenty-four hours, he had completely forgotten that he could now supposedly morph into some kind of animal.

He thought to himself, *How could I possibly have forgotten something like that?*

Maven continued, "Our race have the ability to change from our human form into an animal or animals that are linked to our overwhelming character traits. For example, Axis is loyal, so he can assume the form of a dog – albeit, an extremely large one. He is also fierce and strong, which allows him to take the form of a bear. But our emotions can also have a very strong effect on our transformations."

Maven let this sink in.

"What would I turn into and how does the transformation happen?" asked Eliza.

"It is difficult to say what you will transform into for the first time; it is more likely to be linked to the strongest emotion you are feeling at that time. When you are experienced at morphing, you can quite literally control when you change and what you change into. In terms of how the transformations happen, this is all about focus. You have to close your eyes, clear your mind and picture the change. A word of warning though, if you remain in the form of one animal for extended periods of time, that animal's traits, or in some cases, aspects of their appearance will begin to seep into your human form and character and in extreme cases, you will never be able to morph back."

Alex looked at Axis and said, "You were a dog for as long as I can remember, if what Maven is saying is correct, then surely this must have affected you?"

Axis stared at him. "We used to walk in the woods every day didn't we?" Alex nodded. "When I'd leave you under the safety of the tree, I would disappear to assume my human form for a short time. It was imperative that I changed back every day or as Maven has just mentioned, I would have run the risk of remaining in the canine form for the rest of my life."

"I'm very sorry," said Alex. "I have put you through a terrible ordeal."

"You do not need to apologise for anything, Alex. Your safety has and will always be my number one priority."

"But being in a dog's form every day must have caused some changes. I'm…"

Axis cut him off. "No more apologies. I performed my duty and I would do it again in a heartbeat. Yes, being a dog for so long has caused changes. For example, I wasn't born with black eyes. But on the plus side, I am far more good-natured than I used to be."

Axis looked deadpan as he said this; neither Alex nor Eliza quite knew how to react. After a few seconds, Axis smiled and then let out a booming laugh. Alex smiled as did Eliza and Maven. Before long, they were all laughing. After all that had happened over the course of the last day, this was some much needed levity.

After their laughter had died down Maven announced, "Tomorrow we begin your training. We will teach you how to morph and how to control what you change into. We will also formulate our plan to procure the Muleta. But now it is very deep into the night, I suggest that we all get some sleep."

Even though Alex still wanted to question Maven and Axis some more, he was exhausted and as he quickly glanced over at Eliza, he could see that she was barely able to keep her eyes open.

Maven snapped his fingers and two beds with plump pillows and mattresses appeared on either side of the huge room. Maven then gestured for them to settle down. "Dream well, my young friends," he said. As soon as their heads hit their pillows, both Eliza and Alex fell into a deep sleep.

Alex had very vivid dreams that consisted of being chased by Canly, changing into a variety of different animals, some known to him and some not. He also dreamt that the gems on the face of his father's watch lit up one after another. They then all began to flash and all of a sudden, there was a huge explosion. He awoke with a start. He looked over at Eliza's bed; she was sat upright and looked as if she had only just woken too.

"Are you okay, Alex?"

"I think so," he lied. "How are you?"

"I'm okay, I think. I am just trying to take in everything that has happened and everything that we have been told. Do you believe it all?"

"I don't know what to believe. What I do know though is that Axis has paid a price in protecting me and I trust him."

Just then Maven appeared. "Ah, good morning, you two. How did we sleep – well I hope?" They both smiled and nodded uncertainly.

"Right, up you get. Follow me; I have breakfast waiting for you."

They both followed behind as Maven led them to the part of the room where they had eaten the previous night. Due to the room being located under a tree, no natural light found its way in, though it looked different somehow.

As they approached the table they saw Axis already seated. He was removing the bandage from his arm. He smiled and wished them good morning. They returned the greeting and stared on in astonishment as Axis examined his arm. Mere hours ago, there was a huge bite mark in his arm that went almost down to the bone, now there wasn't even a trace of the nasty wound. Axis rubbed his arm and felt Eliza and Alex's eyes on him.

"Don't look so surprised, you two, this wasn't the first wound that I have ever had. Derma-Regen has come to my aid on many an occasion."

"Indeed it has," said Maven as he joined them at the table. "I am not totally sure how much of your skin is actually original." He chuckled and then said, "Right, let's eat."

They all tucked into a hearty breakfast which seemed to reenergize them all. A few minutes after they had all finished Maven stood up and said, "Okay, are you both ready to learn some new skills?"

They both nodded, but in truth neither of them was even remotely ready.

Maven led them to the foot of the spiral staircase that they had descended hours earlier.

"The Ring of Protection that surrounds the tree extends down here too, so we have to go outside to morph. We will be outside the ring, so will have to be careful. On the plus side, the patrols aren't as frequent in the daytime and where I am going to take you, we can see for a good distance around, so no one will be able to sneak up on us."

They made their way up the spiral staircase. This time Maven led the way followed by Axis, then Eliza with Alex at the rear. As they reached the top of the staircase, Axis told them all to wait inside whilst he made sure that all was safe and clear. He returned a few moments later, indicated that all was well and beckoned for them all to step outside. It was a clear and sunny day. As there was very little tree cover in the clearing, the sun streamed in. They all raised their hands in front of their eyes to shield themselves from its radiance. Alex, who was never a big fan of the sunshine, seemed to struggle with this more than any of them. He continued to squint and cow from the sun long after the others had grown accustomed to it.

"This way, follow me," called Maven, who was incredibly nimble for a person of advancing years. They all fell into step behind Maven with Alex at the rear, still struggling with the pesky sunlight. After a short while, they were back under heavy tree cover, Alex in particular was grateful for this. As they followed Maven deeper into the forest, Alex noticed that there was no longer any kind of discernible path. They were starting to have to battle their way through thick roots and rough undergrowth that was growing continually thicker. The further they walked, the thicker it became. Just when Alex thought that they would need a machete to be able to go any further, Maven broke off to the right and as they followed, they noticed that they had just picked up a new path. As they progressed, it quickly became obvious that the path was starting to climb upward. They continued on. Alex noticed that the tree cover was starting to thin out, but to his relief, the sun was now obscured by cloud cover. Axis had remained very quiet for the entire journey. As they walked, his head was slowly moving from side to side, scanning the entire area. He reminded Alex of a character in a film that he had once seen. He chuckled to himself as he pictured Axis in the place of the actor.

Finally, they reached the top of the hill. As Alex and Eliza caught their breath, it was sucked right back out of their chests. The view that met them was beyond spectacular! They could see for miles! In front of them were a group of hills that snaked their way to the left and then out of sight. A good distance away and to their right, there was a range of mountains. Even though they themselves were high up, the mountains seemed to extend ever upward, until their peaks were lost in the clouds. They looked down to their left, they could see treetops for miles and miles, this green ocean stretched as far as they could see. Looking ahead again and down into the valley, there was a huge body of water that was so blue and clear, Alex could have sworn that even from this height, he could see almost to the bottom. When the intermittent sunlight shone upon the water, it looked like an endless pit of gems twinkling and reflecting back at them.

This all seemed strangely familiar to Alex.

Maven and Axis had remained quiet whilst Alex and Eliza had surveyed the view; they did, however, exchange the occasional look and smile when they saw the astonished reactions on both of their faces. Maven decided that it was time to further educate. He cleared his throat, "Ahem." Eliza and Alex both turned to look at him. "So what do you make of your lands, your home?"

They both looked at each other, but could not seem to find any words. Finally Eliza managed to find a, "Wow!" and Alex summoned up a, "Great!"

"Now for a geography lesson," said Maven. "This area that we are atop is known as the Cragon Hills." He stretched his hand out in front of him and guided it across the area that the hills covered. As they followed the sweep of Maven's hand, they could see rocky outcroppings on the hilltops as they stretched off into the distance. Alex thought to himself that it looked like a huge dormant monster; the rocks were like spines poking up out of its back.

"Now, over here," Maven pointed to their left, "we have the Ensing Forest. This area is so vast that no one knows where it ends as it has not been completely mapped."

Maven allowed them to take in this information for a moment before regaining their attention. "Now if we look down into the valley," Maven pointed to the beautiful clear blue water, "you will see Lake Ancora." The lake stretched for miles and miles, way beyond the horizon. "Now if you look to the left of the lake," he pointed, "just there you will see a place that will interest you in particular, Eliza. That is Kessler, your true home." Eliza stepped forward slightly and looked on. From this distance, it looked like a model village, the buildings were so tiny. "The large building in the back is where you were born and where you spent the first three years of your life." She looked at the building that was partially obscured by the alcove in the Cragon Hills. It was much bigger than any of the other buildings and even at this distance she noticed that it seemed to house a large amount of windows.

"Why are there so many windows?" she asked.

"We as a people are one with nature; your home was designed with nature in mind. It allows for a panoramic view of the beauty that you see before you," said Maven.

Eliza felt an almost overwhelming urge to go there right away.

"What is it like?" she asked.

"What it is like now is a shadow of its former self," said Maven solemnly. "It was once such a happy place, so full of life. There was never any trouble or conflict between its inhabitants, everyone co-existed in perfect harmony. But with Aldar Molia overseeing Kessler and basically doing Magissa's bidding, it has become a cold, soulless place. Between them, they look to break the spirits of all the inhabitants of both Kessler, Arcamedia and beyond."

"To what end?" she asked.

"You want my opinion?" asked Maven. She nodded. "Enslavement! When the spirit is crushed and all hope is gone, people will accept their fate. This makes them more pliable and less likely to rebel against Magissa's rule, makes them more compliant." He had a look of utter disgust on his face as he said this.

Even though she didn't have any memory of Kessler, Eliza felt a wave of sadness hit her. She opened the locket and looked at the picture of her parents and of her younger self. She wished she had known them, had known a life with them.

Maven walked over to her and took her hand. He looked her in the eye. "We will see the real Kessler again, my dear. As long as we have you and Alex, we all have hope. When the time is right, everyone will be made aware of your return and it will be hope rekindled."

This seemed to console her, she smiled and thanked Maven.

Maven, feeling that his work with Eliza was done for now, turned and walked over to Alex.

"Right, my boy, if you look over to the right, we have the Monolithic Mountains. They are as treacherous as they are spectacular; many a soul has been lost to those mountains. Now, if you take your gaze to the west of this point you will see..."

"Arcamedia?" said Alex.

"Yes. Your true home," said Maven.

"Our home," said Axis as he stepped forward. "It has been many years since I was last there." He had a faraway look in his eyes; he seemed completely lost in thought.

Alex stared in awe at the gigantic city that looked as if it were partially carved into the face of the mountain. Then his mind took him back to the daydreams that he experienced and he realised right there and then that they were in fact, more like visions, as this was a carbon copy of what he had seen in his mind on so many occasions.

It was virtually opposite Kessler, but held a more elevated position. There was a huge bridge that spanned Lake Ancora. This was obviously the road link between the two cities. Arcamedia itself was like a huge cake of many layers. It was extremely wide at the bottom and gradually narrowed as the city rose. Each level had houses and other buildings. For every layer, these increased in grandeur. Then at the very top was a fortress that words could scarcely describe. The lower part of it had a walled area that circled its entire perimeter; this gave it the effect of being separate from the rest of the city. In fact from Alex's vantage point, it almost looked as though it were floating above the rest of the city. It had many spires, (Alex counted eighteen in total) all of differing heights. The focal point of the entire fortress was three huge spires that shot skyward. The central one was the tallest with a slightly shorter one flanking both its left and right hand side. It looked like a gigantic trident, breaking out of the ground, being held aloft by some unseen deity.

"It's impressive isn't it?" said Maven.

Alex nodded, "Intimidating as well."

"The intimidating air is the work of Magissa. There wasn't a wall when your mother and father ruled. Although they are royalty, they saw themselves as normal people and as such, they wanted to intermingle, not segregate."

Maven had a nostalgic look in his eyes. "Oh you should have seen the city in its pomp, life was so good. Yes people worked hard, but they also had such fun. Now the oppression of Magissa makes it all feel like a distant memory." Maven looked sombre as he said this.

Alex didn't quite know how to respond to this so decided that it was time to ask a question that neither Axis nor Maven had yet addressed.

"Where exactly are we? Where is Ignius Novus?"

Maven looked at Axis, who met his eye and nodded. Maven gestured for them all to sit. They duly obliged.

"Ignius Novus is basically an alternative Earth. An unspoilt Earth." Alex and Eliza looked at one another but remained silent.

Maven continued, "Igni exists within a different timeline to the Earth that you called home for the last ten years. It is a version of an Earth that has not been ravaged by overpopulation and industry. A version of Earth that has not become consumed and over-reliant on technology. A version of Earth where nature is of the utmost importance and as such has been allowed to thrive, not torn down every time it hampers so called progress.

"This is another reason, if one were needed, why Magissa cannot have access to the power of the Muleta. She would look to create a world where freedom of choice no longer exists, a world where she could completely control the population. She would look to rip down anything that is held in higher esteem than her. As such, she would certainly destroy all that you see before you. The beauty would be gone."

Both Alex and Eliza remained silent as they tried to take in what they had just heard. Maven was correct, it was all so beautiful and unspoilt; for the most part, so unlike the place that they had called home for the last ten years.

Eliza was suddenly overwhelmed by sadness. Alex put his hand on her shoulder, and as she looked up at him, he could see tears in her eyes. He strained to prevent tears forming in his own eyes. The damage that Magissa had done to their homes and their families and the thought that she would try to use the power of the Muleta and the Origin Stones to further drive a stake into this beautiful place seemed to trigger something deep within each of them.

Alex was suddenly filled with a fire, he wanted to act. He wanted to bring back the times that Maven had just eulogised. He wanted to prevent Magissa from adding to the damage that she had already done.

Eliza pulled herself together as she felt her resilience of old start to course through her veins. She wanted to preserve the beauty that was all around her and she wanted to free her city from the evil that occupied it – stifled it.

"We are ready," said Alex.

"Please teach us all that we need to know in order to help overthrow Magissa," said Eliza.

Maven and Axis smiled and nodded. They had succeeded in awakening the inherent spirit that they knew existed in both Eliza and Alex. Great trials and battles lay ahead, but they now knew that the future king and queen of Ignius Novus were ready for all that they were about to face.

Maven led them back down the side of the hill a short way. Here they still had a good view of everything around them, but they would be more sheltered from any prying eyes.

"I am glad that you are ready, because your training starts now," said Maven. "I must warn you, it will not be easy, we will push you to your very limits."

"Are you prepared to do all that we say, without question?" boomed Axis.

"We are ready!" they both bellowed defiantly.

"Good. Then let us begin," said Maven.

9.

Time for Change

"As you are now both of age, we will teach you how to morph," said Maven.

"Normally, you only have the ability to turn into one creature until you are eighteen, but because you are both of royal extraction, this restriction does not apply. What you transform into the first time will give us a strong indication of the level of control you have and how much work we are going to have to put into that particular aspect. For example, if fear is your overwhelming emotion, you will turn into something timid. If it is anger, you will turn into something fierce that you will probably struggle to contain. What we are looking for is control over your emotions. If you have control, you will turn into a creature that is most closely associated to your personality traits. Axis will demonstrate."

Axis composed himself, closed his eyes and a few seconds later, a brilliant white glow consumed him. Alex and Eliza both shielded their eyes from the blinding light. Once it had faded, instead of Axis the man, there stood Axis the dog. Another blinding light and there was Axis in the form of a bear. For effect, he climbed onto his hind legs and let out a roar. Even though they knew that it was Axis, both Alex and Eliza backed up a few foot. He went back down on all fours and after being shrouded again by the bright white light, he was once again Axis the man.

"You made that look easy," said Alex.

"Does it hurt?" asked Eliza nervously.

"It doesn't hurt, but the sensation will feel – unusual," said Axis. He looked over at Alex. "No, it isn't easy. It will take years of focus to be able to morph into the exact creature that you want, at the exact time."

"Okay, who wants to go first?" asked Maven. "Eliza?"

Eliza looked very uncertain as she stepped forward. "Okay, my dear, deep breath, close your eyes and clear your mind. Now I want you to focus on the transformation. I want you to envision stepping outside of your human form and into that of an animal. This will feel strange, almost like an out of body experience."

Alex looked on, transfixed on Eliza. She appeared to be in a trance-like state. All of a sudden, a dull purple glow started to form around her.

"Well done," said Axis. "You are doing fantastically."

"Maintain your focus," said Maven.

The purple glow around her increased in strength and within moments, she was lost from view. Alex shielded his eyes as the light reached its peak. He lowered his hands as the glow began to diminish. To his astonishment, in place of Eliza was a beautiful dog with a long, golden coat.

"Well done, Eliza, such fantastic control for one so young," said Maven.

Axis began to clap his hands and Alex joined in. Maven then walked up to Eliza and patted the side of her neck. He led her towards a nearby stream and as she looked into the water, she saw the form she had taken. She reared back in surprise, but a combination of all three of them managed to calm her down.

"Now, a return to the more familiar Eliza methinks. Close your eyes; clear your mind again and focus on returning to your human form."

She did as instructed, and before long, she was bathed in the purple glow. It peaked and as it died away, there standing before them was Eliza. Alex ran over to her and gave her a congratulatory hug. This took him by surprise, as displays of affection, public or otherwise, were not his forte.

"You were great, well done. How did it feel?" Alex asked.

"It felt strange and fantastic all at the same time."

"Your turn, Alex. Can you top Eliza?" Maven asked with a mischievous glint in his eye.

Alex assumed the same position as Eliza had done moments earlier. He closed his eyes, cleared his mind and began to focus. He could hear Maven's voice telling him to envision the change, but it was distant and muffled, almost as if he was shouting at him from across a field. All of a sudden, a strange sensation started to course through his entire body. He felt as though he was being gently lifted off of the ground and floating in suspended animation. Then everything turned green and he was back on the ground with Maven, Axis and Eliza who were all congratulating him.

"Well done. It seems that we have another natural in our midst, Axis," said Maven.

Alex looked up as Maven guided him away. He looked extremely tall to Alex. *Am I on my hands and knees?* he thought to himself.

As Maven had done with Eliza, Alex was led to the side of the stream. Alex stepped forward and looked into the makeshift mirror. Staring back at him was a large dog, nowhere near as large as Axis, but very similar in appearance, nonetheless. He moved his face closer to the water, very confused to see a dog's reflection staring back at him, the only thing that was familiar to him were his blue eyes.

This was all very surreal.

Maven led him away from the stream and back to the same spot that he had been standing a few minutes earlier. He then talked him through the process of reverting back to his human form. Alex felt the same sensation of floating upward. It went completely dark and silent; it felt as though he were inside a sensory deprivation tank. Then all of a sudden, his whole world lit up in a green light and then he was on the ground again, looking at his three companions from a more familiar vantage point.

Eliza ran towards him, a beaming smile on her face. She hugged him and kissed him gently on the cheek, "Well done," she whispered.

Alex felt fantastic. He wasn't sure whether it was the successful transformation, the kiss, or a combination of the two.

"That's enough for today," said Maven. "You have done superbly, but we do not want to overdo it, besides we need to get back and discuss strategy."

They all started to walk back, their spirits high. They didn't notice but in a nearby tree sat a large raven; it had been silently watching them for some time. It continued to watch them as they headed back into the area of thick undergrowth. Once they had disappeared from view, the raven took flight and headed in the direction of Arcamedia.

****

Dusk was setting in by the time Eliza, Alex, Maven and Axis had made it back to the clearing and passed through the Ring of Protection. They made their way down the spiral staircase into Maven's amphitheatre of a room. As before, Maven performed his elaborate gesticulations and the huge room was bathed in light. He asked them all if they were hungry to which they all replied with a resounding 'yes' and within moments, there was another feast laid out on the table awaiting them.

They all sat around the table and prepared to tuck into the food.

"We need a name," proclaimed Maven.

"What do you mean a name?" asked Alex.

"You know a name. We are a team; we have a common goal that we need to achieve. We need a name."

Alex thought back to the name of sports teams from back on Earth: *Hotspur, Rovers*. Derma-morph United crossed his mind, but that was just stupid.

Maven was becoming more and more animated. "Come on, people, ideas. Throw out some ideas."

Axis seemed a little annoyed. "What does it matter, Maven. Let's eat!"

"Not yet! We must have a name for our collective." Maven stroked his beard and began to pace. He then started to mutter to himself.

Eliza, who had been thinking quietly to herself throughout, finally spoke. "Well, we are all connected and have the same purpose which makes us kindred spirits I guess. So what about – The Kindred?"

Maven stopped pacing and stared at her.

"What did you say, my dear?"

Eliza could feel all of their eyes on her and suddenly felt uncertain. "It doesn't matter, it was silly really."

"No I'm sure it wasn't. We'd all like to hear it. Wouldn't we?" Both Axis and Alex nodded.

"Well, I thought that we could be called The Kindred," she said shyly.

Maven looked at Axis and then at Alex. He then turned back to Eliza, a huge smile on his face.

"Fantastic! We are The Kindred." Axis and Alex nodded approvingly.

"That was cleverly conceived, my dear. Well done."

Eliza smiled coyly.

"Now can we eat?" said Axis disgruntledly.

"Oh alright, Axis!" came Maven's impatient response. "Alex was right, you were a dog for too long, you are always thinking of your stomach. You'll be wanting a walk afterwards I suppose?"

Axis fixed him with a hard stare but then smiled and laughed as he began to load his plate with food.

They were all very animated as they tucked into their food. They discussed all that had happened during the course of the day. A strong bond had already formed between the four of them. Little did they know, but this would soon be tested to its limit.

****

The raven passed over the clear blue waters of Lake Ancora as it approached Arcamedia. Three thunderous beats of its wings allowed it to alter its trajectory. The huge black bird arrowed its way towards the fortress. No people or animals were visible and most of the homes had their windows shuttered. Magissa had imposed a curfew on the city. Anyone caught out after dark without her authorization would suffer severe punishment. Many of the residents spent most of their time inside, it just wasn't worth risking Magissa's ire. The raven was now flying over some of the lower spires of the fortress. It seemed to be making a beeline for the central and largest tower. The raven flew through a window and into a well-lit room. As soon as it had passed through the open window, there was a red flash. The raven was gone and in its place stood a man. He was in his late teens and dressed completely in black. He was of medium build with long, greasy black hair that stuck to his shoulders, seemingly clinging on for dear life. He had cold black eyes, like those of a shark and to the side of his left eye he had a long scar that stretched down the side of his face and disappeared somewhere under his chin. He exuded an arrogance that you could cut with a knife.

"Mother!" he shouted out. "Mother! Where are you?" His voice sounded sickeningly obedient. He scanned the room. "I have some information that will be of interest to you." He walked over to a table in the corner of the room and fixed himself a drink. He gulped it back and then fixed another. He started to turn around ready to call out to his mother again, but as he turned, a stern looking woman was already standing there. The man was startled and dropped his drink.

"Sorry, Mother, I didn't realise that you were there."

Magissa Veil was a tall, thin woman with jet black hair that was pulled back so tight that it seemed to be pulling her facial features higher up her face than they should be. She had a very pale, gaunt complexion that only served to accentuate her cold, green eyes. They say a person's eyes are the windows to their soul, well if that was the case, Magissa Veil did not possess one. Everything about her was emotionless – rigid. The way she spoke, the way she looked and even the way she moved.

"Clean that up, you fool!" she hissed. The disdain in her voice was evident. "What information do you have for me?"

Varios Veil finished cleaning up his mess and then apologised once more.

"I'm sorry, Mother."

"Yes, yes, yes, just tell me what you know and then be on your way."

"I was on the edge of the Ensing Forest, near the Cragon Hills this afternoon and I saw that crackpot Mystic, Maven."

"Maven! He is of no concern to us; he hides away in the forest. He lost his mind right about the same time as his king." She looked towards another room as she said this and her lips curled slightly at the edges and formed the most sinister of smiles. "This isn't news. If there is nothing more, then be on your way."

She started to walk away.

"He wasn't alone," said Varios.

Magissa stopped in her tracks and her smile faded away.

"What do you mean he wasn't alone?"

"He was with the exile."

"Axis!" she spat. "It couldn't have been, Canly disposed of him back on that overpopulated rock that he was hiding on."

"No it was definitely him; he is not someone that I would quickly forget." He traced his finger down the entire length of his scar as he said this.

"Axis," she said more to herself than Varios. "Your loyalty to your king and your city is noble, but it will ultimately be your downfall."

"There is more, Mother."

Magissa glared at him, her pale complexion reddening slightly.

"More?"

Varios stared at her; he could see that what little patience she possessed had petered away. He backed up slowly.

"Well?" she asked impatiently.

"There were… er… two others with them."

"Who?" she demanded.

"A boy and a girl." Varios cowered as he said this, almost as if he were expecting something to be thrown in his direction.

But Magissa did not launch anything; she just stood there, seemingly processing what she had just heard.

"It cannot be!" she hissed. "Ah, Axis, you must think yourself very clever. You did a good job protecting them while they were worlds away, but now you bring them here, to the devil's front door. Maybe you aren't so clever after all."

"Who are they, Mother?" asked Varios.

"The boy is the king's son and the girl is heir to Kessler. Axis has obviously brought them here so they can try and claim their birthright. We cannot let the Arcamedians or the Kesslerites know of their existence. They are all but drained of hope because, as far as they know, both of them are dead and it must stay that way. In fact, we must make it a reality."

Varios nodded along with his mother's last sentence, a sinister smile adorning his face.

"What can I do?" asked Varios.

"Nothing right now. Tomorrow we will send out additional patrols to bring them all before me. But for now, I have things to do – leave me."

Varios bowed and made his way out of the room.

Magissa looked on, lost in thought as Varios disappeared from view. She had convinced herself that by taking control of Cordium, the subsequent banishment of Axis and the removal of any who hadn't sworn obedience to her, she had eliminated any threat to her and her claim to the throne. Locating the Origin Stones was the toughest task that had stood before her, but with no one to rival her, she knew that she had time on her side. But now that the exile had returned with the king's son and the heir of Kessler in tow, this could complicate matters.

As she considered the ramifications of this and began to plot her next move, her mind drifted off to a place that she hated it to go. She looked visibly pained as her mind conjured up the image of a pretty, young girl. The girl was walking in the woods with her family who were all besotted with the beauty and nature around them. The girl could not understand their infatuation. "It's just a tree. What's so special about it?" Her mother and father looked at her, openly hurt that she didn't share their love of the greenery that surrounded them.

"Now, my dear, you may think it is only a tree but it is a beautiful living thing. Were there no trees, there would not be any people or creatures," her father chided.

"Would you really want a world without either?"

The young girl did not respond. But the idea of this seemed to awaken something in her. She had never really considered before that the removal of something would have an effect on something else. The type of smile that one would not associate with one so young, crept across her face. She couldn't explain it, but the idea of controlling the fate of a species, really appealed to her.

The voice of her mother pulled her away from her thoughts. "I don't understand. Why would the thought of that cause you to smile? Why can't you accept and enjoy this like the rest of us, Margaret?" She pointed to herself, her father, as well as a young boy and girl, who were both a few years older than the young girl.

"I despair of you, I really do."

Margaret, oh how she hated that name, she could feel an anger starting to build within her. She glowered at her perfect brother and sister. All her life, she had struggled within the dynamic of her family. She had always been jealous of her brother and especially of her sister. Their similarities to her mother and father saw to it that they received all of the love and affection. In her opinion, she was not even an afterthought.

She did not have a single thing in common with any of them, in fact she hated all that they loved and right at this particular moment, she hated each and every one of them.

"Well maybe it would be best if I were no longer part of this family!"

"Margaret! How could you say that?" cried her mother.

"Easily! I hate you all! I wish that I was no longer part of this family!"

"You should be careful what you wish for, young lady. It may just come true," her father warned as he tried to console his distraught wife.

"That's good! I want it to come true! I want to be with a family who will let me be me. I wish it to be true!"

Magissa no longer looked in pain; she now had a familiar reptilian smile painted on her face. As she looked back on it now, this really was the turning point in her life.

Not too long after this revelation to her family, she had been 'taken' and her new life, the life that she had wished for, began.

****

The Kindred had just finished their meal and had now moved into another part of Maven's huge room.

Maven walked in carrying some large rolled up pieces of parchment.

"Before we turn in for the evening, we must discuss our plan to obtain the Muleta," he said.

"Why can't we search for the stones first, harness their power and then take the Muleta from Magissa?" asked Alex.

"A good question," said Maven. "The trouble is the stones are volatile, they need to be housed in the Muleta or the damage could be catastrophic."

"If they are so volatile, then why are they not causing damage now?" asked Eliza.

"Another good question, at the moment they are dormant. When they were scattered, they will have tethered themselves to something that is an associated element. For example, the Waterstone will be in or very close to a body of water. Once we find and remove one of the stones, it will awaken and must be contained within the Muleta. The stones are all connected, so once we find the first one and it is removed from its resting place, we are against the clock."

"What do you mean?" asked Alex.

Maven looked at him and then beckoned all three of them over as he began to unfurl the smaller of the two parchments that he was holding and laid it down on the table. Eliza and Alex moved in for a closer look but the light was poor, so they couldn't really make out what they were looking at and then it grew darker still as Axis appeared behind them. His huge frame cast a shadow across the parchment and seemingly, the entire room. Maven rolled his eyes and glared at Axis. Looking slightly flustered, he held up his right hand and rubbed his thumb and index finger together, it looked almost as if he were playing the world's smallest violin. All of a sudden, just the right amount of light for them all to see clearly radiated down from above their heads.

The entire perimeter of the parchment was covered in strange symbols that neither Eliza nor Alex understood. On the left-hand side of the page were drawings of four identically sized gemstones. One was yellow, one was green, one was blue and the last was orange. There was writing and a symbol under each one that told the reader which colour represented which element.

Just to the right of the four gemstones was a much larger gem. This one was red and had the word 'Pana' beneath it. Underneath the pictures of the gemstones, there was a picture of an ornate, platinum medallion. It was circular with symbols around its circumference, similar to those that adorned the edges of the parchment. If you imagined the medallion as a compass face, there were small circular grooves cut into it at the points north, east, south and west. Platinum braid linked the points together and this created a diamond shape on the outer edges of the medallion. In the centre was a much larger circular groove and at the same compass points, more platinum braid created a cross symbol that linked this larger circle to each of the smaller ones around it. This was quite clearly an illustrative depiction of the Muleta and it was impressive to behold.

Maven turned to look at them all. "So here are the element gemstones – the

Origin Stones." He pointed to the four smaller gems. He then pointed to the larger stone. "This is the Panastone." He then scrolled his finger down the page and pointed to the platinum medallion. "This is the Muleta which houses and contains the power of the five gems." He then explained their positions within the Muleta. "Yellow represents Air and it goes here." He pointed to the north point. "Green represents Earth and it goes here." He pointed to the east point. "Blue represents Water and sits here." He pointed to the south point. "Finally, orange represents Fire, which goes here." He pointed to the west point. He then pointed to the larger red gemstone. "This is the Panastone which sits in the centre. What you need to understand is these stones are all linked magically," to emphasise this he traced his finger around the platinum braid that joined all of the points together. "The stones were by-products when our world was created so they are also linked organically. When we remove the first stone, the next stone on the Muleta will activate. For example, if we were able to find the Airstone first, then the Earthstone would awaken. So we would have to focus all of our efforts on finding this next, because if we don't, the unchecked stone could cause untold devastation."

"Why would this happen? I thought that these stones were about life and balance?" said Eliza.

"They are," said Maven. "But without the Panastone and Muleta, the balance does not exist. Wherever they are now, they are dormant, in a symbiotic trance with their associated element."

"Why don't we leave them wherever they are then?" said Alex. "We can focus our efforts on taking down Magissa. Surely if she is not around to find them, then everything is safer this way?"

"Two very important reasons. Firstly, we need the power that the stones bestow to overthrow Magissa," said Maven.

"What is the other reason?" asked Alex.

"There are very few on Igni who know about the Origin Stones or the power that they hold. Consider this, if we were by some miracle, able to eradicate Magissa without the stones, then yes, they will be at one with their element and remain in their dormant state. But one day and it may be years, decades, possibly even centuries from now, what if someone unearths one of the stones? They have no idea of the need for the Muleta or the Panastone. All they see is a beautiful gem. They may turn it into a piece of jewellery, unaware that they will have inadvertently doomed the planet. There would be floods, tidal waves, hurricanes and earthquakes. Igni's very core would boil!"

Maven let all of this sink in.

"So you see that this is our only course of action. We need to liberate the Muleta from Magissa's tower and then we can set our minds and efforts on locating the gems."

"You say that we need the stones to defeat Magissa, so if she is as powerful as you say, how can we hope to be able to take the Muleta from her?" asked Eliza.

"We need to create a distraction so that Alex can enter the fortress," said Maven.

"Me!" Alex cried. "Why me?"

"Because none of us will be able to enter. Magissa is sure to have magical shielding in place, but as powerful as she is, she can't shield against one of the fortress' true occupants," said Maven.

"That is why I am certain she was responsible for your mother's death," said Axis.

"She would not have been able to shield your mother from re-entering the fortress. She would have never been able to control your father if your mother was still around. Their bond was too great."

"I don't think that I can," said Alex.

"This is not going to be a full frontal assault," said Maven. "It will be a stealth mission. If all goes to plan, Magissa will be nowhere near the fortress. We will lure her out of there and you will be able to enter undetected, obtain the Muleta and then disappear into the night."

Alex was panicking, but then thought back to his earlier transformation. "Could I morph into an insect of some kind and sneak into the fortress undetected?"

Maven looked him in the eye. "Unfortunately, it doesn't work like that. We cannot turn into just anything. It has to be something that shares a personality trait or that we have an emotional connection to: a dog, a cat, a large bird. You should not try to push the boundaries of what you morph into. It would be unwise even for the most experienced."

Axis moved over to Alex and placed a comforting hand on his shoulder.

"You are not alone in this, we will be with you."

Maven flipped open his pocket watch.

"Tomorrow night we will set this in motion. But for now, I do not want you to concern yourself, Alex. It is late and it has been a long day. We must all get some rest, for tomorrow our mission truly begins."

10.

Dogged Determination

Alex didn't sleep well at all. He kept turning everything over in his mind. When he did finally manage to drift off, his sleep was fitful, due to more vivid dreams. When he was awoken by Maven the next morning, he felt anything but refreshed.

They ate breakfast in virtual silence. As keen as they all were to begin their mission, there was also a sense of foreboding. *What if Magissa doesn't leave the fortress? What if I can't get the Muleta?* thought Alex. *It will be all over before it's even begun.*

After they had all finished their meal, Maven told them all that they were going to go out and train some more. They would come back to his home early in the afternoon to complete their preparations for the plan to call out Magissa and for Alex to gain access to the fortress and take the Muleta.

The Kindred made their way back up the now very familiar spiral staircase and out of the tree, into the daylight. The brilliant sunshine that had greeted them the previous day was today replaced by cloudy skies that threatened rain. Maven led them deeper into the Ensing Forest today rather than towards the Cragon Hills.

After a while they came to a place where the roots of the huge trees that flanked them on both sides, broke out at random points into the pathway. At some points, the roots from both sides met in the middle completely taking the path away.

Maven cleared his throat. "Right, we have established that you can morph; now we need to test your speed and agility whilst you are in your animal state. After a while the instincts and abilities of the animal that you morph into will become second nature, but early on, these instincts and abilities will need to be honed.

"The path ahead of us stretches for approximately one and a half miles, before it becomes impassable. You will both assume your canine forms and you will run to the end and back as quickly as possible. It is rough terrain and at points you are going to have to jump some distance over roots and rocks to be able to regain the path. For an added incentive, Axis will be chasing you down. He will give you a two minute head start, but keep in mind he has never been beaten on this course. This will really test your mettle." Maven had that familiar glint in his eye and a sly smirk on his face. "Any questions?" Alex and Eliza both shook their heads. "Good! Let's see how you get on."

Alex looked at the path, if you could call it that. There were so many tree roots and rocks. At some points, it looked as if the trees on each side were almost touching – was there even enough room to get through? It was a daunting prospect. It reminded Alex of an assault course on a sadistic gameshow where the contestants were sent in to be tortured and ridiculed. Would there be a fake floor that would collapse the moment it was stood upon? Or a place where some kind of ejection device would send him flying into the stratosphere?

As they had been taught twenty-four hours previously, both Alex and Eliza closed their eyes, cleared their minds and focused on the transformation. After their respective glows had diminished, there they stood in their canine forms. Maven congratulated them, as he knew that they were both nervous but had managed to keep their emotions in check and morph into the correct animal. They looked behind to see Axis morph into the huge black dog that had been Alex's companion for as long as he could remember.

Maven cleared his throat. "Are you ready?

"Go!"

Alex and Eliza both tore off the mark. The early part of the path was quite easy going, so they managed to eat up the ground in no time at all. This was so exhilarating, their nerves washed away almost immediately. Alex thought he was fast in human form, but it just did not compare. They came upon the first obstacle on the path, a set of tree roots that knitted together in a misshapen plait. It looked like a little girl's first attempt to style her own hair. They both leapt off of the ground and cleared the roots with consummate ease. Two more full extensions of their legs and rocks loomed ahead, another leap and they were clear. Another set of tree roots cleared and as soon as they landed, they immediately leapt again, to clear some more. Another clear stretch of path allowed them both to accelerate. They were level with each

~ 64 ~

other as they approached the narrow area of path that Alex had spotted before they had set off. If it were possible, it was even narrower up close. There was no way that they could pass through it side by side. Alex looked across at Eliza, who was showing no signs of slowing down. He decided that he would ease off slightly at this point and let her go through first. Eliza disappeared into the narrow opening with Alex right behind. The opening was so tight that Alex had to go down on his haunches slightly in order to get through. Once through, he took the opportunity to peer back to see where Axis was and was stunned to see that he had just cleared the last set of roots and was devouring the stretch of clear path that led to the narrow opening. With teeth bared and jowls flapping in the wind, he looked truly scary as he bore down upon them. Alex turned back around to see Eliza slaloming through some rocks that littered this part of their course. Conscious that Axis would soon be quite literally, on his tail, Alex pushed on. The path started to open out again as they approached a slight curve. They were neck and neck again as they reached its apex. They both turned at this point to see Axis gaining on them. As they turned back they could see a wall of thorns looming just ahead. This must be the end of the path.

Just before they reached the thorns, they turned and started to run the reverse of the route. They were still neck and neck, so close to each other, they could almost touch. Then they saw Axis heading straight for them. Alex was sure that he would move to the side so that he and Eliza could stay on their current line, but he was heading straight for them down the gut of the path. It was then that Alex realised that he and Eliza were two small cars playing chicken with a juggernaut. Eliza must have realised the same thing because just as they were about to collide, Alex broke left and she broke right. They barely avoided contact and such was the speed and power of Axis, they both almost got sucked backwards into his wake. They powered on and slalomed through the scattered rocks and went through the narrow opening, this time Alex was first through. They then cleared the two sets of close proximity roots and then over rocks and more roots. They now realised that they were on the home straight. Alex looked back and was surprised that he couldn't see Axis, but then he was there, flying through the air as he leapt over the last set of tree roots. As fast as they were running, Axis was gaining on them rapidly. They looked ahead and saw Maven. They were both side by side, neck and neck and there wasn't any space for Axis to pass.

They were going to make it! They were going to beat Axis! The finish line was there. Then, all of a sudden, they felt a rush of air above them and as they looked up, they saw a huge black shape airborne above them.

Axis, knowing that there wasn't a passing lane had leapt over them. He came crashing down just in front of them, kicking up some leaf debris into their faces. Without breaking stride, he crossed the finish line. Alex and Eliza were a split second behind and crossed at precisely the same time as each other. Maven was applauding and saying well done.

Alex, who was extremely competitive, thought of a few choice words that he would never actually say.

Axis morphed back to a man and Alex and Eliza morphed to their true forms.

Axis walked over to them. "That's not very sporting of you, Alex."

Alex stared, mouth wide open. "How could you hear that? I didn't say it, I just thought it."

He looked nervous. "You can't hear all of my thoughts can you?"

Axis thought he'd let Alex squirm a little, so did not say anything, he just continued to smile.

Alex was sweating and it wasn't to do with the race he'd just run. Eliza too was looking somewhat uneasy.

Maven, deciding that they had been held in suspense long enough, spoke up. "Don't worry. When you are in animal form, the part of your brain that you communicate with is split in two. When you speak, your mouth doesn't move, but your brain makes it feel as though it does. Your thoughts are still your thoughts, the only reason that Axis heard you is because there was a part of you that wanted him to hear it and hence, he did."

Alex and Eliza both looked relieved. But from that point on, they made a note to be very conscious of their thoughts when in their animal forms.

Axis then broke the silence. "Still, that was some race. You both did superbly. Don't feel too down, I have never been beaten. To your credit, nobody has ever run me that close. You should be proud."

Eliza and Alex both still felt annoyed to have been pipped at the post, but Axis' words did make them feel a little better.

"We should be heading back, we need to prepare for this evening," said Maven.

They all agreed and made their way back to the old tree that led to Maven's home.

After a short time, they reached the clearing. They were just about to enter when they heard voices.

"Get down," whispered Axis.

Maven, Alex and Eliza all did as they were told and ducked out of sight behind some thick ferns. Axis crouched down and making sure to remain in the brush, stealthily made his way to the right-hand side of the clearing. Three men all dressed in a dark blue uniform with silver trim that bore the same emblem as that on Alex's pocket watch, entered the clearing not ten foot from where Axis was crouched. They were each carrying a long staff that had a blade on one end and a metal hoop on the other. They were deep in conversation and seemed quite distracted. One was saying that he had won fair and square and that they each owed him ten pieces of silver. Before the other two could retort, their heads crashed together and they crumpled to the floor like ragdolls. Standing in their place was Axis. Confused, the remaining man turned around only to be confronted by this giant of a man. As all of this was happening, Maven had come out of hiding and was coming up behind the man. Axis looked at Maven who gave him an 'okay' signal. Axis then leant in close to the man and said, "Boo!" This wasn't what the man was expecting, but it still seemed to startle him and he fell backwards, right at the feet of Maven. Realising how foolish he looked, the man tried to regain his feet but before he could, Maven touched his temple and the man was immediately unconscious.

Eliza and Alex came out of hiding.

"Wow that was lucky," said Eliza. "If we had been a little later, they would have seen us."

"I would say fortuitous rather than lucky," said Maven.

"What do you mean?" asked Alex.

Maven motioned to the three unconscious men. "We were looking for a distraction, a ruse to get Magissa out of the fortress were we not?" Both Alex and Eliza nodded. "Well, these three will give us our opportunity."

"I still don't understand. How are they possibly going to get Magissa out of the fortress?" asked Alex.

"With the help of this." Maven rummaged in a pouch that he had attached to his belt and pulled out a clear gemstone.

"What is that?" asked Alex.

"It is called a Lepmoc Stone," said Maven. "It allows us to extract a memory and implant a new one. We will take away what they have just seen and experienced here and implant a false memory, a story that you and Eliza were seen on the outskirts of Kessler. If all goes according to plan, Magissa will be drawn out by this information, giving Alex the opportunity to enter the fortress and take the Muleta."

"Do you really think that it will work?" asked Eliza.

"I don't know," said Maven, "but it is the best chance that we have."

Maven then wandered over to the first of the three men. He held the Lepmoc Stone just in front of the man and then chanted several inaudible words. The other three members of The Kindred watched on as the clear stone began to fill with a grey mist. Maven held up the stone and watched the mist swirl around inside, it looked just like a storm was brewing inside the stone. He then held the stone close to his mouth and spoke more words that neither Eliza or Alex could make out, though they did think that they each heard their names in amongst the gibberish. The grey mist inside the stone stopped swirling and then it dissipated, leaving behind a pearlescent glow. Maven then brought the stone back in front of the man and they watched as the contents seemed to be syphoned out until it was back to its original clear state. He repeated this process with the other two men. As the mist from the stone cleared, he asked Axis to move the three men to a suitable spot, under a shady tree on the outskirts of the forest.

As they watched Axis hoist two of the men up and place one on each of his massive shoulders, Maven looked at Eliza and Alex and said, "They will wake up in a few hours with a pressing need to get back to Arcamedia and to tell Magissa of your sighting. If my instincts are correct, she will leave for Kessler as soon as she hears this news, so we need to be on the outskirts of Arcamedia, just before dusk. If my calculations are correct, Alex will have about one and a half hours to get in, find the Muleta and then get out again before she returns."

Alex was definitely starting to feel the pressure of the burden being placed upon him. He wanted to ask Maven if there was another way, another person that could go instead of him, but then he remembered the shielding and the fact that he was likely to be the only one of them who could enter the fortress.

Just then, Axis reappeared and unceremoniously dragged the last man to his feet and then slung him over his shoulder like a sack of potatoes. He walked away, disappearing from view behind a cluster of trees.

Alex picked up one of the weapons that the soldier had been carrying and studied it. The staff was approximately four foot long with a twelve inch razor sharp blade at one end and a thick metal hoop at the other. Maven approached.

"This is an unusual weapon," said Alex as he rolled it over in his hands.

"Be very careful with that," Maven warned as he took the weapon from

Alex. He pointed to the spear tip. "The purpose of this end is obvious." He then pressed a hidden button that caused the blade to retract. He spun the staff over and pointed at the metal ring. As Alex looked closer he could see that the inside of the ring was serrated. It looked like a coil of razor wire.

"This end is used to subdue, torture and control when one is in the form of an animal."

"That's inhumane," said Alex, totally disgusted.

"Indeed." Maven had a faraway look in his eyes as he threw the weapon to the ground.

Alex looked at him quizzically. Maven met his gaze and slowly removed the scarf that he always wore around his neck. There was a raw looking scar that went all of the way around and was cut deep into Maven's neck. It looked like it had only just happened.

"That looks really painful," said Alex.

"It is," said Maven. "But you do get used to it."

Alex knew immediately that Maven was downplaying the situation.

"When did it happen?" Alex asked, expecting him to say a few days ago.

"The night that you and Eliza left Igni."

Alex and Eliza, (who had since wandered over to listen to the conversation) both looked shocked.

"But that was ten years ago!" said Alex.

"That wound looks awfully fresh," said Eliza. She took a sharp intake of breath as she grimaced and recoiled slightly.

"I can assure you, it has been ten years," said Maven. "I ran interference for Axis and Aurora the night that they evacuated you. The leader of one of Magissa's patrols caught on to what was happening and tried to ambush you all. I took the form of a fox and managed to lead them away from you all long enough to allow your escape. Unfortunately, I was eventually caught and one of these awful devices adorned my neck for a good few hours." Maven stroked the scar gently.

"But how can the wound still be so fresh?" asked Alex.

"If the device isn't torturous enough, Magissa has her men rub the sap of the Scalium plant on the inside of the ring. This plant's sap basically causes the tissue to continually breakdown. The only reason that it didn't pick all of the flesh off of my neck is due to the daily application of Derma-Regen."

"But this healed Axis; surely it should do the same for you?" stated Alex, almost outraged.

"Unfortunately not," Maven conceded. "Every part of the Scalium plant is poisonous. I was exposed to its poison for far too long, thus I will have to apply Derma-Regen every single day, for the rest of my life." There was a sense of resignation in his voice.

"You must understand that Magissa is evil personified, she does not have an iota of compassion for another living thing. You are only of use to her through service and devotion. If you stand against her… he rubbed his neck again, well let's just say that I got off lightly."

Just then, Axis returned. He saw the three weapons on the floor and picked them up. He looked disgusted and at once, broke all three across his knee.

"Evil devices," he muttered.

One by one, they passed through the Ring of Protection and then disappeared into the opening of the deformed tree.

11.

Morphing and Entering

The sun was getting low in the sky as they all re-emerged from the tree opening. Since they had gone back into Maven's home earlier that afternoon, they had been over the plan one more time. Alex was still feeling nervous about everything. Maven assured him that he wouldn't have to go until they were sure that Magissa had vacated the fortress and Axis continued to reiterate the fact that he would be there for him. He would come as close to the fortress as the shielding would allow. Alex started to feel a little more at ease.

They exited the forest and were only about half a mile from Arcamedia. They made their way along a path that ran parallel to Lake Ancora.

It was almost dark as they all pressed up against the outer wall of Arcamedia. A few minutes passed, and then somewhere up ahead, they heard the creak of a huge gate opening followed by the pounding of horses' hooves speeding away. Axis morphed into an extremely large eagle owl and flew up high and in the direction of the horses. He returned a few moments later and confirmed that Magissa had indeed taken the bait.

"It is time, Alex," said Maven. "You need to change, but your dog form is no use in this situation, you need to approach from the air. I suggest an owl of some form, as your approach needs to be a silent one." Maven pointed towards the city beyond the wall. "Make for the highest accessible window on the central spire of the fortress. Good luck."

Alex closed his eyes, preparing to morph when Eliza came over to him. She squeezed his hand. "Good luck. I know that you can do this. See you soon." She released his hand and walked back over to Maven.

Alex smiled hoping that it would conceal the fear that he was feeling. He closed his eyes and cleared his mind. He then focused on where he needed to get to and the creature that would get him there. The glow surrounded him and as it died away, Alex the person was gone and hovering in his place was a large barn owl. He looked back at Eliza and Maven and then towards Axis, who was hovering just above him and then set off towards the fortress.

The experience of being a dog was one thing, but this was a whole other level. The exhilaration of being airborne was greater than anything else Alex had experienced up to this point in his young life. Gliding effortlessly above the rooftops, feeling the stroking sensation of the wind passing over and through his feathers, was a wonderful experience. A silent spectre skimming through the night sky. Alex had to refocus. He could not fully enjoy this experience; he had to concentrate on the job at hand.

He and Axis continued to drift silently above the rooftops of buildings of all shapes and sizes. They were now nearing the top level that housed the fortress behind the high perimeter wall. Alex passed over the wall but then heard a muted crash just behind him. He turned back to see Axis trying to join him on the other side of the wall, but an invisible barrier was keeping him out. He tried flying higher, but he was still being blocked.

Alex could hear Axis' voice in his head. "You need to carry on alone. I will wait for you here. Listen for my call; I'll alert you if Magissa returns."

Alex hovered, unsure of what to do next. "You can do this, Alex; I have every faith in you. If anything goes wrong though, you get out of there immediately."

Alex looked at the central spire of the fortress, there was a dim light emanating from the highest window. Silently, he flapped his wings and then like a ghost, he disappeared into the darkness.

He touched down silently on the window ledge and looked inside. The room was completely empty. He hopped off the ledge, but before he landed on the floor, he was surrounded by a red glow and then he realised that he was no longer an owl, he was back in his true form.

Magissa must have a Ring of Protection of her own making in place, he thought to himself. Unperturbed, he looked around the room all the while thinking, *If I were hiding a talisman, where would I put it?* He surveyed his surroundings. It was a large room but had very little furniture save for several high backed chairs and a small table in the corner that was home to a number of bottles, each with a different coloured liquid inside along with several drinking vessels. There was also a large fireplace that was home to a fire that was starting to die down. This was what had created the dim light that he could see when he was flying towards the window. On the far wall hung a huge tapestry that bore the same emblem as the one he had seen on his father's pocket watch – his family crest. It covered the entire wall, floor to ceiling. He looked to his left and could see a large doorway. He moved towards it and as he stepped through he found himself in a long corridor that seemed to stretch for as far as he could see. Dozens of closed doors ran parallel to one another down both sides of the corridor. *The Muleta could be in any one or indeed none of these rooms.* He started to panic. *How am I possibly going to be able to check all of these rooms before Magissa returns?* He tried to put the negative thought to the back of his mind and grabbed the handle of the first door that he came to. There was a click and the heavy wooden door opened. The hinges whined in protest as he pushed the door just far enough to allow him to enter. The light from the fire in the previous room seemed to stretch in here too. On closer inspection, he could see that the lower part of the wall had been hollowed out to allow for the fireplace from the adjacent room to extend through into this room too.

He looked around. Shelves covered two of the walls, one side housed nothing but books and the opposite wall was covered in glass vials that contained liquids of every imaginable colour as well as a variety of different coloured crystals. On the wall opposite the fireplace was a huge cushioned chair that looked like a very big, very elaborate Chez Lounge. As he approached, he noticed that there was a rolled up parchment on a table off to the side. He unrolled it and saw a picture of the Muleta and the four Origin Stones. It was similar to the information that they had looked at the previous day with Maven. He looked all over it and though he couldn't make out any of the text, he did notice that there was no illustrative reference to the Panastone. Could Magissa be unaware of this piece of the puzzle? Surely, if what Maven said was true, the Panastone would have also left the Muleta the moment that Magissa tried to take it from his father?

He pondered this whilst continuing to look around the room. Once he was satisfied that there was nothing else to be found in there, he started to make his way back to the door. As he reached for the handle he heard a noise coming from behind him that sounded like the clinking of glass. His immediate thought was that he had dislodged one of the vials on the shelf. He braced himself for the smash of glass on the hard stone floor, but it never came. As he turned around, he heard the clinking noise once again. It seemed to be coming from the elaborate chair at the other end of the room. Curiosity got the better of him and he made his way back towards the chair. Although he could still hear the clinking sound, he could not locate its source. He looked all around the chair but could not find anything so decided to look underneath. He placed his hand on the arm of the chair to steady himself, and as soon as he made contact with the chair, he was hit by an ill feeling. He tried to stand but his legs felt like jelly. After several attempts, he finally achieved a vertical base, though he still felt faint. He then became aware that his hand was still on the arm of the chair. He tried to lift it off but it wouldn't budge, it was as if it were attached by a powerful epoxy. Again he tried to free his hand and still it remained attached. He could feel his legs starting to buckle again and he could feel a debilitating weariness start to wash over him. He was starting to panic. With his last remaining strength, he used his free hand to grab the wrist of his trapped hand. He pulled with all the might that he could muster, and after about ten seconds of pulling, his hand finally came free.

His exertions had sent him off balance and he fell backwards hitting the hard stone floor with a sickening thud. He cursed as he slowly got to his feet. He took one final look at the chair, confused yet grateful that he had gotten free. He imagined still being trapped, unable to defend himself and Magissa returning. He shook this thought from his mind. Still feeling groggy, he made his way to the doorway as quickly as he could. As he was about to exit, he could have sworn that he could hear a disembodied, ghostly voice behind him. After what had just happened in this room, there was no way he was going to go back in to investigate. Quickly, he made his way out making sure to close the door behind him. Where the hinges had whined when he opened the door, they let out what sounded to Alex like a sigh of relief as he closed it. The voice was gone.

Feeling slightly better, he stepped across the corridor to the door on the opposite side. He extended his hand and grasped the handle. He was just about to turn it when he felt pressure against the handle. Someone or something was trying to open the door from the other side.

Was Magissa back already?

Had his experience in the previous room caused him to miss the warning call from Axis?

His head darted from left to right, unsure what to do or where to go. He thought about jumping back into the room that he had just exited but after what he had just experienced, he was very reluctant to re-enter. Besides this, he was sure that the whining hinges would alert whoever or whatever was on the other side of the door to his presence. He released the handle and darted into the room where he had first entered the fortress. He heard a whine and realised that the door was opening. He looked around, frantically trying to find somewhere to hide. He heard the sigh of the door hinges and then heard the door click shut. He could not hide behind the high backed chairs as he would have to run past the doorway and whoever or whatever it was that was now in the corridor, would undoubtedly see him. There was only one other option. He ran towards the back wall and dived behind the huge tapestry that bore his family crest.

The light from the fire struggled to stretch this far, such was the size of the room. He dared to not even breathe as he hid behind the huge fresco. He hoped that the entity that left the room had gone into one of the dozens of other rooms that littered the corridor. All was quiet. He was just about to peer out from behind the tapestry when he heard the clink of iron – he froze. Then he heard a dull thud and another scrape of metal on metal. He steeled himself and slowly, quietly, he clutched the side of the tapestry and peered out.

He could see a figure in front of the fire. Even though they had their back to him, he was sure that he was looking at a person. The person then started to ramble incoherently – judging by the sound of the voice, it was a man. All of a sudden, the man spun around. Alex ducked back behind the tapestry, hoping that he hadn't been spotted. He heard footsteps coming towards him – he had been seen! He held his breath. Could he overpower the man? He was sure he could outrun him, but where would he go? He had no idea of the layout of the fortress, even the first corridor he had entered with all of the doors was disorientating. It was like a labyrinth. The footsteps were almost upon him. He braced himself expecting the man to pull back part of the tapestry and expose his hiding place – but it didn't happen. The footsteps veered off to his right and then stopped. Spread-eagled against the wall, Alex sidestepped towards the far edge of the tapestry. Carefully and not making a sound, he pressed himself as tight to the wall as he could. He was on tiptoes now, craning his neck to see where the man was and then he spotted him. He was approximately five foot away and was fumbling with the lid of one of the bottles that contained a purple coloured liquid. He was at a forty-five degree angle to Alex so this allowed him to see the man's face for the first time, albeit from the side and in a poorly lit part of the room. He looked familiar somehow. The lid finally submitted and the man tossed it down on the table, grabbed a goblet and began to fill it with the purple liquid. Who was this man? Why was he so familiar to Alex? Then it hit him, this was an older, more hunched, more gaunt looking version of the man in the picture inside the pocket watch that he had been given by Maven. This was his father!

The man drained the contents of his glass and quickly refilled it. He then passed very close to Alex as he made his way towards the open window that Alex had used to enter the fortress. Alex sidestepped his way to the other end of the tapestry. He was very close to the man now and thanks to the light of a full moon streaming through the window, he could see his face clearly. The man had a look of someone who was being crushed by far too many troubles to list. He looked old beyond his years and where Alex had seen a glint in the man's eyes in the picture, this had been extinguished from the man in front of him. Alex didn't know what to do. He had not achieved his objective and the man, his father, was standing right in front of his only realistic exit. He had to get out. But this was his father, a man he had no memory of. He needed to talk to him, tell him who he was. He could hear Maven's voice somewhere in his head. *His mind is gone, Alex. He doesn't remember anything of his old life, he doesn't even know himself.* Alex shut this out, he decided that he was going to talk to him; after all, he may never get an opportunity again. He stepped out from behind the tapestry.

"Father?" he asked timidly.

The man spun around so quickly, it took Alex by surprise and he stumbled backward slightly. He regained his composure and said, "Father, it's me Alex – your son." The man did not move; he just stared blankly at Alex.

"Do you remember me?" asked Alex.

Still nothing, the man just stared. Somewhere in the distance, Alex heard the screech of an owl, but he didn't react, he was trying to get through to his father, trying to see if there was any sort of recognition, but the man just stared blankly. All of a sudden, he dropped his goblet. This seemed to wake him from his trance, as he reached down to pick it up, Alex noticed a metallic flash under the man's shirt, just beneath his neck line. The man clutched at the goblet but it was just out of reach. He stretched down a little further and then the metallic object slipped right out of the top of his open shirt. It was the Muleta!

Alex heard the owl's screech again and suddenly remembered Axis' words: "*Listen for my call. I'll alert you if Magissa returns.*" The man had finally managed to grab the goblet and was making his way back towards the table that housed the purple liquid. Alex ran over to him. "Father! It's Alex; do you not recognise your own son?" He looked straight into his father's vacant eyes, hoping for even the faintest reaction. He then heard a nearby door slam and a woman's shrill voice. He reached for his father's neck and snatched at the

Muleta. It broke free. "Sorry, Father, but we need this. I *will* see you again soon." He turned and sped towards the open window. Alex didn't see it, but there was the faintest flicker in his father's eyes.

Just as he got to the window, Magissa Veil burst into the room; she was flanked by her son. Her cold, green eyes found Alex immediately. "Ah, you must be Alex, it has been so long. It would be *so* nice to catch up," she said with mock affection. "Come, sit down and talk with me a while." She and Varios both had the look of two vultures that were about to pick over the remains of a carcass.

Alex, who had the Muleta behind his back, slowly slipped it into his belt and let the back of his shirt drop back down, covering it. He looked back at his father who seemed to not notice that anything was going on.

"It's no use looking to him, he does not know you. He does my bidding and through the goodness of my heart, I allow him to continue breathing."

Alex found his courage and shouted, "You have poisoned his mind! You have turned him into a virtual zombie! What gives you the right to take away a person's free will?"

"Ha!" she spat. "Free will is an illusion. I am Magissa Veil. My will is the only one that matters. In time, all who dwell on Ignius Novus will come to see this. Now, you have nowhere to go and no one to help you, so come and sit down," she motioned towards one of the chairs – "I shall not ask again."

Alex didn't know what to do. He knew that he would be as good as dead if he took another step towards her and her deranged son. There was only one thing for it; he dived for the open window. There was a thunderous crash behind him and for a moment, the whole sky glowed red. Magissa had tried to hit him with some sort of spell that had only found the thick stone wall that surrounded the window that he had just dived through. He was clear of the fortress, clear of Magissa's Ring of Protection but he was in free fall. Even in the darkness, the ground was growing clearer by the second. He needed to eradicate the panic and find his focus. He closed his eyes and tried to dismiss what was sure to be his imminent death. He pictured the other three members of The Kindred. He pictured his father as he should be and then he pictured himself taking flight and re-grouping with his companions. Suddenly, everything went white – was he dead? Slowly he opened his eyes and saw the world from upon high. He had morphed! He leant forward and went into a dive. As he crossed the perimeter wall, he was re-joined by Axis.

He heard Axis' voice in his head. "Are you okay?"

Alex tipped his wing in affirmation. Within moments, they were clear of the city and had touched down alongside where Eliza and Maven were hiding.

Quickly, Alex and Axis returned to their human forms. None of them spoke, there was no time. They made for the nearby tree line that would take them to the comparative safety of the forest, which in turn, would lead them back to Maven's home.

They heard a huge creaking sound in the distance, somewhere behind them and they realised that people or creatures of an unknown number had left Arcamedia, most likely in pursuit of them. They picked up the pace, but then all of a sudden Axis stopped. It took the other three a little while to realise that he wasn't there.

Maven looked back. "Axis, what are you doing?"

He didn't answer.

"Axis!" Maven called. "What on Igni are you doing? We need to get back."

"I need to buy you time, I need to slow our pursuers down," he replied.

"There are too many of them, they will take you – or worse," Maven's voice trailed off.

"Take Eliza and Alex and get back, I'll slow them down."

They then heard howling and it was close.

"No, Axis, don't be a fool!" Maven shouted. "We need you! We are close; we will be safe as soon as we pass through the ring. I doubled the protection before we left. Now come on, let's go."

Axis looked towards his companions and then looked back in the direction of the howls, they were getting closer. The wolves must have their scent. He looked torn and then suddenly, he broke into a run and caught up with his companions.

"Good choice, my friend," said Maven as they all sprinted in the direction of the safety of Maven's home.

Alex wished that there had been time for them to morph, because as fast as they were running, the wolves were gaining. Two hundred yards ahead was the clearing which was bathed in moonlight. They were going to make it. All of a sudden they heard the crunch of undergrowth and there, behind them was a wolf. Its eyes were fixed on Alex. It sprung into the air, hooked claws and teeth bared, heading straight for him. He froze and then he heard Axis yell, "Duck!"

He dropped to the ground as instructed and rolled out of the way. Axis jumped over him and met the wolf with a flying lariat. The wolf went down hard in a crumpled heap. It did not get back up.

"Let's move!" shouted Maven.

They didn't need telling twice. They were in the clearing now and heading towards the old tree, towards safety. Maven ushered Eliza through the Ring of Protection. She was consumed by the blue flash and was gone.

"Your turn, Alex, go!"

Alex looked to see Axis just enter the clearing. There was a huge dark shape behind him. He shouted, "Axis, look out!"

Axis spun around to see the wolf in midair. He caught it by the throat; it struggled and thrashed about trying desperately to clamp its jaws on some part of Axis' body. But he was too clever for it, he kept it at arm's length and then he lifted it as high as he could and propelled it with all of his considerable might into the trunk of a nearby tree. There was a sickening crunch of bone cracking and the wolf yelping in pain.

"Come on, Alex – in!" Maven grabbed him and pushed him through the Ring of Protection. A blue flash later and he was with Eliza. They could see Maven and Axis on the other side, everything was muted and it was like watching the scene through multiple layers of thick cellophane. Maven was encouraging Axis to get to the ring. As Axis started to run, Alex and Eliza could see another wolf enter the fray behind the men. It was approaching silently to the left of Axis, meaning that Maven could not see it from where he was standing. They tried frantically to let them know by shouting and screaming, but it was no good. You could barely hear anything through Maven's standard Ring of Protection, but with the increased warding that he had applied to this one, nothing on the other side of it could hear them.

Axis was nearly there but the wolf was almost upon him. Eliza and Alex could do nothing but watch the scene unfold. Maven ushered Axis towards the ring and then he saw the wolf about to pounce on Axis' blindside. He twisted the top of his staff and a razor sharp blade extended from its base. The wolf pounced and Maven drove his staff deep into its chest. It was dead before it hit the ground. Axis dived into the ring and was enveloped by the blue flash. He met Eliza and Alex on the other side and a split second later, they were joined by a breathless Maven.

"Well that was too close. Is everyone okay?" They all nodded.

Axis looked Maven in the eye. "Thank you, my old friend; I thought that my time had come."

"You have done the same for me, many times. Now quickly, let's get inside."

One by one, they disappeared into the opening in the tree and made their way down the staircase.

****

Magissa, who had sent a squad out in pursuit of Alex and his companions stood in front of the damaged window, that minutes earlier had been Alex's escape route. She stared into space as she contemplated what had just happened. She was angered by the fact that she had been so easily duped, but was more concerned that her shielding had not been strong enough to keep Alex from entering the fortress – *Why was this?* She looked down at the floor; it was covered in the rubble of the window frame that her spell had crashed into.

She called out to Cordium and he idled his way across the room. "Clean this up," she ordered. As commanded, Cordium reached down and started to clear away the stones. Magissa looked down at him disdainfully, but was then distracted as she heard a howl in the distance. She generated a smile as she took this to mean that her charges had caught up to their quarry.

Her thoughts then returned to finding Alex in the fortress. *Why had he even taken the risk to come there?* Her assumption was that he must have been trying to get through to Cordium.

Her gaze returned to Cordium who was on his hands and knees clearing the rubble. *Brain addled fool,* she thought to herself. "Your son risked his life for nothing."

She continued to stare at him and then suddenly the disdain was gone and was replaced by concern. "Cordium, get up!" she demanded. Right on cue, he got to his feet. Magissa swooped in on him immediately and ripped open his shirt. Cordium stood there as if nothing had happened. Magissa stared in disbelief and then everything became abundantly clear. Out of nowhere she let out an ear-piercing scream.

Varios ran into the room to see Magissa staring at Cordium in a state of shock. "Mother, whatever is wrong?

"Mother?"

Magissa managed to tear her eyes away from Cordium to look at her son.

"They have it." Her voice was strangely muted.

"Have what, Mother?"

"They have it... They have the Muleta."

****

Once they were all down the stairs, Maven stood at the foot of the staircase and began to chant under his breath. Right before their eyes, the staircase started to collapse upon itself until it was no longer there. Then Maven performed some intricate gestures with his hands and where the stairs had been, was now being closed off by a nest of tree roots. He then nonchalantly tapped his staff on the base of one of the huge bookcases that circled his home and it extended itself to totally conceal what had a few moments earlier been their exit. Finally, he performed his elaborate routine that lit the room.

Alex looked horrified.

"You have trapped us down here! Why would you do that?"

Maven had a weary look on his face but he managed to produce a half smile.

"We had a full pack of wolves on our tail that now know where we reside, so that route was always going to be closed off to us. I have just made sure that it is not open to them."

"But they couldn't get past the Ring of Protection... could they?" enquired Eliza.

Maven looked across at her. "They couldn't, but if they are able to give Magissa this exact location, I fear that she could."

He then looked across to Alex. "We are not trapped, my boy, do you think that I would be foolish enough to have not planned for all eventualities? There is a network of tunnels that will bring us out at the far end of the forest."

Alex felt a little silly for questioning what was obviously an extremely astute mind.

"I'm sorry," he said. "I did not mean to question you."

"Think nothing of it, the important thing is, we are safe. The unfortunate thing is that our first mission was unsuccessful."

Maven slumped down in a nearby chair, exhausted.

"I wouldn't say that," said Alex as he produced the Muleta from behind his back.

Maven drew himself up in the seat and had a stunned look on his face. As

~ 81 ~

he moved towards Alex, he rubbed his thumb and index finger together, and a split second later, there was an orb of light that followed him. He then asked Alex to hold his prize up higher and began to study it. After a few moments, a huge smile started to creep across his face.

"Well done, my boy, you do not disappoint. Axis look at this."

Axis made his way over and Alex held the Muleta up for him to inspect.

Axis smiled and came over to pat Alex on the back, the force of which nearly knocked him off of his feet.

"This is fantastic, Alex," continued Maven. "Whilst they are distracted trying to find a way in here, we can get a head start on them and start looking for the stones. For the first time, we have the advantage."

"There is more," said Alex.

"Oh yes?" said Maven, looking very interested.

"I took the Muleta from around my father's neck, so Magissa might not yet be aware that it's gone."

Maven smiled, "This is good, we…"

Axis interrupted, "You saw your father? How was he?"

Alex's head dropped. "He looks old – old beyond his years. He did not recognise me; he didn't react in any way, not when I told him who I was, not when I took the Muleta. Not even when Magissa threatened me."

"Do not judge him too harshly, he has been bewitched. His thoughts and mind are completely under Magissa's control," said Maven.

Alex sat down looking saddened.

Axis came and sat beside him and put a soothing hand on his shoulder.

"Your father loves you, Alex and if we are successful in our mission, you will know that love again."

This seemed to cheer Alex up slightly. He thought about telling them of his strange experience in the room with the chair, but enough had already happened, so he thought better of it.

Maven, who had disappeared deeper into the room, returned holding something in his hand.

"Here, take this," he said to Alex.

Alex held out his hand and Maven placed a silver chain into it. Alex stared at it and looked quizzically at Maven.

"It is for the Muleta," he said. "It will be safer if you carry it around your neck."

Alex smiled and proceeded to attach the Muleta to the chain. He lifted it over his head and allowed it to drop onto his chest. He tucked it under his shirt and patted it, indicating to Maven that it was safe.

With that, Maven and Axis went off to prepare some food. Eliza came over and sat beside Alex.

"You did brilliantly today, you were so brave. Seeing what you have been through makes me surer than ever that together, we can do what needs to be done."

"Thank you," said Alex. "We need to. We cannot allow Magissa to use the Muleta and the Origin Stones to do to others what she has done to your parents, my mother and what she continues to do to my father."

Just then, Axis came back over to tell them that the food was ready. When they got to the table, they noticed a map laid out that Maven was poring over.

"Ah, you two, grab something to eat and let's look at this map. We need to decide on the first stop of our journey."

They both did as instructed and positioned themselves at the table, opposite Maven and Axis.

Alex looked at the map; he could not believe how vast the forest was or how huge of a body of water Lake Ancora was. He felt a slight surge of despondence. *What if the Waterstone is at the bottom of the lake? It could be lost forever.* He saw the Cragon Hills with the city of Kessler nestled in their protective embrace. He then saw the vast range that was the Monolithic Mountains with the city of Arcamedia lying obediently, like a pet, at their feet. His eyes then traced to a massive area that went to the edge of the map. This had the word 'Malustera' running across it.

"What is this area?" he asked, pointing to the word 'Malustera'.

"This is a largely unchartered area that few wish to enter," said Maven.

"Why? What would stop them from going there?" Eliza asked.

"From what can be seen from the outskirts, it appears to be largely desert. The inhabitants have had to evolve to adapt to this seemingly harsh environment and are thought to spend more time in animal form than human. As explained before, too much time in animal form can bleed into your human side, both in temperament and appearance. If the area is as barren and unforgiving as legend tells us, then the creatures that they would have to adopt to survive it wouldn't exactly be… friendly. They are also said to be cannibals, or so the story goes," said Maven.

"Story? So what do you believe?" Eliza asked.

"I believe that those who reside there are best left to themselves. I believe that it is an area that we should avoid at all costs," said Maven, with a hint of fear in his voice.

"So where to begin?" Maven mused. He studied the map and traced his index finger across it and stopped at Lake Ancora. He was aware that they may have picked up on a fearful tone in his voice from the last comment, so he tried to sound more authoritative. "It is the only known body of water on Ignius Novus, so we know that the Waterstone will either be in it or near it. So, I think that this makes it our obvious starting point. I think that we should leave before dawn, so it would be wise for us to take some rest."

"What about the wolves outside?" asked Alex.

"We are safe in here overnight; we will leave before first light. Now to bed."

They all agreed and said goodnight to one another and went off to their respective beds.

Maven could not sleep though. He knew that once they had found the Waterstone, it would activate the Firestone. He did not want the others to find out that he did not know of anywhere charted on Igni that the Firestone would have gravitated to. He turned it over in his mind all night and eventually came to the realisation that they would have to enter and search the unknown of Malustera in order to find it.

12.

Watch where we're going

Maven woke with a start. He had only managed about an hour or so of fitful sleep. He looked around the room to see that the others were all still asleep. He decided that he would prepare the provisions for their trip before waking them all.

Just as he had packed the last of the items, they all awoke. They had a light breakfast and then made their way to the far end of Maven's gigantic room. They had not ventured to this part before but it was very similar to the rest of the room, with its intricately carved bookcases that were fully stocked with all manner of books. They came to a halt in front of one of these large bookcases. Maven tapped the base of it three times with his staff; there was a gentle rumbling as the bookcase slid to the right exposing an opening. Maven stepped into the darkness of the tunnel and beckoned the others to follow. "Don't mind the dark," he said. "Our movement will activate the lanterns as we go."

They all stepped inside and as Maven had promised, a lantern sprung to life. The light that it provided was dull but it was just enough to see the way ahead. Maven tapped the ground three times with his staff and the bookcase slid back across closing them inside the tunnel. He tapped the back of the bookcase in its four corners and once in the middle. He then drew a line from the centre to each of the corner points and then pushed his staff into the central point, which connected them all to one another.

Alex and Eliza looked on and Maven pre-empted their question.

"If by some chance they find their way in through the tree, this will conceal our exit. As powerful as Magissa is, it would take her a good deal of time to find this and more still to break it."

They made their way single file, through the narrow tunnel. It snaked its way under the forest floor, the dull light of the lanterns coupled with the tree roots that sprouted out at all angles above their heads created apparitions on the tunnel walls that on more than one occasion, made both Alex and Eliza jump in alarm.

After what seemed like hours, they reached a dead end. Once again, Maven used his trusty staff to draw a doorway in the dirt wall. He then tapped the centre three times, and an opening appeared. They stepped inside to see a staircase that corkscrewed its way upward. Axis led the way followed by Eliza, then Alex, with Maven bringing up the rear. As they reached the top, they could see daylight breaking through up ahead. Axis told them all to wait whilst he checked the coast was clear. After a short while, he returned and gave them the thumbs up.

They all stepped into the bright daylight.

Although they had been walking for some time, it was still very early in the day. The sun was out but there was a cold wind that bit at their necks. Alex looked around and could see that they had exited at the very edge of the forest. There were very few trees in this particular area but a quick glance behind them showed the vast ocean that was the Ensing Forest. It really did seem as though it went on forever. Looking over to the northeast they could see the Cragon Hills undulating their way across the landscape. Lake Ancora, the first objective of their journey was located on the other side.

"The quickest way to the mouth of Lake Ancora is over that hill." Maven pointed with his staff to a lower lying hill that looked to be at least half a day's walk away. "My instincts tell me that the Waterstone will be very close to the shoreline, so we will start by working our way from the mouth, around. I assume that you have your father's watch, Alex?" Alex reached into his pocket and withdrew the watch. "Excellent, my boy. Even with this though, we are still looking for the proverbial needle in a haystack, but at least it will place us on the right path and will give us an indication when we are close to this particular needle." He gave a wry smile. "This is why Magissa's efforts have been futile so far; she has no way of knowing if she is even remotely close to finding the stones. For all she knows, her men have passed by the stones on multiple occasions." He stretched out both of his arms, encouraging them all to come closer. He stared at them all intently. "I know we have a tumultuous task ahead of us, but we do have an advantage. We should be thankful for that at least."

With a modicum of hope in their hearts, they started on the path that would lead them to Lake Ancora.

****

Back at the tree that sat atop Maven's home were a group of Magissa's guards. Those who had survived had been joined by some others. Some of them were removing the now human bodies of the wolves that had attacked The Kindred the previous night and the others were examining the area leading up to the tree. The tallest of them and judging by his more elaborate uniform, the leader, picked up a stone and threw it in the general direction of the tree. There was a blue flash and a loud crack as the stone was ejected skyward and out of sight.

The man who had thrown the stone called across to one of the guards who was helping with the removal of the bodies.

"Falmus! Over here." The guard's voice was deep and guttural.

The one named Falmus immediately jumped to attention and sprinted over to where the huge man was standing.

Falmus crouched down in front of him, an obvious subordinate gesture.

"Yes, Captain."

The larger guard gestured for him to get to his feet.

"I need you to get back to the fortress immediately. Magissa needs to see this."

"Right away, sir." Falmus saluted and then morphed into a wolf and powered his way through the forest towards the fortress.

The captain turned his gaze back towards the old tree, he had a very intense look on his face as he rubbed at a deep looking, partially healed wound on his neck.

****

The Kindred followed the tree line of the forest's edge the entire way. This allowed Axis to disappear into the trees every so often. At certain points, he would backtrack to ensure that they weren't being followed and at others, he would scout ahead on the lookout for any potential ambushes or traps. It made the journey very slow going as the other three had to stop every time he would perform his reconnaissance. He was a mountain of a man but Alex was amazed at how light on his feet he was. More than once, he silently reappeared alongside or behind them which caused Maven to jump and call him a few choice words.

It was about mid-afternoon when they finally reached the foot of the hill that Maven had pointed out so many hours earlier. The tree line that they had been following all day carried on to the edge of the hill but as its progress was hampered by the inconvenient mound, it broke off to the left and continued its never ending march into the distance. This area was very sheltered so it was decided that they would rest a while and take on some food and water before continuing over the hill.

Once they were all sated, they then began their ascent of the hill. It was not an easy climb. From the distant vantage point that they had viewed the hills earlier that morning, this one had looked like a veritable molehill compared to the others, but now that they had to climb it, it was anything but. Finally they reached the top and looked down into the valley. The wind that had whipped at them earlier that morning had died away so the waters of the lake were completely still. It looked like a huge piece of translucent blue glass as it glistened up at them. They made their way down the hill into the valley. They finally arrived at the mouth of the lake and all looked on at the spectacle before them. Alex had viewed the lake from a distance, but now that he was at its edge, he was more in awe than ever. He stole a quick glance over at Eliza to see her awestruck face. With the Cragon Hills shrouding one side and the Monolithic Mountains shrouding the other, it created a sense of detachment from everything else and gave them the feeling that they had just set foot into a secret valley. This truly was the land that time forgot.

Their sightseeing was interrupted by Maven's voice, "Yes, yes it's all very beautiful but we have no time to admire the view, we need to search for the Waterstone."

Both Alex and Eliza nodded. The seclusion and beauty of this place had made them feel so at ease that for a moment the purpose of why they were there had completely escaped their minds.

Maven looked up at the sky; the sun was starting to set. From where they were standing, it looked like the sun was starting to submerge into the lake.

"This is perfect," he said. "It is still light enough to allow us to search for a few hours, but not so bright that we can be easily seen. Alex, it's time to open the watch."

Alex did as he was instructed and looked at the gems on the dial. He half expected the blue gem to be glowing back at him, but immediately felt silly at this naive notion. Maven stepped over and studied the watch.

"We need the secondary hands to give us a bearing. May I?" He took the watch from Alex and pressed down on the crown twice. He then twisted the crown and as Alex looked on, he saw the secondary hands move. Maven continued to twist the crown until the two secondary hands pointed directly to the blue gemstone which was located where one would normally expect to find the number six on a standard watch face. He then clicked the crown again twice and after a second or two, the secondary hands started to spin wildly. He then held the watch out in front of him and slowly started turning on the spot. He resembled a penguin as he shuffled in a circular motion to the right of where they were all standing. The hands on the watch continued to spin. He continued to turn until his back was to the lake, still the hands spun wildly. There was a slightly concerned look on his face as he was drawing very close to returning to his starting position. But then, all of a sudden there was a loud click. The concern left Maven's face immediately and was replaced by a wry smile. "We have our heading and the good news is it is leading us alongside the lake rather than directly towards it."

Axis seemed visibly relieved to hear this news and although he was just hoisting the heavy pack back onto his shoulders, another, less tangible weight was leaving them.

Maven handed the pocket watch back to Alex and pointed to the dial.

"Keep this outstretched in front of you and if the hands start to spin again, we need to stop and regain the heading. We cannot linger in one area for too long as the risk of being seen or captured will increase. If fortune is with us, we will find the Waterstone quickly and be able to move on."

They started walking. Alex had the watch in his hand which he held out in front of him, just as Maven had instructed. It looked like he was holding a simple compass, trying to get a northerly bearing. This was anything but a normal compass and their northerly bearing was in the form of a blue gemstone that was hidden somewhere in or around this vast body of water. They continued to walk the water's edge as the daylight started to fade. They all had their eyes fixed on the dial of the watch as they went.

Finally, they were defeated by the lack of light. Maven led them into a concealed area, close to the foot of one of the hills and indicated that they would be making camp there for the night. Axis had taken the huge pack that he was carrying off of his back and started to unpack and then erect a large tent. Maven then used his staff to draw a Ring of Protection.

There was a despondent air in camp that evening as they sat in silence around the fire and ate their food. How many more days would they be searching for the elusive stones? How many more nights would they be sitting around the campfire, disillusioned that they had yet to find them?

****

Magissa arrived in the clearing and was greeted by the large captain.

He bowed.

"My queen."

Her voice was cold and shrill. "What is so important that I should be summoned out here, Canly?"

Canly drew himself back to his full height and pointed towards the old tree.

"I believe that they may be hiding in there."

As before he picked up a stone and threw it in the direction of the tree and as before, there was a blue flash followed by a loud crack as the stone was ejected skyward.

"The Mystic obviously has some kind of shielding in place," said Canly.

"Well obviously," she replied sarcastically. She may have rolled her eyes but it was impossible to tell as the skin on her face was pulled up so tightly, nothing could really move.

"Step aside!" she hissed.

Canly obeyed and Magissa lifted her staff and touched the ground just in front of where the stone that Canly threw had impacted. From there, she very slowly started to trace a curved line. As Canly looked on, he could see that a light blue ring was starting to form.

Some while later Magissa had exposed the entire blue Ring of Protection. Looking pleased with herself, she delved into one of her pockets and withdrew a clear gemstone which she affixed to the top of her staff. Then she pointed the end of her staff at the ring and said, "Syphonous." The blue ring was being pulled towards the end of her staff. After a few moments, there was no longer any trace of the ring. With a twisted smile on her face, she gestured to Canly that it was safe to enter. Canly bent down to pick up another stone but Magissa placed her staff across his arms and shook her head.

"It *is* safe to enter," she said.

Reluctantly, Canly made his way towards the tree. He carried the weapon with the blade at one end and the noose at the other, so he decided to walk in with the weapon in front of him. He stepped through, half expecting to be shot skyward like the earlier stone, but his feet remained firmly on the ground. He was now right in front of the tree that used to have an opening that led down to Maven's home. He looked back at Magissa and gave her an 'I never doubted you' look. Walking extremely rigidly, she joined him at the tree. Not saying a word, she studied it for a while.

"What do you think?" asked Canly.

She didn't respond. She pressed her hand against the trunk of the tree and uttered the words "Tricio Oculus." In her mind, she could see all that used to be there, the opening, the stairs and then she could also see down into Maven's home. She then removed her hand.

"My queen?" said Canly.

Magissa looked at him and said, "They were hiding here, but no longer. The Mystic is a misguided fool, but he was not unprepared. He would have had an alternative exit, an escape route. This means that they have a head start on us."

She pondered this a moment.

"This is a good thing though."

Canly frowned. "How is this a good thing?"

Magissa gave him a chastising look; she did not like to be questioned. "Our attempts to find the stones have so far been futile. We can use them, they can do the hard work of finding the stones and once the time is right, we will take them away."

Her lips curled into a smile.

"Take three of your best men and track them. Track only – do not engage them. Report back to me regularly."

Canly bowed and then took his leave.

13.

A Feeling in the Water

The next few days followed a similar pattern for The Kindred. They would wake, eat breakfast, pack up their tent and remove all indications that anyone had camped in the spot. Then they would then set off on the path that ran alongside the lake. Alex with pocket watch in hand would take the lead, watching the dial closely, hoping beyond hope that the blue gem would illuminate. Then at the end of another unsuccessful day, they would set up camp somewhere very secluded and Maven would draw his Ring of Protection. Then they would eat dinner in virtual silence, after which, they would turn in for the night.

Alex awoke with a start. His dreams were getting more and more vivid. Though this dream was more of a re-enactment of his time in the fortress, the strange experience in the room where his hand was stuck to the chair, meeting his zombie-like father, Magissa and Varios trying to capture him and the consequent daring escape.

He peered through a small gap in the door of the tent and noticed that it was still dark outside. He wondered what time it was and fumbled around for the pocket watch. He was trying hard not to wake the others, so decided he would slip outside and check the time out there. Once he was outside, he flipped the lid of the watch open and was met by the beautifully illuminated dial. He hadn't seen the watch in total darkness before so was surprised to see it like this. The area of the face that didn't have the gems inset glowed a silver-ivory colour and as the hands swept around their ever repeating three hundred and sixty degree journey, they left a silvery slipstream that made the whole thing look alive with energy. He walked around outside the tent, mesmerized by what he was seeing. He was so distracted that he wasn't watching where he was walking and ended up tripping over a half exposed rock and dropped the watch in the process. He cursed as he fell and rubbed his shin before getting back to his feet. He bent down to look for the watch, expecting to see its magical glow, but it was nowhere to be seen. Panicked, he started to look around frantically. How could he lose this? It was their only hope of ever finding the Origin Stones. Even with the watch, the odds were against them but without it, they may just as well go back to Maven's subterranean home and wait for the inevitable.

He was now on his hands and knees scrabbling about looking for the watch. Though his eyesight was sharp, his only real light source was the intermittent moonlight that, just to add insult to injury had now disappeared behind a thick cluster of clouds. Still Alex searched. How was he going to explain this to the others? Maven and Axis had built him up as the saviour of Ignius Novus and in one distracted moment, he may have helped seal its fate! His search had now led him right to the water's edge. Then a terrible thought snuck its way into his mind. *Please don't let it have gone into the lake*, he said to himself. Just then, the moon fought its way out from behind the cloud to aid him. Out of the corner of his eye, he caught the briefest glint of platinum. He jumped to his feet and headed in that direction, hoping beyond hope that his eyes weren't playing tricks on him. He arrived at where he thought he had seen the platinum glint, but there was nothing there. The moon had deserted him yet again. He remembered what Maven had told him about how his eyesight would be heightened if his eyes could draw in enough, consistent natural light. His mind flashed back to how easily he had been able to see on the night that he had first arrived on Igni. If only the moon would stay visible, he could surely find the watch. He got down onto his hands and knees, patting the floor, hoping to feel something other than grass or sharp stones. His heart was in his mouth now and he could hear the flow of his own blood gushing through his ears. He couldn't find it. He sat down, cradling his knees and rested his head sideways on his thighs. Hope was starting to leave his body. He was in the process of psyching himself up to get to his feet just as the moon won the current battle of its ongoing war with the clouds. Its light streamed down on Alex whose head was still on his thighs. There it was, a glint about four foot from where he was sitting. He had undoubtedly seen it this time. He jumped to his feet and shot towards it. It was there! Two thirds of it was hidden from view by the long grass. He picked it up, relief coursing through his body. He cradled it in his hands as if it were a fledgling that had fallen from its nest. *Please don't let it be damaged,* he said to himself over and over. He closed his eyes and very gently, opened the lid. He couldn't bring himself to look at it but knew that he must. He squinted through partially opened eyes. He could see a glow – the dial was still intact! He now opened his eyes fully and looked down at the watch. If he had thought it was beautiful earlier, it was nothing compared to how good it looked now. He closed the lid and decided to head back to the tent, before any other misfortune befell him. He put it in his pocket and took a step back towards the tent. But then he came to a standstill, his brow furrowed, and he reached back into his pocket and pulled out the watch. He flipped the lid open and was once again greeted by the magical glow, but this time, there was something else. The stone in the number six position was exuding a blue light. The Waterstone was close! His heart was racing again, but for a different reason this time. He took a deep breath and tried to compose himself. He thought to himself, *Should I wake the others? No, what if I lose the location?* He looked at the watch, the blue gem was still lit but the secondary hands were spinning, he needed to re-establish the bearing. He mimicked what Maven had first done with the watch. *Wow, that seemed like weeks ago*, he thought to himself as he slowly turned anti-clockwise on the spot towards the edge of the lake. He had now drawn parallel to the water but the hands were still spinning. He continued on his turning curve, but was conscious that he was moving away from the water. He kept his eyes firmly fixed on the watch face. Suddenly, there was that same click that he had heard when Maven first established a bearing. The hands locked and were pointing. In this light, they seemed to pulsate. He smiled and gave the air a small uppercut. He looked up and saw that the hands were pointing at a rock formation that crept along the side of the lake, part of it seemed to actually head out into the water. Cautiously, he moved towards the exact place that the pulsating hands were pointing. As he drew close to the rock formation, he noticed that there was an opening. He knew that he was going to have to go inside and wondered if the small amount of light that the watch gave off was going to be enough for him to see once he was inside.

He stepped through the opening.

To his surprise, the light emanating from the watch seemed to intensify as he ventured inside. Its glow was strong enough for him to see as walked down the sloping path that descended into the cave. He kept a constant check on the watch face as he walked, ensuring that the blue gem was still illuminated. The path then started to level out and he could hear lapping water and was that light up ahead? Cautiously, he continued on and as he rounded the corner he was met by a stunning sight. He was now in a large, well-lit area that looked like it could have been Poseidon's holiday home. The water was crystal clear and it seemed like it was being illuminated from underneath, but this was an illusion because as he looked up, he could see clear sky with the moonlight streaming in. The moonlight reflecting off of the rippling water created stunning patterns and effects on the stalagmites and stalactites that adorned the cave. He looked at the watch face again; the blue gem seemed to be brighter than ever. Was it because his eyesight was being assisted by the moonlight that streamed into the cave? Or was it trying to tell him that he was very close to the Waterstone? Alex chose the latter and with a rush of excitement, he started to search every square inch of the cave.

After some time and no success, he decided that the stone was going to be in what he had, (while searching) dubbed 'The Moonpool'. He took off his shirt, shoes, socks and he carefully removed the Muleta that was hanging on the chain around his neck. As he prepared to enter the Moonpool, it briefly crossed his mind to go and wake the others. But no – he had come this far – he could finish the job. He sat on the edge of the pool and put his feet into the water. It was icy cold. He closed his eyes, took three deep breaths and then jumped in. It was so cold; it felt like he had been hit in the stomach by a sledgehammer. He swam for a moment, hoping to get feeling back into his body and out to his extremities. After a few moments, his body did start to become a little more accustomed to the extreme change in temperature. He could now search. He decided that the most likely resting place for the stone would be on the bed of the pool, so with that, he took two more deep breaths and dived for the bottom.

Thankfully, the pool was so well lit by the moon, (it had obviously won its war with the cloud) that he had a clear view of the bottom. Another bonus was that the bed of the Moonpool was rock rather than sand or silt, so he would not have to sift through this in order to find his prize. He swam to the bottom of the pool and scanned the entire area, but found nothing. He started to feel along the rocky sides of the pool, hoping to find a recess that might house the stone. Again nothing. At this point, he needed to come up for air. He swam for the surface and sucked in the precious oxygen, before heading back under the water to make sure he hadn't missed any possible hiding places. Several minutes later after deciding that he had explored all of the options, he made his way to the surface. Despondent, he reached for the watch, which he had left in his shirt pocket, and opened the lid. The blue gem was still glowing.

It must be here, but where?

Alex set the watch back down and decided that he had better get out of the water. As he reached for the side with his hand in order to pull himself out, it slipped and he cursed as he caught it on the sharp rocks. A quick examination of the wound showed that it was bleeding; as he looked down into the pool he saw his blood trailing into the water. Something was strange though, whilst watching the misty red shapes spiralling in the water, he noticed that rather than dissipating, they were being pulled from his view under the shelf that he was leant against.

There must be an air pocket, he thought.

He intentionally squeezed his hand to release some more blood into the water. A soft clinking sound momentarily distracted him. Deciding that it was nothing, he took a deep breath and dived back under. He was now about halfway from the bottom, looking at the rocky shelf. The last wisps of the blood disappeared, seemingly into nothingness. He moved in closer to examine the area, but couldn't see where it would have gone. He pressed his hands against the shelf and swept them gently across the area where the blood trail had exited. As before, all he could feel was the smooth, pumice-like rock that he had felt earlier. But just then he felt a slightly spongy area, which he pushed this with his finger and it gave way. Now adjusting his position in an effort to see the area that he had just exposed; there was definitely something in there. He reached in and pulled out a stone – was it the Waterstone? Eager with anticipation, he swam to the surface. Holding the stone aloft and as the bright moonlight hit it, there was no doubt in his mind that he was holding the Waterstone.

Carefully, he exited the Moonpool, throwing on his shirt and just picking up his shoes and socks. He ran up the slope that had taken him down into the cave and exited through the opening in the rock face. The now constant light of the moon was being filtered into his eyes, which fully triggered his heightened sense of sight. The tent was clearly visible now. Exhilarated, he ran towards it, eager to tell his companions of his find.

He dived through the tent door. "Axis, Maven, Eliza. Wake up! Wake up!"

Maven sat bolt upright and reached for his staff, and pointed it menacingly in Alex's direction.

"What the… who goes there?" he shouted, still brandishing his staff.

"Maven, it's me."

Maven rubbed his eyes; all he could see were the two floating blue orbs that were Alex's eyes. "Alex. Is that you? What's with all the kerfuffle?"

Eliza and Axis both stirred awake at this point.

"I've found, I've found it!"

"Found what – the insensitivity to wake us in the middle of the night?" retorted Maven.

"No! I've found the stone. Come outside and see for yourselves."

They were all wide awake now. They got to their feet and followed Alex out of the tent. The moon shone brightly upon them and within moments, their eyes had filtered enough of its light to be able to see almost as clearly as if it were the daytime. Alex reached into his shirt pocket and pulled out the stone and held it up for all to see. When the moonlight hit it, the resulting refraction made it look as though there were silvery blue waters swirling inside. It seemed to be split in two, divided by a misshapen S. One side had what looked like still waters and the other side looked like rolling waves. Eliza, Axis and Maven looked on, their faces agog. Maven stretched out his hand and Alex passed the gemstone to him. Without saying a word, he held the stone aloft to allow the full force of the moonlight to hit it. He studied it much like a jeweller would inspect a diamond to determine its authenticity. At the conclusion of his inspection, he looked at Alex with an almost sombre look. "Where did you find this?" he asked.

"In a cave down near the water's edge," explained Alex.

Maven, still looking solemn studied Alex's face. Then a huge smile broke out on his own face and without warning, he ran to Alex and gave him a huge hug.

"Fantastic, my boy! Absolutely fantastic! You have done us proud!"

Alex was taken aback by Maven's unrestrained emotional response but returned his embrace and smiling, willingly accepted all of the adulation that he was receiving.

Axis came over and congratulated him and extended his arms. Alex tried to brace himself for what came next, but it was no use, Axis gave him an almighty embrace that he was sure realigned his spine. He gave Axis a thumbs up as he tried to disguise the fact that he was trying to refill his lungs with the air that had been so unceremoniously driven out of them. As he recovered from this display of 'affection', Eliza walked over to him.

"Well done," she smiled and hugged him. Axis' hug had redefined pain to him, but Eliza's hug drained all of the pain away and it was as if it had never happened.

"Thank you," Alex smiled back.

He then proceeded to tell them all how his dropping the watch had inadvertently aided in locating the Waterstone. When he had finished, Maven spoke.

"We have had some good fortune here, but do not let it detract from what you have achieved, Alex. However, as we continue our search for the other stones, we cannot rely on good fortune alone."

Maven continued to study the Waterstone. Perhaps it was a trick of the moonlight, but it seemed like the side of the stone that housed the rolling waves was starting to breach into the still water side.

"Now, Alex, you need to add the Waterstone to the Muleta."

After exiting the Moonpool, Alex had put the Muleta back around his neck. He lifted the chain over his head and then held the talisman in the palm of his hand. Maven passed the Waterstone back to him. Alex took it and frowned as he could see it starting to change before his eyes. He looked at Maven. "What's happening to it?"

"Don't worry. It is just an indication that we need to bond it with the Muleta."

Reassured, he looked for the correct segment on the Muleta.

Maven then said, "You need to hold the stone just above its place on the Muleta and it will be drawn in. You will likely feel a strange force or sensation as you do this; you must not release the stone until you see its segment light up. Oh and be careful to not actually touch the segment." Alex shot Maven a questioning look, but no response was forthcoming. Maven was trying to sound matter of fact, but in reality, as much as he had studied the Origin Stones and the Muleta, he didn't really know what to expect – no one did. Alex, who was now holding the Muleta by the chain, carefully held the Waterstone above the south point on the Muleta.

Suddenly, he could feel an unseen force trying to draw his hand into the Muleta. The force grew and it now felt like his entire body was going to be pulled in. Axis could see that he was struggling with this, so went over to him and grabbed him around the middle in order to anchor him down. The pressure that was building was getting too much. He could hear Maven shouting at him to hold on and not to release it until the segment lit up. He could see Eliza with her hands clasped to her face looking extremely concerned. He could also feel the powerful arms of Axis holding him down. He was grateful to Axis for doing this, because without him, he felt sure that he would have been pulled in by the intense force. Why was the Muleta not glowing? Just when he didn't think he could stand it any longer, a blue glow finally emanated from the Muleta.

"Let go now, Alex!" Maven shouted.

He did as instructed and the stone shot into the Muleta as if drawn in by some sort of powerful magnet. Then there was a sound like water breaking on rocks, the stone glowed and the insignia underneath flashed. As Alex looked on, a blue light made its way along the braid that connected the Waterstone segment to the Firestone. The light continued along the braid but faded just before it reached the Firestone segment. Alex looked at the Waterstone and noted that the initial separation of the two halves had been restored.

Everyone breathed a collective sigh of relief.

"I'm sorry that I couldn't prepare you better for that, Alex. I had an idea of what would happen, just not the extent of it," said Maven.

Alex nodded and smiled.

"It's safe to place it back around your neck," said Maven.

Cautiously, Alex placed the chain over his head and let the Muleta fall around his neck and nestle under the neck line of his shirt.

Maven looked at the sky, dawn was breaking. "The clock is now against us. The Firestone will awaken from its slumber. We need to find it and find it quickly."

They packed up the tent and cleared the campsite so it was as if no one had ever been there. Maven asked Alex for the pocket watch, he handed it to him and looked on as Maven pressed down on the crown twice and then he twisted it to move the secondary hands into position. They pointed at the orange gemstone that was in place of the number nine. He clicked the crown twice which caused the hands to spin wildly. Maven's mind was on their next objective as he moved on the spot to get a bearing. Deep down, he knew the direction that the hands would point but hoped beyond hope that he was wrong. He looked at the watch face to see that the hands had locked themselves in a northerly direction. Maven swallowed, his mouth suddenly felt as dry as the location that he knew the watch would take them. He forced a smile and said, "We have our bearing, we need to move faster than these forms can carry us so while the day is still young I suggest we adopt four legs rather than two."

They all nodded in agreement. Axis changed into the black dog almost immediately; he looked quite odd with the large pack attached to his back like some sort of beast of burden. Maven placed his staff into the pack and secured it in place. He then morphed into the guise of a fox, followed closely by Eliza and Alex who both took on their canine forms. Without looking back, they all tore off along the path that ran parallel to the lake.

On an outcropping, just above where they had been camping, hiding in some brush, were four wolves. In the blink of an eye, three of them suddenly changed, but even in their human forms, there was still more than a slight resemblance to the animals that they had just changed from. One of them was Canly. The man to his right spoke. "Let's go! We can run them down easily – attack them when they least expect it. They won't know what hit them."

"No, Falmus!" growled Canly. "We are to track, not engage. Magissa gave specific instructions. We must get a report back to her."

Without taking his eyes off of the four shapes speeding towards the horizon, Canly shouted "Lunitas!" The lone wolf looked at him. "Go back to Arcamedia and inform Magissa of all that you know. We will continue the pursuit." The wolf bowed its head and then turned tail towards Arcamedia. The remaining three men returned to their wolven forms and jumped off of the outcropping on which they had been standing. They landed in the abandoned campsite and thundered after their quarry.

14.

Tracking and Trepidation

The Kindred had covered a good amount of ground since they had left their campsite just before dawn. The sun was now high in the sky. As they came to a standstill under the shade of a large tree, Maven morphed back into his human form. The other three all followed suit.

Axis removed the heavy pack and set it down. Alex immediately checked the watch. Unfortunately, there was no orange glow, but at least the secondary hands were locked in position, indicating that they were still on the right path.

"We can take a short break," said Maven. He looked behind him, "But we mustn't linger here too long though." He seemed very distracted as he stared off into the distance.

"Where do you think we are headed?" Alex asked.

"Where the watch takes us!" Maven replied, somewhat abruptly.

Alex wanted to ask if Maven had any further insight on their destination, but based on the previous response, he thought better of it. Even before the curt response, he was aware that Maven's mood had changed significantly. His childlike enthusiasm had been replaced by trepidation. This was not an emotion that Alex had experienced from Maven, despite his kooky demeanour, he always seemed to be in control and knew exactly what to say or do. Alex wasn't sure how to deal with this change.

They all remained silent whilst they rested. Eliza noticed that Maven kept looking in the direction that they had come from. He looked edgy and nervous. She looked across to Axis, who, judging by the look on his face, had noticed the same thing.

"Are you okay, Maven?" he asked.

Maven didn't respond; he seemed lost in thought.

Axis stood up, walked over to Maven and placed a hand on his shoulder. Maven was startled by this and recoiled.

Axis was concerned. "What's wrong?"

"Nothing – nothing, I'm fine."

Axis was unconvinced and gave him an incredulous look.

"I'm fine, Axis, just a little tired that's all."

After one more look back, Maven said, "Okay, that's enough rest, we need to get back on the path."

"Should we stay in these forms?" asked Alex.

"No, time is of the essence, we need to change."

With that, they all reverted back to the animals that they had assumed prior to their break and continued apace along the path.

****

Magissa looked on stone faced as the man named Lunitas explained to her that they had tracked their prey along the Northern Lake Road. He also explained that a blue gemstone had been located only hours earlier. Magissa's lips curled into a satisfied smile. "Good – good. Go and re-join Canly and await further instructions."

Varios entered the room and Magissa turned her attention to him.

Lunitas bowed but stayed where he was.

Magissa turned back around.

"Is there something wrong?" she said. Her voice sizzled like hot oil landing on a cold surface.

"No, my queen. I-I was just thinking that we have the upper hand, we should take them out while they least expect it."

Magissa looked straight through Lunitas. She raised her staff and pointed it in his direction -he was immediately wracked with pain.

"Did I give you permission to think?"

Varios had an evil smile on his face; he seemed to be taking great pleasure in the pain that Lunitas was enduring.

Lunitas was spread-eagled and being lifted off of the ground. It looked like he was being stretched out on an invisible torture rack.

"N-No. Argh! I am sorry, my queen!" screamed Lunitas.

"I didn't think so." She lowered her staff and Lunitas fell on the hard stone floor with a heavy thud.

"Now get back to Canly before I send another in your stead and *reassign* you."

Lunitas didn't need to be told twice. He winced as he bowed and half-limped, half-ran out of the room.

"Well done, Mother, they need to know their place," said Varios.

"I did not send for you to hear your feeble attempts at positive reinforcement." Varios cowered. "I sent for you as I have a job for you."

"As you wish. What is it?"

"I want you to fly above the Northern Lake Road and see if you can either spot or anticipate where the insurgents are heading. Report back to me as soon as you know."

"Yes, Mother. Consider it done."

Varios exited the room.

****

It was late into the afternoon as The Kindred continued to speed along the Northern Lake Road. Just then, they could all hear Maven's voice in their heads. "We are drawing close to the walls of Kessler. I do not want to pass directly in front of the city, the path will break off to the left in a few moments, we need to take this and head up into the Cragon Hills. We will pass Kessler from behind the hills. I know that we will lose our bearing, but we can pick up the route again once we are clear of Kessler."

The other three bowed their heads in affirmation and followed Maven as he suddenly broke left and started to climb the hill road. There was an element of truth in Maven not wanting to pass directly in front of Kessler, but he had another motive for taking the hill path. He had the sense that they were being tracked for much of the day. He didn't want to alarm the others, particularly Eliza and Alex, but he really wanted to try and throw any potential pursuers off of their scent. There were patches of trees that broke away from the main forest and climbed up into the hills behind Kessler. Maven would lead them all into these in the hope that if they were being followed, it would seem as though they had headed back down into the forest.

A large black raven was flying across Lake Ancora. Its keen eyes were scanning the road on the lake's western shore that headed north. It had now cleared the lake and was directly above the Northern Lake Road. From its elevated position, it could see for a good distance, but there was no sign of any people or animals on this road. The raven was now flying parallel to Kessler and then beyond. It thought to itself based on what Lunitas reported, there was no way that they could have gotten beyond this point yet. It decided to backtrack, so dipped its left wing and circled back and headed south along the road. After a short time it spotted three wolves powering their way along the path. It swooped down and as it landed, its true form was assumed. Varios Veil now stood in the road. The wolves spotted him and immediately came to a standstill. The largest of the three wolves morphed into his human form.

"Ah, Canly," said Varios with an authoritative air. "How goes the hunt?"

Canly, who didn't care much for Varios, fixed him with a stare and said, "It was going well until we were interrupted."

Varios recognised the insubordinate tone in Canly's voice and decided to try and make him squirm.

"Well where do you think they are then? I have scanned the Northern Lake Road well beyond the borders of Kessler and there is no sign of them."

Canly was surprised at this news, as they still had a scent that continued along that path. He composed himself and said, "Well, darkness is drawing in, perhaps they have made camp for the night. The Mystic's shielding makes them untraceable."

Varios smiled, liking the fact that he had the inside track on them. Though he did agree that they had probably made camp for the night and warded themselves. "I suggest that you follow the scent for as long as you can and once it is lost, make camp yourselves. Lunitas is on his way back and this will give him time to catch up. You can then attempt to pick it up again at first light. In the meantime, I shall report back to Magissa."

Canly was not happy at being dictated to by this sycophant who he felt was only in the position that he held due to who his mother was. But at this point, he just wanted to be rid of him so he nodded his head. With that, Varios reassumed the raven's guise and took off, heading back towards Arcamedia.

"Worm," muttered Canly as he watched the large black bird flying across Lake Ancora. With that, he became a wolf once again and he and his pack sniffed the ground to regain the scent of their quarry and once they had it, they resumed the hunt.

Night was now closing in as Maven, closely followed by the others, zig-zagged their way through the scattered patches of trees. At one point he told the others to continue along their current path as he disappeared down the side of the hill and into the sea of trees at its base. Twenty minutes later, he returned.

The others all gave him quizzical looks which he didn't react to, instead he pointed out that they would be clear of Kessler soon and as it was now very dark, as soon as they were clear, they should find a suitable place to camp for the night.

They decided to camp away from the Northern Lake Road and found a hollow in the side of the hill. They all filed inside and Maven administered the now very familiar shielding. Conversation did not flow that evening, just the occasional words followed by awkward silences. Alex was grateful when Maven, stating that they would be leaving before dawn, suggested that they all turn in for the night. Alex, who had now become quite used to his sleep being blighted by vivid dreams, actually slept quite well as did Eliza and Axis. This was not the case for Maven. Although he was confident that their choice of hideout could not been seen or found, he was still conscious of the fact that they were being tracked. But the overwhelming fear in his mind was that they were drawing ever closer to Malustera. What evil awaited them there? He did not know, but the stories that he had heard as a child all came flooding back to him. He had heard tales that it was like entering a netherworld, that the soul was literally ripped from a person's body as soon as they set foot in the place and they would be left to wander the desolate wasteland, trapped in their own private hell for the rest of their days. Other tales that he had heard were of creatures out of myth that would hunt, kill and consume anyone who dared enter. He did not know if these stories were true, but what he did know was that no one who had ventured into Malustera had ever returned. Would he and his three companions be the next to fall victim to this perdition?

It was still dark when Maven woke them. "We must be on our way. Let's pick up the Northern Lake Road and use the watch to regain our heading."

Axis and the others all started to pack up their bedding and once again, make it look as though they had never been there. Whilst they did this, Maven silently disappeared over the hill.

He saw a small herd of deer grazing in the early morning light. Quietly, he headed towards them. The deer didn't seem too concerned by his presence; he managed to walk right up to them. As he stretched out his hand to touch the largest of the deer, it reared back slightly which in turn, spooked its companions. Maven managed to settle it down and gently stroked the side of the deer's neck whilst speaking to it in a hushed voice. This instantly calmed the deer down. Slowly, he removed his coat and placed it on the now very placid deer's back and gently pressed it down into the animal's fur. He then removed the coat and took his hand off of the deer's neck. This caused the animal to come out of its trance. It took one look at Maven and along with its companions, scattered in the direction of the forest that lay at the foot of the hill. Maven watched them disappear into the tree line.

"I'm sorry, my friends, but we need the time that this will afford us." Feeling totally disgusted with himself, he made his way back to the camp.

"Where have you been?" asked Axis.

"If you must know, I had to take care of some business." Maven gestured towards a small cluster of trees on the hilltop just above them that suggested a call of nature.

"Ah, I see," said Axis.

With that, still in their human forms, they headed down the side of the hill back towards the Northern Lake Road.

Canly and his pack had lost the scent quite soon after Varios had left them the previous evening. But they were now back on the road and desperately trying to regain it.

They were now four again as Lunitas had caught up with them during the night. They continued down the Northern Lake Road, stopping to occasionally sniff the ground and air. Suddenly, Canly stopped. The odour that he had been searching for entered his many scent receptors. He tore off down the road, closely followed by the rest of his pack. The road forked and he shot off to the left and along a path that started to climb. He stopped again once they reached the hill's summit. He looked all around, sniffing loudly. He drew the air into his highly attuned nose, his head then jerked left towards the forest. The trees seemed like a huge congregation, jostling for position at the foot of the hill. Without acknowledging his pack, he arrowed his way down the hill and into the clamouring trees.

The Kindred had made good progress along the road. They had used the watch to regain their heading and as Maven had expected, it pointed in a northerly direction.

They had stayed in their human forms and after some time had passed Alex asked Maven if they should morph.

Maven responded with a resounding, "No!"

"But I thought that time was of the essence?" said Eliza.

"It is, but for now we remain as we are," Maven replied.

In reality, Maven knew that they should morph and speed on along the

Northern Lake Road, but his reasoning, which he kept to himself, was that as their scents differed in both human and animal forms it would confuse their pursuers, and of course the overriding reason was the fear of actually reaching Malustera.

The sun was now high in the sky as they continued along the road.

They were blissfully unaware that high above with its eyes firmly fixed on them and the path that they were taking was a large, black, bird. It followed them for some time and then suddenly adjusted its flight path and headed southwest back over Lake Ancora.

As the raven flew in through the window of the central spire of the fortress, there was a flash of red and there stood Varios Veil.

Magissa was there waiting for him.

"Well?"

"They are heading north along the lake road. I fear that they are heading towards Malustera."

Varios saw the faintest hint of something in his mother's eyes, something that he had never seen her display before – if he didn't know better he could have sworn that it looked almost like fear.

Magissa aware that she may have looked slightly ruffled, composed herself and thought for a moment. "Of course, it makes perfect sense that the Firestone is in Malustera. The fools are walking to their death. We must apprehend them before they enter Malustera and take the Waterstone from them, otherwise that stone will be lost too and we will be back to square one."

She paced the room, pondering her next move. "Varios, go to Canly and inform him of where they are and that he must intercept before they reach Malustera. He is not to harm the children, but the other two are expendable."

Varios bowed and turned on his heel, and then he stopped and turned back to his mother. "How can we hope to recover the Firestone though? Nobody in their right mind is going to enter Malustera." He cowered as he said this as he fully expected one of his mother's patented tirades.

Magissa, knowing that he was correct but not wishing to acknowledge the fact, thought for a moment and then an evil smile started to extend onto her face much like a crack forms in ice.

"We will use them to our advantage. Tell Canly that they are to be apprehended but unharmed. We will take the girl captive and hold her until the others return from Malustera with the stone. If that isn't an incentive to succeed, then nothing is."

Varios smiled and nodded in agreement. He jumped up onto the window ledge and seconds later a raven appeared in his place, it took flight and headed back towards the Northern Lake Road.

The Kindred, guided by the watch, continued along the path. Though Axis had not travelled these lands for over ten years, he was starting to get the sense that they were being guided somewhere off the map – so to speak.

He was noticing that Maven was becoming more and more agitated. He was continually looking behind and when he looked forward, he had a look of dread etched on his face. Axis could not contain his concern any longer. Maven turned around to inspect the path behind only to be met by a stern, yet concerned Axis. He motioned for Maven to join him at the side of the path as Alex and Eliza – who were both studying the watch, continued on.

"What is with you?" Axis asked Maven. "And don't tell me that it's tiredness."

Maven sighed deeply, "I fear that we are being tracked, my friend. I didn't say anything as I didn't want to alarm the children."

"I've sensed it too. But if we are, I feel that they are some distance behind," Axis replied.

"Yes, I took measures this morning to throw them off of our scent."

Axis nodded knowingly. "That would explain your disappearance then?"

Maven nodded and smiled, though it was quite half-hearted.

"There is something more that you need to tell me isn't there?"

Maven looked sheepish as he replied, "I believe that the watch is leading us into Malustera."

Axis looked like he had taken a heavy punch to the stomach. He thought that they were being guided to an unfamiliar destination, but had not considered for a moment that it might be Malustera.

"We cannot take the children there, Maven! You know the stories as well as I do."

Eliza and Alex must have sensed the other two had fallen back, as they had stopped and turned around. They were surprised at how much farther ahead they had travelled and were even more surprised to see both Maven and Axis in a heated exchange. Wondering what was wrong, they both started to backtrack.

"I do know the stories – believe you me. But we have no choice, have you forgotten that we cannot handle the Muleta? We need them with us, Axis."

Axis pondered this for a moment. "You and I can go in and retrieve the stone and bring it back for Alex to place it into the Muleta."

"That will not work, my friend. The Firestone has already awoken. The only way that we can contain its power is to find it and place it in the Muleta as quickly as possible. You saw what happened with the Waterstone. Its balance was affected very soon after Alex had removed it from its resting place. Based on this, it is unlikely that we would be afforded the time that we would need."

"We are supposed to be their protectors, Maven, by doing this we are likely to be leading them to their deaths!"

Just as Axis uttered the last word of his sentence, Eliza and Alex appeared alongside them. They both looked extremely concerned.

Maven and Axis had become so absorbed in their conversation, they had not realised that Eliza and Alex were standing there.

"How much of that did you hear?" asked Axis.

"Enough," said Alex.

"What's going on? Where exactly are you taking us?" asked Eliza.

Maven and Axis looked at each other.

"Tell them," said Axis.

Maven turned towards them both with a resigned look on his face.

He then said as casually as he could, "It would appear that the watch is leading us into Malustera."

Eliza and Alex had a mixture of fear and confusion painted on their faces.

"But I thought you said that we needed to avoid that place at all costs?" said Eliza.

Maven sighed, "Yes, I did. But the watch is leading us there and upon reflection, Malustera is the only logical place that the Firestone would be."

They all stood in silence as this news sunk in.

Finally, Alex spoke up. There was a reverence about him as the words exited his mouth. "Well, the choice is clear. We must press on to Malustera and retrieve the Firestone. We have overcome all obstacles that have been placed in our way so far. I don't see why we can't overcome this."

Maven, admiring Alex's resolve, patted him on the shoulder. "You truly are your father's son, Alex."

Maven did not say anything but he somehow felt energised, bolstered by Alex's words. *Indeed, a king in the making,* he thought to himself.

Maven, suddenly seeming more like his old self, started to organise his colleagues.

"Right, we must assume our animal forms and push on. We do not know what awaits us, but if we remain united, Alex is right, there isn't anything that we cannot overcome. If fortune is with us once again, we will be able to enter Malustera undetected and hopefully find the Firestone quickly and exit without incident."

Eliza and Alex both smiled and nodded in agreement. Axis said nothing but smiled to himself and in his mind said, *Welcome back, old friend.*

Alex looked at the watch to see that their heading was still set – due north. With that, they all reverted back to their animal forms and tore away with all haste towards the unknown of Malustera.

High above them, the raven watched as they sped along the road. It turned south, searching for Canly and his pack. He flew all the way back to Kessler, but to his surprise, he did not encounter them. *Where is that incompetent fool?* he thought to himself. *Why would he leave the road?* He decided to fly towards the Cragon Hills as this was the only other route open to Canly. He flew over the city of Kessler, smiling to himself as he looked down to see its occupants trudging along, mundanely going about their business. From his vantage point, it looked almost rhythmic, mechanical. He smiled to himself. *Every last one of them is under Mother's control.* He cleared the final and most impressive looking rooftop that was once Eliza's home and then proceeded to scan the surrounding area for Canly. Still no sign. *They have gone off mission,* he thought to himself. *Mother will hear about this.* He was just about to head back to Arcamedia, when he sensed movement at the edge of the forest. He flew around for a closer look.

Crashing its way out of the throng of trees was a massive wolf, closely followed by three slightly smaller comrades. The four wolves were speeding their way up the hill, almost as if their tails were on fire. The raven landed on the branch of a lone tree near the top of the hill and let out a screech. The largest wolf looked up in the raven's direction and slowed a little but did not stop. The raven screeched again, louder this time. Canly came to a standstill near the tree, but remained in the form of a wolf. He could hear Varios' voice in his head, "Get lost did we, Canly? I thought that you were an expert tracker? Evidently not."

If he didn't know better, Canly was sure that he could see a sneer on the raven's face. He bared his teeth. "I suggest you stay up in that tree if you know what's good for you."

"Are you threatening me, Canly? I certainly hope not, because my mother would be most displeased to hear of that in my report."

Canly backtracked slightly, but was still baring his teeth. "No. I never make threats, *not idle ones anyway.*"

"Good. I am glad to hear that."

"Those that you hunt are a good distance ahead. Where have you been?"

Canly did not like being questioned but felt the need to explain. "They obviously realised that they were being tracked and must have created a diversion," he growled. "We tracked their scent into the forest but all that we came upon were a herd of deer. I would have slaughtered every last one of them had time permitted." He bared his teeth menacingly. Despite this, Varios could not resist the urge to goad him further.

"The great Canly being so easily out-foxed. Based on your reputation, I really would have expected better."

Canly snarled under his breath but did not respond.

Varios was disappointed by this, so decided to prod further.

"You obviously drew too close to them during the pursuit and this alerted them to your presence. This really is amateur hour. So very disappointing," he oiled.

Canly was primed, ready to explode. Varios smiled to himself as he could see that his comments were having the desired effect.

"I am obviously the better tracker as I know where they are as well as where they are heading and they did not have the slightest inkling that they were being watched."

Varios went silent as he allowed his latest slight towards Canly to sink in.

"Well?" growled Canly.

"Well what?" said Varios, feigning ignorance.

Canly was seething. "Where are they?"

Varios was silently revelling in playing Canly.

"They are still on the Northern Lake Road."

"And where are they heading?"

"Towards Malustera," said Varios as casually as he could.

Canly seemed to shrink ever so slightly.

"What are our orders?" His level of aggression had all of a sudden diminished, he seemed almost sheepish.

"Magissa wishes you to intercept them before they can enter Malustera. Her plan is to hold the girl captive whilst sending the others into Malustera to gather the Firestone. This will then be their bargaining chip for her life."

Canly took all of this information in.

"I suggest that you get a move on, because if they cross the borders of Malustera before you intercept, you and your pack *will* be joining them."

As much as Canly hated being spoken to like this, it paled in comparison to the unknown evil that lurked in Malustera. His mind wandered back to his childhood. Against all advice, his father had ventured into Malustera and that was the last he had seen of him. His mind snapped back to the present. "We will take them before they cross."

"Good," said Varios. "You three carry on. I need a word with Falmus, he will catch up."

Canly threw his head back and let out a howl. He, closely followed by Artemas and Lunitas powered up the hill back towards the Northern Lake Road. Such was the pace that they set, one would get the impression that their very lives depended on it.

Falmus heard a voice in his head as he looked up at the raven. "I need you to do something for me."

"What?"

Varios looked behind him to see that the other three wolves were some distance away.

"I need you to take the children out of the picture."

"But we were told to intercept, not kill."

"Well things change! Do as I say or my mother will hear of how you disobeyed a direct order and intentionally sent your pack off course."

"I did no such thing!" Falmus protested.

"Oh come now, Falmus. I will tell Mother that you are a sympathiser to their cause. Perhaps you can explain things to her, as you know how understanding she is."

Falmus, knowing that he was in a no-win situation nodded and tore off after the rest of his pack.

Varios, satisfied that he had adequately motivated Canly, Falmus and the rest of the pack, took flight and headed back towards Arcamedia.

15.

The Borders of Malustera

Varios arrived back at the ledge located on the highest window in the central tower. Once again, Magissa was waiting for him.

"Well? I assume that you have news?"

"I do. Canly and his pack are heading to intercept with all haste."

"What! They have not intercepted already? What have they been doing?"

Varios knowing that he had a further opportunity to trample on Canly and attempt to raise his own profile in the process, smiled smugly.

Magissa glowered at him. "What are you smirking about? You consider this situation to be amusing?"

The smile disappeared from his face immediately. "Of course not, apologies, Mother. Canly and his pack drew too close to their quarry, which alerted them to their presence. Then to add further incompetence into the mix, they were easily outwitted and sent on a wild goose, actually in this case, a wild deer chase." The smug smile once again crept across his face, but it was far less pronounced this time.

Magissa was simmering with rage.

"Canly is an incompetent fool, Mother. I don't know why you put so much stock in him."

"He is my best and most loyal soldier, not that I have to explain myself to you!" she hissed.

Varios would normally retreat into himself at this point, but felt an unfamiliar bravery course through him. "How can you think he is your best soldier, Mother? If he was a good soldier and had disposed of Axis when he was off world as you had ordered, then we would find ourselves in a much stronger position."

Magissa stared in silence. Varios braced himself for the explosion, but it never came.

"He has been disappointing of late," she mused. "Maybe I should reassign him? Do you know of someone worthy enough to replace him?"

"Indeed I do, Mother."

"Who?"

"Well, me of course."

Without even the slightest change to her demeanour, Magissa let out a high-pitched noise that was somewhere between a laugh and a scream.

"You! You! No, Varios, you are not at all worthy. You are a slinking coward. You are lucky that you are my son otherwise you would be residing with the braindead zombies that are found in the lowest level of Arcamedia."

Varios did not say anything but could not hide his dismay at this affront.

"I think that it is time that I take a more hands-on role in this," said Magissa. "Prepare a regiment and my horse. We ride for the borders of Malustera."

Varios nodded, bowed and still smarting from his mother's slight, exited the room.

Magissa thought to herself, *I cannot rely on weak-minded fools. If I want this handled properly, I need to do it myself.*

****

The Kindred could see a shimmering light on the horizon. They all heard Maven's voice in their heads. "Malustera, dead ahead!"

Next, they could hear Axis' voice. "You could have chosen your words more carefully, Maven."

"Ah, yes. Forgive me. That was in poor taste."

Alex looked ahead and wondered if the shimmering was indicative of heat in the air or was there was some sort of spell or force field in place, designed to stop unwanted visitors from entering. He didn't ask Maven, but continued to turn this over in his mind as they all drew ever closer to their shimmering destination.

Canly, flanked by his three comrades, continued to devour the ground as they tore along the Northern Lake Road. He had now regained the scent of their quarry and knew that they were closing in. At this, he afforded himself a smile even though he was still angry about the way Varios had spoken to him and lauded his supposed superiority over him. But this paled in comparison to the other thoughts that had been spinning around his mind. He had not thought about his father for years, but the mere mention of Malustera had immediately brought the memories flooding back.

He looked ahead and in the distance he could see a shimmering light that descended across the horizon. It was imperative that they intercept their quarry very soon, as he had no desire whatsoever to enter Malustera, lest he meet his father's fate. He and his pack were already moving at great speed, but inexplicably, Canly found another gear, tearing on ahead and leaving the other members of his pack in his wake. They all looked at one another and then heard Canly's voice, "You'd all better keep up. We need to take them before they cross into Malustera."

"We can't go any faster, Canly, we have been running flat out for hours, we need to rest," came the response from Falmus.

If he had time, Canly would have stopped and shown Falmus the error of his ways, but instead, he just offered a warning. "We do not have time to rest, if we don't catch them before they cross, the last one of you to arrive will be the first into Malustera."

This was the greatest incentive that they could have been given as simultaneously, they all found that other gear and drew level with Canly.

He grinned menacingly at them. "You see, we all have hidden reserves, it is just a case of pressing the correct button to reveal them."

They didn't respond to this, they all just focused on keeping up with Canly. None of them wanted to enter Malustera and certainly didn't want to be the first to enter, alone.

Canly's voice came through again. "The road being so exposed does not allow us to attempt a stealth attack, so we need to hit them at the same time. Though it still calls for a probing, synchronised attack. Falmus, you and I will take the big one as he is the main threat. Lunitas, you and Artemas can deal with the Mystic and the two children. Do not underestimate the Mystic, he may appear a feeble old man, but he is far from it."

His companions all tilted their heads slightly to confirm that they understood.

"Remember, we are to take them hostage, no maiming and no killing or we will have to answer to Magissa which will make Malustera the very least of our concerns." Once again they all tilted their heads, though it was much more pronounced this time. "Good, I am glad that you all understand. We are drawing very close, I can smell it."

The Kindred had drawn to a halt and had morphed back into their human forms. The lush path that had been their road for so many days had come to an abrupt end. The lands that lay behind them epitomised beauty, but what lay in front of them was the polar opposite. It was the most desolate looking landscape that any of them had ever seen. It was arid, barren, and seemingly bereft of life. There were what appeared to be former trees that were so scorched, that in reality, they were nothing more than reconstituted ash. There were the occasional bushels, but these had fallen foul of the environment and now all but blended in with the sand that made up ninety-nine percent of the panorama. One more step would take the band into this would-be purgatory.

"Surely nothing could live in there?" said Alex.

Nothing friendly, thought Maven.

"I'll enter first and scout around," said Axis.

"If you insist," said Maven. He was half relieved and half concerned. "First, let me just ensure that there isn't any shielding in place." Maven removed his staff from the pack that Axis had been carrying and cautiously, moved it towards the threshold. All of a sudden, there was a huge crackling sound followed by an orange flash of light and Maven was thrown back a good distance.

Axis ran to him. "Maven! Are you okay?"

Maven opened his eyes and murmured before reaching out a hand which Axis took and pulled him to his feet with such ease, he may as well have been a ragdoll. Maven's hair was on end and his normally perfectly coiffed beard had splayed out at the edges and now looked like an upside-down Christmas tree.

"Maven?"

"Um. Oh yes, I'm fine – I'm fine. Well, I think that answers our question regarding shielding." He mustered a cheeky smirk before heading back towards the threshold.

"Careful," said Eliza.

Maven looked at her and smiled.

"Don't worry, my dear, I believe that there is a saying on Earth: twice bitten, once shy. No, no, that's not it. Ah yes. Once bitten, twice shy." With that he took his staff and drew an oblong that was approximately seven foot tall and four foot wide. It stood just a few inches in front of the threshold. He then muttered the word 'Apertios' and touched the outline of the doorway with his staff. Slowly, it moved towards the threshold. Alex and Eliza both stepped back slightly and braced themselves for the crackling sound followed by the orange flash of light, but neither happened. Instead, the doorway moved into position and as it clicked into place, a white light traced around its perimeter. Maven moved in closer. Once again, he took his staff and moved it towards the threshold, parallel to the doorway that he had just created. This time, his staff continued past the threshold without incident.

Alex studied the barrier and then turned towards Maven.

"Who do you think put this here?" he asked.

Maven thought about this for a moment and then said, "I don't know. But maybe the more pertinent question is why was it put there? Were they trying to keep people out, or keep something in?"

Maven then turned to Axis. "It is safe to enter, old friend. Good luck and be careful."

Alex and Eliza moved alongside Maven. Axis smiled and said, "I'll be fi..." As his voice broke off, his expression changed from soothing to horrified. "Look out!" he shouted and he pushed all three of them to the side of the path just as a pack of four ravening wolves descended upon them.

The one called Falmus attacked first. He seemed to break protocol by running ahead of Canly and pouncing in the direction of Axis. Axis did not have time to morph, but he was more than formidable in human form. He sidestepped Falmus' attack and as the wolf tried to adjust to compensate for the feint from Axis, he was caught in the side of the face by one of Axis' huge fists. He yelped and fell down in a crumpled heap. Axis looked over to check on his companions. The wolves called Artemas and Lunitas had the three of them pinned down. Canly was circling Axis, teeth bared, ready to attack. To the left of Axis, Falmus was starting to stir.

"We have been here before, Canly, have we not?" said Axis.

Canly opened his steel trap of a mouth wider to further expose his huge fangs.

"Indeed we have. I must say, the taste of your flesh was pleasing to my stomach. Though last time, I just took a morsel, this time, I intend to tear myself a steak!"

With that, Canly launched himself towards Axis, the speed and force of which, knocked Axis onto his back. Canly was grappling with Axis, using his front paws to try and pin Axis' shoulders down to the ground. As they were so evenly matched in the strength department, this contest went on for some time. After what felt like hours, Axis' shoulders started to sink towards the earth. Canly seemed to be gaining the upper-hand. Little did he know this was an intentional ploy by Axis. As Canly drove his weight forwards, it enabled Axis to free up his tree trunk like legs. Canly's face was now inches from Axis'. He could feel the hot breath of the wolf hit his face in intervals. It was like somebody was rhythmically opening and closing the door to a furnace. It was stifling! Axis sensed his opportunity. Slowly he started to draw back his huge legs, careful not to alert his foe to this. Canly, still not realising that Axis was allowing him the impression that he was being overpowered, started to get overconfident.

"I am disappointed, Axis. The head of the king's guard, undefeated in the Arcamedian Trials, your reputation is legendary. Perhaps you are just another example of the stories far and away exceeding the reality. I expected... no, I wanted a better fight."

Axis looked him square in the eye. "You really should be careful what you wish for."

Axis, now with his knees almost parallel to his sternum, pushed out with all of his immense leg strength, sending an unsuspecting Canly on a short, sharp journey that culminated with him crashing headlong into both Artemas and Lunitas, scattering them like skittles. Maven, sensing an opportunity, got to his feet and encouraged Eliza and Alex to do likewise. They made their way towards Axis who was just starting to get to his feet. Canly was enraged. He hated being made to look foolish. He got back up and started to cajole Artemas and Lunitas to do the same. There was no methodical, probing attack this time. The three wolves all started to run towards The Kindred. Axis was poised in the stance of an experienced fighter; Maven brandished his staff in the direction of the wolves. Alex and Eliza both looked uncertainly at each other, but repositioned their feet so as to dig in and hold their ground. Maven looked over at them and realising that they were unarmed, pointed his staff at them in turn and uttered the words, "Apt Armar." Eliza and Alex, who moments earlier had their hands balled into fists, now had a black club-like weapon in each hand. They both looked quizzically at Maven.

Maven pre-empted the next question, "They are called Impulse Batons."

They still looked confused.

"What?"

"Shock Sticks," said Maven hurriedly. "I'll properly explain at a less perilous time. Now use them! Defend yourselves!"

The wolves had picked their targets. Lunitas had Maven in his sights. Artemas had his eyes fixed firmly on Eliza and Alex, with Canly once again, homing in on Axis.

Maven was firing bolts from his staff towards Lunitas, but the wolf was able to dodge the Mystic's attempts to slow him down. He was drifting expertly from side to side and now was once again, squarely in front of Maven. The Mystic managed to get another bolt away that exploded into the ground just to the left of the wolf, this caused him to drift right just as he was about to make contact with Maven. This was Maven's opportunity, he repositioned himself slightly and with the help of Lunitas' own momentum, he used his staff to sweep the legs out from under him. The wolf sailed through the air and then tumbled head over tail, unable to control himself. Alex, who was in the path of this, had to dive out of the way. A split second later, there was a loud cracking noise, followed by an orange flash and the wolf was being propelled in the direction from whence he came – a fur covered projectile that landed unceremoniously, smouldering and unconscious.

At the same time, Artemas was bearing down on Eliza. Her heart rate was increasing rapidly, she was starting to panic. She fought the urge to run and continued to hold her ground. Artemas was now airborne with one of his huge paws drawn back, poised to strike.

"Disable, not maim!" roared Canly.

Artemas kept his paw in the striking position, but immediately retracted his claws. Everything seemed to slow down for Eliza, she could see the huge wolf airborne, heading directly for her, but she seemed to have time to assess her options. Just as the wolf was upon her, she drew back one of the batons and cracked the wolf right on the snout. There was a loud buzzing noise as the Impulse Baton made contact, followed by a pained yelp from the wolf and the smell of burning fur.

Eliza looked at the baton and smiled, *I like these.*

Artemas was enraged; he rounded on Eliza and once again left the ground to attack her. As before, everything slowed down for her. Without realising it, she was now moving towards Artemas' attack. At the last possible second, she slid on her knees underneath the wolf and held both of the batons above her head. As the confused wolf passed over her, the buzzing noise started again as the batons impacted against the wolf. This built to a crescendo that sounded like a buzzsaw. The power of the batons seemed to affect every single nerve ending in the body of the wolf. Artemas cleared Eliza and landed on the ground in a crumpled, convulsing heap. Eliza couldn't believe what she had just done. Was it her, or were the batons imbued with some sort of spell that ensured each of her blows were true? At this point, Alex had regained his feet and was rushing to Eliza's aid. When he reached her side, he was amazed to find that the wolf was unconscious and that she was on her feet, seemingly unharmed.

"Did you do this?" asked Alex.

Eliza was looking back and forth between the wolf and the Impulse Batons in her hands.

"Of course," she smiled. "I've got skills!" She twirled both of the batons in her hands, and blew on the ends like a gunslinger from the Old West.

He smiled back at her. "I am impressed, well done."

Alex was relieved and full of admiration for Eliza. He was also aware that his feelings for her were intensifying.

Across to their left, Falmus, who had been conscious and aware for some time, decided that the time was right to make his move. As Maven, Eliza and Alex were making their way across to assist Axis with Canly, Falmus on his haunches, crept towards Alex who was at the back of the group. Falmus, remembering his conversation with Varios, was poised, ready to take out the heir to Arcamedia once and for all. He was right on his prey now. Alex was unaware, as his focus was on assisting Axis. The wolf, with jaws parted was about to attack. Then there was a shrill voice behind them, "Restrix!"

Falmus was frozen; he could not move anything other than his eyes that were desperately scanning in an effort to find out what had happened to him. The sound of the voice had caused Axis and Canly to break off from the latest battle and Maven, Eliza and Alex all looked around for the source of the voice. As he turned, Alex was startled to find Falmus virtually on top of him; he almost fell over as a result. As he composed himself, he noticed that the wolf was unable to move, except for his eyes that were darting around frantically searching. They didn't need to search much longer because the source soon became apparent. Magissa Veil, flanked by Varios, came into view. They had a small army behind them.

16.

A Vulgar Display of Power

"Well, Alex. What do you say?" oiled Magissa. With her now customary tightened features her mouth barely seemed to move, she was almost like a ventriloquist. This was quite apt as Varios, astride his horse alongside her, certainly looked like her dummy.

Alex said nothing; he just stared at her with a burning hatred in his eyes.

"The children of today, no manners at all." She looked at Varios who was smiling at his mother's comment.

"Thank you is what I was looking for. Had I not arrived when I did, Falmus would certainly have killed you."

Alex found his voice. "Why would you help me, they are obviously doing your bidding, so why stop him?"

Magissa looked at him. "Well, that is where you are wrong, my dear boy. My four charges were sent to capture you, not kill you. I don't want you dead…well, not yet." Her lips quivered as she tried to generate a smile. When it came, it was suitably menacing.

She dismounted her horse and headed towards where Alex was standing. The way that she walked was so mechanical, Alex thought that she would only get so far before Varios had to run over and rewind her before she could progress any further. His entire body tensed as she drew nearer, but instead of coming to him, she stood alongside Falmus. Methodically, she extended a hand. Falmus' eyes widened, even though he couldn't move, the fear in his eyes was evident. She then brought her hand down onto his head, pausing for effect and then proceeded to stroke him.

"Falmus. Falmus," her voice was uncharacteristically soft. "You have been a loyal servant to me." She continued to stroke his head, almost affectionately. "But you would have killed Alex had I not arrived and this act could have jeopardised everything. I cannot let this go unpunished." A menacing tone had returned to her voice. Veins were breaking in Falmus' eyes as he was frantically trying to use the only part of his body that would move, to offer an apology.

Her tone then softened once again. "But I can see in your eyes that you are sorry."

Falmus seemed to relax slightly.

"Perhaps I'll just send you on a holiday."

She stopped stroking his head and uttered the word, "Destrix." He could move again.

He bowed his head. "Thank you, my queen," Falmus continued, "I'm so sorry. I did not want to do this." He looked across at Magissa's entourage. Varios shifted uneasily in his saddle. "It was Va…"

Magissa cut him off. "Please let me know how Malustera is at this time of year."

"No! My queen! Please!"

She pointed her staff at the panicked wolf. "Expedex!" she screamed.

Falmus was wrenched upwards and moved apace towards the opening that Maven had created in the barrier on the border of Malustera. Falmus was pleading and screaming as he passed into Malustera. Magissa's spell carried him until he was just a speck on the horizon and they all looked on as he was dropped unceremoniously to the ground.

Magissa looked at each of The Kindred in turn, and a self-satisfied smile slowly made its way onto her face. She was obviously revelling in her show of power. Maven and Axis stood resolute, ready to resume the battle. Magissa recognised this.

"I admire your courage, but you are ridiculously outnumbered." She gestured to the horde behind her. "I suggest that you stand down before any blood is needlessly shed."

She started to make her way towards Eliza. She tousled Alex's hair as she walked past him. Alex felt a coldness penetrate his scalp as if someone had poured ice cold water onto his head. He grabbed her hand and shoved it away aggressively, she seemed to not notice; her eyes were fixed firmly on Eliza.

Eliza felt extremely uneasy, she dared not meet Magissa's gaze. Instead she looked all around, seeking an escape route.

"Get behind me, my dear," called Maven as he stepped forward. "She will have to go through me to get to you."

"Oh don't be so dramatic. I have no intention of causing her harm," said Magissa.

"Besides, you are no match for me and you know it!"

"Harm one hair on her head and we shall see," threatened Maven.

"The delusion in you runs deep, Maven. Think yourself lucky that I do not make an example of you right here and now."

Once again she turned her attention to Eliza. "I knew your parents very well, I am sure that you have many questions, we could discuss this during the time that we will soon be spending together." Once again her face began to twitch and spasm as a smile crept across it. She looked positively reptilian.

Eliza thought that she would rather follow Falmus into Malustera than spend a single moment with this awful woman.

How dare she speak of my parents! she thought to herself. She suddenly felt a rage begin course through her.

"What do you know of my parents?" she demanded. "The only question I have for you is why did you kill my mother?"

The smile on Magissa's face vanished. "Is that what this fool has told you?" She pointed to Axis. "He has no proof of this and neither do you. I have had enough of being reasonable; here is what is going to happen. You will stay with me, Eliza, whilst your friends enter Malustera and retrieve the Firestone. Once they return with it, we shall make a trade; the Origin Stones and the Muleta for you. Should they be unsuccessful... well, let's just say that failure is not an option."

Alex, whose head was just starting to get back to normal, spoke up. "What good is the Muleta to you? You cannot wield it!"

Magissa slowly turned to look at him.

"Congratulations on obtaining the Muleta by the way. You must be very pleased with yourself."

Alex did not expect this reaction at all.

"But don't be too quick to pat yourself on the back, as it is just on an unsanctioned loan. You are going to keep it warm as well as populating it for me. All you have really achieved is proving yourself to be a thief."

Alex made to retort, but Magissa cut him off.

In response to your original question, you forget, I don't need to wield it."

"Varios!"

Varios Veil jumped off of his horse and disappeared into the mass ranks behind him. A few moments later, he re-emerged clutching the arm of a shorter, older man and dragged him into view. Alex immediately recognised the shell of a man that was his father. Maven stared in disbelief.

Axis gasped and called out, "Cordium! My king! What has she done to you?"

The frail-looking man gave no indication that he had even heard Axis, let alone recognised him. They had known that Cordium was no longer himself but they were shocked at just how different he had become. Axis made to run towards him but Canly with teeth bared, cut him off.

Magissa was clearly enjoying the effect that seeing a man that they once so revered reduced to the husk that stood before them, unaware of who they were, where he was, or even what day it was, had on them.

She decided that another display was in order. "Cordium!" she shrieked. Slowly, the man turned his head to face Magissa. "Show these people how obedient you are? Get down on all fours and crawl over to me." She snapped her fingers and slowly, methodically, the man proceeded to lower himself to the ground until he was on all fours. He then crawled his way towards Magissa.

"I have someone who can wield it for me and as you can see, he is extremely well trained."

Axis looked horrified. "Cordium! Get up! Don't let her do this to you!"

The man seemed not to hear, he just continued to crawl towards Magissa.

"He cannot hear you, turncoat. He only hears me and even if he could hear you, he would not recognise or respond to your voice. You and all of his past life has been vanquished from his mind. He will do anything that I say."

"You are vile!" yelled Alex.

Magissa fixed him with a cold stare.

"It's pronounced 'Veil' and very soon it will be the only name that any of you will know. Now enough of this! You have a Firestone to recover and a girl to save," she glowered at them all.

"Artemas! Bring the girl here."

Maven stepped forward. "You cannot take her!"

Suddenly Magissa's entire visage changed. Her face darkened and her green eyes seemed to burn like emerald fires.

"I am warning you, Mystic!" she shrieked. "You are not critical to this mission, if you try to get in my way one more time, I will put an end to your pitiful existence! Now stand aside!"

Maven stood resolute.

"Maven! Stand down!" cried Axis. "It wouldn't make sense for her to harm Eliza." He looked across to her reassuringly. "We will get the stone and make the trade."

"You should listen to the turncoat," said Magissa. "He offers sound, life-extending advice."

Axis looked at him imploringly. "Please, Maven. We need you."

Reluctantly, Maven backed away allowing Artemas to usher Eliza away.

"A wise choice," said Magissa slimily, her rigid demeanour returning. Artemas manoeuvred Eliza alongside Magissa; she looked down at her and grabbed her by the wrist. In a show of defiance, Eliza snatched her arm away and tried to move out of Magissa's reach but Artemas was circling, keeping her within arms-reach of Magissa.

She grabbed Eliza by the wrist once again.

"Your stay with me will be far more pleasant if you fall into line, my dear."

Eliza looked across at her companions. Axis nodded and forced a smile in an effort to reassure her.

"Stay strong, we'll be back before you know it," Alex called out.

"That's the spirit!" said Magissa condescendingly. "Now no more stalling. The three of you need to cross the border. Canly, Lunitas and Artemas will also be joining you."

The three wolves stared at Magissa in disbelief. Canly morphed into his human form. "My queen? What need is there for us to enter? We did as you asked; we apprehended them before they crossed."

"Had I not arrived to intervene, they would have overpowered you and slipped through my fingers. You will accompany them to ensure that they do not try any tricks and you will also aid them if the situation calls for it."

"Very well," came Canly's reluctant response. "We will accompany, but I have no intention of fighting alongside them. They are my enemy, why would I aid them?"

Magissa's face flushed. "I grow tired of this insubordination! You will do as I ask or you will find that the doorway back will be closed off to you. Besides, you will very well face unknown dangers in Malustera; your only hope of returning will be to work together. This is a situation whereby your enemy's enemy is your friend – temporarily of course."

Canly looked resigned to his fate. "As you command, my queen."

Artemas and Lunitas morphed into their human forms and along with Canly, they lined up alongside Axis, Maven and Alex. They all stood just in front of the barrier. Axis and Maven turned to face Magissa who had Eliza on one side and Cordium on the other. Both men then placed their left hand on their right shoulder and grabbed their left wrist with their right hand. Alex looked on confused by the makeshift 'A' that both men had made. "What are you doing?" he whispered.

"It is an Arcamedian mark of respect that we are directing towards our king," said Axis.

Cordium didn't react at all. He had the same vacant expression on his face, seemingly unaware of where he was or of anything that was going on around him.

"Very touching and noble of you both, but in vain. What part of 'he does not recognise you' do you not understand?" Magissa drawled.

"That salute means absolutely nothing to him. Now, Malustera awaits!"

The six *companions* turned to face the barren nothingness that was Malustera. Alex looked towards the horizon, wondering what dangers awaited them. Then he noticed that there was a black shape moving at great speed heading in their direction. As Alex watched the speck draw closer, he realised that it was Falmus. *He must have come to and started to head back to the border to plead with Magissa*, he thought to himself. He continued to look on, puzzled by what he was seeing. *He is moving awfully fast though.* He looked across at Axis and Maven; both men were squinting at the rapid black speck that was heading towards them.

"What are you waiting for? Get in!" screamed Magissa.

"My queen," said Canly. "That is Falmus and he seems to be heading back this way."

Magissa looked at the black shape in the distance. "Forget him. Just get in!"

Just as she had uttered these words, they all became aware of a large number of additional black shapes coming over the rise of the large sand dune that was on the horizon. They were too far away to make out what they were, but they were unquestionably moving at high speed. They were already gaining on Falmus.

Everyone on the Northern Lake Road looked on in disbelief at the scene that was unfolding in front of them. As the shape in the lead drew closer, it became clear that it was Falmus. He had a look of pure dread on his face and looked like he was literally, running for his life. As he drew closer still, Alex soon realised why Falmus looked so scared. He was being chased by a pack of creatures that bore some resemblance to lions, cheetahs and coyotes but as he looked closer, he noticed that there were some significant differences. Their teeth were more like tusks as they protruded from their gaping maws. Also, their hind legs were ridiculously overdeveloped, which explained the huge speed that they were travelling at. They were now virtually on top of Falmus.

They could hear him scream, "Somebody help me! Please!"

"Get out of there, Falmus!" yelled Canly.

But it was too late. The first wave didn't break stride and ran straight over the top of him. He was lost from view by the plumes of sand that had been kicked up by the rampaging pack. As the dust started to settle, they all saw the now human body of Falmus lying motionless in the sand. It was in this moment that everyone on the other side of the barrier realised that these creatures were heading straight for them and had no intention of slowing down.

Many of Magissa's entourage started to panic and were beginning to scatter. In the ensuing chaos, Axis saw an opportunity. He grabbed Alex by the arm and said, "Follow me."

Axis, Alex and Maven headed off to the side of the road, away from the melee. They looked on as Magissa was trying to regain control of her troops.

"Get back into formation!" she shouted.

"Assume your animal identities, stand your ground and await my order to attack." She had a look of confidence on her face. "These fools will have to come through the doorway single file; we can pick them off one by one."

No sooner had she said this than a particularly large lion inexplicably, picked up more speed and broke away from the pack. He sprung towards the doorway that Maven had created and when he landed on the Northern Lake Road, he still bore a huge resemblance to a lion, but was standing on his hind legs.

Alex stared at the Lionman. He was huge, a good three inches taller than Axis – at least. Most of his body was covered in fur and his wild hair and beard, looked just like the mane of the lion that he had been seconds earlier. Alex thought that he made Canly look positively warm and friendly. The Lionman grabbed a staff that was attached to his back. It extended as he held it aloft in front of him. He then drove it hard into the ground. The ground shook and there was a discernible whooshing sound and the barrier was no more.

Magissa's eyes widened as she watched the shimmering barrier disappear. Moments earlier she smugly thought that she and her charges had the upper hand, but now the rampaging throng of creatures had the ability to attack as one. Once again, she found herself having to regain control of those around her.

"Hold your positions!" she screamed.

"Every single one of you will fight to your last, or there will be consequences!"

17.
Let Battle Commence

The Lionman turned to face Magissa. As he stared directly at her, there was no discernible emotion on his face. She remained stoic, trying not to show any sign that she felt even remotely threatened. The Lionman then raised his hand and the mass of animality behind him came to an immediate standstill.

Now that all of his charges were on the Northern Lake Road, the Lionman once again drove his staff into the ground which caused the shimmering barrier to reappear. Maven looked on and noted that the doorway that he had created earlier was still open.

They stared in silence for some time, Magissa with her army flanking her and the Lionman with his behind him, creating an additional barrier to the entrance into Malustera.

Finally, Magissa decided to break the silence, her authoritative air had returned as she spoke.

"What is transpiring here does not concern you. I suggest that you move on."

The Lionman said nothing, he just continued to stare.

Magissa looked slightly ruffled.

"Who are you and what do you want?"

He continued to ignore the interrogation as his stare fell onto Eliza whose arm was still being clutched by Magissa. His eyes softened ever so slightly as he nodded to her. He then looked across to where Axis, Maven and Alex had positioned themselves and once again nodded at Alex and smiled at the other two.

Alex looked at Axis and Maven. "Do you know him?" he mouthed as he pointed at the Lionman. They both stared back blankly and Axis shrugged his shoulders. In actuality, there was something mildly familiar about him but Axis just could not place him.

Magissa was growing impatient.

"I am addressing you, creature! I suggest that you make yourself known and answer my questions."

The emotionless look returned as the Lionman's stare found Magissa once again, but still he said nothing.

Internally, Magissa was beside herself. *Who does he think he is? Does he not know who I am?*

"You do resemble a creature more than a man, perhaps you have lost the ability to verbalise?" she said, her tone demeaning.

Still the Lionman just stared.

"Speak! Or so help me, I shall make you scream out in pain!"

The Lionman looked unperturbed by this threat; he just looked on as a nonchalant smile broke out in the corner of his mouth, displaying a huge set of fangs. He had an obvious under-bite that only served to further accentuate his fangs as they splayed out of his mouth at twenty-five degree angles.

Finally, he spoke. After each word there was a resonating rumble from deep within his chest that almost made it seem as if he were growling more than speaking.

"My name is Leomas Exelcor. I speak for the people of Malustera. We are here for the two children."

The realisation suddenly dawned on Axis. "That's Leo," he whispered to Alex and Maven.

"I thought he was dead," said a stunned Maven.

"Who is Leo?" Alex asked. Neither responded; their attention was once again directed to the conversation between Leomas and Magissa.

"Really?" The sarcasm in Magissa's voice was apparent. "Well what are they to you?"

"I do not have to answer to you. That is between them and me," rumbled Leomas.

This riled Magissa further. "How dare you speak to me in that manner! Do you know who I am?"

"I know who you are Magissa Veil and I also know who you were," he growled.

Magissa did not outwardly show it but she was a little taken aback by this comment.

"I do not know you, creature and you only know of me through my renown. Now I ask again, what are they to you?"

"None of your concern, witch. You hold no sway over me or my people. Now I suggest that you let us take the children and there will be no need for any further unpleasantness."

"Unpleasantness," she sneered. "You do not dictate terms to me, creature. You will not take the children. If you stand down now, I will allow you all to return to your sandpit, unharmed."

Once again Leomas smiled, exposing his crooked fangs. "I don't think that you understand. We will be taking the children and are quite prepared to use force if necessary."

"You do not threaten me, creature. You have had your one chance to return unscathed, you now leave me with no choice." With that she raised her staff and screamed, "Acermors!"

A large red bolt erupted from the end of the staff and struck the creature directly to the left of Leomas. It was dead before it hit the ground. Leomas was incensed as he looked at his fallen comrade.

"Attack!" he roared and in unison, the creatures that had been guarding the border bore down on Magissa and her army.

"Varios!" yelled Magissa.

He appeared, "Mother?"

"Where have you been hiding?"

"I haven't be…"

"Never mind! Get these two out of here now!" She thrust Eliza and Cordium in his direction and then continued to fire the red bolts out of the end of her staff at the enraged creatures that were descending on them.

Varios grabbed Eliza by the wrist and started to drag her away from the battlefield. She tried to wrestle her way free, but Varios was too strong and he knew it. He sneered at her futile efforts. He then turned his attention to Cordium who was meandering along completely ignorant to the conflict that was raging not far behind. "Move your worthless carcass." Varios lifted his right foot and used it to push him in the lower back. Cordium staggered forward a few foot, it looked as if he would lose his balance and fall face first to the ground. Eliza reached out with her free hand and grabbed Cordium's belt. This was enough to steady him and help him regain his balance and as if nothing had happened, he once again resumed the same meandering pace. Varios dragged Eliza back into step.

She glared at him. "You are a coward and like all cowards, you prey on those who cannot defend themselves. You disgust me!"

Varios grinned at her. "Well thank you *so* much for that assessment, if only your opinion meant something to me. Now move!"

The battle was in full swing now; many had already fallen from both sides. Alex was frantically searching for Eliza. He sensed that she was in danger and was desperate to run to her aid.

Maven and Axis had now both joined the fray and resumed their battle with Lunitas and Canly respectively. As Axis was clashing with Canly, he noticed Alex moving closer to the throng of Malusterans and Arcamedians. "Alex! Where are you going?" he yelled. "Get yourself to safety." Alex didn't seem to hear him. "Alex!" Still no response. Axis tried to side step Canly so that he could pursue Alex, but Canly had anticipated this and closed the route off. Axis looked up to see Alex disappearing from view. "Alex!" he roared but he knew it was in vain, there was no way that he would be heard over the din of the battle. But someone had heard. He saw Artemas weaving his way through the battle. He had a sinister smile on his face as he looked back at Axis. "Don't worry. I'll get him."

"No!" Axis yelled. He continued to clash with Canly, desperately trying to overpower him so that he could tackle Artemas before he got to Alex.

Alex had successfully navigated his way through the worst of the battle; he could now see three figures some way ahead, making their way along the road. The two shorter figures were being pushed and shoved by the larger one. He realised that Varios was leading Eliza and his father back towards Arcamedia. He thought that if he could take Varios by surprise, he could possibly catch him off guard and overpower him just long enough for Eliza and his father to escape. Silently, he ran along behind them. After fifty yards, he came to a recessed area on the side of the path. He looked ahead, Eliza and his father were still being manhandled by Varios and although he had reduced the distance between them, they were still some way ahead of him. He slipped into the recess and realised that he couldn't be seen, even if Varios were to look behind him. He needed to cover the ground quicker, with the ability to not draw attention to himself, but also be large enough to tackle Varios. He closed his eyes and focused. He then realised that this was the first time that he had attempted this alone. He thought back to his training and remembered Maven's words, *"Clear your mind. Envision the change."*

He took a deep breath and focused fully on what he needed to do and what he needed to become in order to achieve it. Nothing happened. He could hear the battle raging some distance behind him. He closed his eyes tighter and tried to tune out the sounds of the fracas. He could still hear it. He took another deep breath and as he exhaled, he heard – nothing at all. It was like he had entered a soundproof room. Then he had the feeling that he was being lifted off of the ground and in his mind's eye, he saw himself shrouded in a green glow. As it died away, he opened his eyes and was immediately aware that he was on all fours. He had morphed! But had he morphed into the desired creature? He stepped out of the recess and looked ahead. Even though Varios, Eliza and his father had moved on some distance, he could see them much clearer than before; it was almost as if he had binoculars strapped to his eyes. He stepped towards the edge of the lake and leant over. Looking back at him was a huge black cat. He looked closer and saw subtle spots dotted about its face. He had become a black jaguar.

On a rare excursion with his parents, or should he say, the people who posed as his parents, he remembered going to the zoo. He was fascinated by each and every creature he saw that day, but none fascinated him more than the black jaguar. He looked at this beautiful creature as it stared straight through him; it had an almost spectral presence. He had read the facts associated to the animal and he clearly recalled there being particular emphasis placed on its stalking ability and ambushing prowess. Perfect skills for the situation before him. Pleased that he had managed to achieve this, he focused on the hunt. Silently, he started to pursue.

Although he was now a two hundred pound animal, his footfalls did not make a sound. He was gaining rapidly. Varios was so preoccupied with his domineering behaviour towards Cordium and Eliza, that he was completely unaware that a huge predatory cat was drawing ever closer. Alex was thinking about how to tackle Varios. He was playing out the various scenarios in his mind. Although he was in the form of a huge cat, his mind was still that of a thirteen year old boy, complete with a thirteen year old's uncertainties. *What if he hears me? What if he knows I am behind him and he is luring me in? What if I hesitate? What if I am not strong enough to overpower him?* All this and more was spinning around in his mind. Before he knew it, he was approximately ten foot behind Varios, who still seemed to be unaware of his presence. He was too busy pushing Cordium. He would shove Cordium who would stagger a few steps forward and then stop, only to be shoved again. Varios was like a cruel child tormenting an injured creature. Even though he couldn't see his face, Alex knew that Varios was taking a twisted pleasure in this. This enraged him further. Now was the time to strike! He decided that he would jump on Varios' back and pin him to the ground, allowing Eliza and his father to get away. He lowered himself onto his haunches and inched closer to Varios. He was primed and ready to pounce when he heard a noise behind him. He spun around to see a wolf sneaking up on him. He had been so focused on taking down Varios that he was completely unaware that he too, was being followed. Varios had heard the noise too, he jumped into the air and as he did, he pushed Eliza and Cordium into Alex's path. Eliza was on her hands and knees, face to face with the black cat. She looked petrified.

She froze, unsure of what to do. Then she heard a very familiar voice in her head, "Don't worry, Eliza. It's me."

"Alex?" Eliza relaxed. "You came for us?"

"Of course."

Eliza had pure adoration in her eyes. "Thank you."

Alex was momentarily distracted, but managed to refocus. He looked behind him, the wolf just stood there, barring his way. He looked ahead, expecting to see Varios, but he wasn't there. He looked up to see a large black raven, hovering just out of harm's way.

He could hear Varios' voice in his head. "What are you waiting for, Artemas? Take him!"

Artemas, who had expected this order, was primed, ready to pounce. He took Alex by surprise and knocked the wind out of him as he sent him crashing to the floor. Alex had no time to catch his breath; Artemas was on him, clawing and biting.

Whilst all of this was going on, Varios had lowered himself to the ground and assumed his human form. He was cajoling Cordium and Eliza. "Move! Now!" Eliza was rooted to the spot; her only concern was for Alex. She wanted to morph into something suitably ferocious so that she could help him. Varios must have anticipated her thoughts. "Don't even think about it! This is an evenly matched fight. I'd hate for you to try to tip the balance in your boyfriend's favour. Now let's go!"

She stood resolute. "What if I don't? What are you going to do about it?"

The omnipresent sneer had temporarily left Varios' face and was replaced by a look of pure anger. He stepped over to Cordium. "Would you like to be responsible for something happening to this mindless fool?"

"You wouldn't harm him. Magissa needs him. She would punish you, or worse."

"She would never know. He is unaware of his surroundings. He could so easily fall into Lake Ancora." He grabbed Cordium and frog-marched him to the lake's edge and began to enact a story for the benefit of his mother. "I'm so sorry, Mother. She tried to escape and whilst I was preoccupied with her, Cordium wandered to the lake's edge and must have fallen over the side." He leered at Eliza. "You would be the one to incur her wrath, not me." She started to retort, but Varios cut her off. "What! You think that she would believe you over me? You are more stupid than I thought. Now move!" Eliza did not move; she looked at Alex who was still wrestling with Artemas. She then looked at Varios. "Don't test me, girl!" Varios grabbed Cordium by the collar and dangled him precariously over the edge. The look on Cordium's face was the same as ever, he had no idea that he was in a precarious position.

Eliza felt so sorry for him. Reluctantly, she did as she was told and started walking away from Alex. The sneer had returned to Varios' face. He drew Cordium away from the water's edge and got back on the path. He lined him up in the correct direction and pushed him forwards. Moments later, he stopped and turned back to Artemas. "Keep him busy. Oh and if you happen to get a little over-zealous with your bites, then so be it." With that, he turned away, his laughter filling the air.

Although Alex was in peril, he had the awareness to know exactly what was happening. Varios had just basically given Artemas the go ahead to kill him. He was prone on his back, desperately trying to block Artemas' bites. His jaws clanged like a steel trap. Every attempted bite resonated through Alex's entire body. Before, Artemas was just trying to waylay him, but now he was focused on trying to hit Alex's jugular. He couldn't keep blocking these; he had to get off of his back. Still the steel trap clanged and the resulting shockwaves travelled down his paws as he continued to block the wolf's attempts to finish him. He tried to summon up some strength. He focused. He could feel the shockwaves but no longer heard the clanging of the steel trap. Then he felt a power surge through him. Was it adrenaline or something else? It didn't matter, he felt empowered. He blocked Artemas' jaws with one paw and smashed him across the face with the other. The wolf yelped as it was knocked sideways. Alex quickly rolled over and pushed himself up onto all fours. Artemas had recovered and was circling, preparing to attack again. He mirrored the wolf's movements as they faced off with one another.

Alex was aware that he needed to attack first; he couldn't afford to let Artemas get the upper hand on him again. He sprung forth, his claws exposed and his jaws bared. Artemas managed to dodge to the side and avoid his claws and teeth, but with quick thinking, Alex lashed him across the face with his thick tail. This startled Artemas long enough for Alex to bat him across the face with his paw. Artemas was knocked to the floor. Now Alex was in the ascendency, he had the wolf prone on the floor. He stepped over the wolf and used his huge paws to pin down its front legs. Artemas thrashed about in vain, he was at Alex's mercy. Alex was convinced that Artemas would have killed him, and he wanted revenge. He felt an almost serene rage start to build inside. Artemas could obviously see the blood lust in his eyes and he began to plead.

"Please. Please have mercy. I would have shown it to you. No matter what Varios ordered, I would not have killed you!"

"Liar!"

Alex went into a trance. His conscious mind was gone. It felt like he was viewing this as if it were a dream. He leant in towards Artemas' neck, his jaws open wide.

"No!" screamed Artemas.

"No! Stop! What are you doing?"

Alex was drawn partially out of his trance. That wasn't Artemas' voice.

He looked down at the look of horror on the wolf's face. He wasn't sure why he looked quite so scared.

He turned to look behind him. Axis, in his canine form, was powering towards them. "Get off of him!" he yelled. Alex still had an overwhelming urge to finish what he had started but slowly, reluctantly, he stepped off of Artemas. The wolf got to its feet and without looking back, tore off towards Arcamedia.

A split second later, Axis arrived on the scene.

"Alex. What were you doing?"

Alex, unsure as to exactly what had just happened was trying to collect himself.

"Protecting myself," he said.

"You were doing more than that. You had Artemas beat, you were looking to kill him."

"No I wasn't. It was self-defence," Alex protested.

Axis looked him over. "I think that you have been in this guise long enough. Morph back now!"

Alex, still feeling discombobulated did as instructed. He closed his eyes, focused on changing back into his human form and as the green glow died away, he opened his eyes to see that he was standing next to Axis the man. He suddenly felt overwhelmed. He threw himself into Axis and began to cry. "I'm so sorry, Axis. I don't know what happened. I tried to rescue Eliza and my father only to be attacked by Artemas. I felt so angry, anger like I've never experienced before."

Axis hugged him tight and let him cry himself out.

After some time, Alex had pulled himself together. Yet he still had a pleading look in his eyes. "What happened to me, Axis?"

Axis looked at him. "It wasn't you, Alex. You are still inexperienced when it comes to morphing. I understand why you chose the animal that you did, but it was too difficult for you to control. I think that the creature's natural instincts overtook your own." Alex was still in a state of shock. Axis tried to reassure him further. "Ultimately, there was no real harm done. In time, we will work on this, Alex and you will learn control."

Alex thanked him and they both looked in the direction that the wolf had retreated. In the distance, they could just about make out Artemas who was still running flat out. But Eliza, Cordium and their sadistic captor were nowhere to be seen.

"They are out of our reach for the time being," said Axis. "Come on, we need to get back to the border. This time, please do as I say and keep out of harm's way and I suggest that for the time being, you refrain from morphing."

Alex nodded and they both turned tail and headed back towards the battle that was raging on the borders of Malustera.

18.

Three Heads are Better than One

The Malusterans were starting to gain the upper hand as Axis and Alex re-joined the fray. Axis guided Alex off to the side, away from the main battle and told him to stay out of sight. Alex was still shaken by what had just happened between himself and Artemas, so he did not put up a fight.

Maven had managed to temporarily get the better of Lunitas who had retreated. Between them, he and Leomas were managing to use their staffs to deflect Magissa's kill shots out of harm's way. The Malusterans were converging on Magissa's position. She had a look of concern on her face now as she looked around and realised just how few men she had left. She was starting to back away as Leomas and Maven moved within a few yards of her. They both brandished their staffs in her direction.

"You are defeated, witch," said Leomas. "I suggest that you lay your staff down and surrender, we shall spare your life."

Magissa looked almost sheepish as she dropped her staff to the ground. Slowly she lowered herself to the ground, in what was seemingly a show of surrender.

Both men lowered their staffs. Leomas looked down on her. "You have made a wise choice," he said.

Magissa looked at him; the sheepish look that had been there moments earlier had gone. It had been replaced by the more familiar smug, self-satisfied look.

"Oh, I know that I have," came her contemptuous reply. "Unfortunately for you, you have not."

Before either Leomas or Maven could react, she grabbed her staff and disappeared from view. She was shrouded in an oily green-black cocoon. Maven immediately thought that she had concealed herself in order to open a portal that would allow her to steal away. Leomas didn't wait for any explanations; he raised his staff high above his head and brought it down axe-like, with all of his might. It did nothing; he may as well have dropped a feather on the cocoon. He looked at Maven bemused.

Maven pointed his staff at the cocoon and uttered the word, "Extricas." It remained intact and Magissa was still concealed. They both continued to inspect the cocoon, looking for an opening. After some time had passed Maven looked at Leomas. "I think that she has used this to escape, she certainly can't still be inside as her air would have run out by now."

Leomas took one more look at the cocoon and then looked at Maven. "Agreed."

They both turned away from the cocoon and made to aid Axis and the remaining Malusterans. As he was walking away, Maven thought he heard a noise coming from behind. He turned around; there was nothing there other than the cocoon that was just as they had left it a few moments earlier. Leomas looked quizzically at Maven. "It's nothing, I just thought I heard something," he said uncertainly. They continued towards the skirmish. Then there was another noise, louder this time. Leomas must have heard it too, as he had spun around at precisely the same time as Maven. They both stared at the inanimate looking cocoon. Nothing. Between them, they decided to head back over to it just to be certain. There were no sounds; it just sat there as before.

Both feeling somewhat foolish, they turned around, fixed on aiding Axis and the others. Then they heard it clear as day, a loud cracking sound followed by what sounded like the release of steam. Cautiously, they moved in for closer inspection. Something was definitely happening to the cocoon. They could still hear the hissing sound and there was a visible release of vapour. The cocoon then started to pulsate and expand. The cracking noise returned. Initially, it was intermittent.

As they studied the cocoon, they couldn't actually see any cracks or breaks. Right at that moment, the cocoon stopped expanding and everything went quiet. Leomas and Maven looked at each other, each man had a look on their face that suggested a hope that the other would have an explanation for this strange phenomena. Once more the cracking noise returned, but this time it was far more consistent and intense. It sounded as though someone or something was inside and that they were running an ice-pick through the seam of the cocoon.

Leomas and Maven could now actually see the cocoon starting to breakaway. They both started to back up. Then they saw a spike break its way through the tough skin on top of the cocoon. For a moment, it really did resemble an ice-pick, albeit, a very large one. But as it broke through fully it was clear that it was something else entirely. The 'spike' which had now reached the apex of the cocoon, suddenly paused its work. It was perfectly still. It almost seemed to be assessing, taking in its surroundings, like some sort of bizarre sensory organ.

As they continued to look on, it suddenly sprung back into action. It started to rip downwards through the cocoon as easily as a razor blade would cut through tissue paper. It was almost fully through now and just before it touched the ground, the spike disappeared from view. Once again, everything went extremely silent.

The few remaining battles had now petered out as the participants had joined Maven and Leomas in staring in stunned silence at the bizarre sight unfolding in front of them. Even Axis and Canly's blood feud had ceased.

The silence was broken by a low rumble that at first sounded like distant thunder. As it started to build it became apparent that it was emanating from within the cocoon. It was now a deep growl and was still growing in intensity. As if this wasn't strange enough, they started to hear competing noises, as if there were several things inside the cocoon. Magissa's remaining men were backing away rapidly at this point. Leomas looked around at his people; there was uncertainty on most of their faces.

"Stand fast!" he commanded.

Just as the sounds from the cocoon built to a crescendo, the air was suddenly silent again.

Night was setting in at this point and there was an awful lot of mist starting to descend, that added an extra eeriness to the proceedings.

"Maven!" Axis called.

Maven spun around to see Axis staring intently at him.

"I really think that we need to get out of here... Now!"

Maven nodded in agreement and he along with Leomas started to head towards the doorway into Malustera. Axis grabbed Alex, who still seemed to be suffering from the effects of his earlier encounter, and followed.

The air was suddenly filled by three of the most blood-curdling noises imaginable.

All at once, there was a roar so deep and loud it literally made the ground shake. This was followed by a shriek that was so high-pitched and piercing, everyone had to cover their ears through fear that their very eardrums would explode. Finally, there came laughter. This was unexpected after the two previous noises that they had heard, but such was its sinister nature, it arguably induced more fear in the men than the other two sounds put together.

Magissa's remaining men were running back in the direction of Arcamedia. Axis, Maven, Alex, Leomas and the remaining Malusterans headed towards the doorway. Then there were two large thuds that sounded like boulders being dropped onto the ground from a great height. Every one of the fleeing men knew that whatever was inside the cocoon wasn't friendly, but it was pure morbid curiosity that made each one of them stop in their tracks and turn around to look once again at the cocoon.

The scene had now changed. The cause of the large thuds now became clear; the cocoon was now completely broken in two with the pieces laying either side of what appeared to be another oily green-black cocoon! This one though, inexplicably appeared to be much larger than what had just covered it. Every onlooker had varying degrees of confusion etched on their faces. As they continued to look on, there was activity from the new cocoon, though it was completely different. Where the previous one had pulsated and cracked, this one was actually moving and expanding before their eyes. Still they stared, rooted to the spot as the shape grew. It looked like it was being inflated. For the briefest moment, something appeared at the back of it and the resulting noise sounded like a crack of lightning followed by a heavy thud indicating that whatever it was, it had made contact with the ground.

Although Alex and all on the Malustera side couldn't make out what it was, Magissa's men on the other side would have had a clear view and judging by the fact that they had all turned tail and started running again, it obviously wasn't good. There was now a low thrumming sound emanating from behind the shape. As Alex listened more closely, he realised that it was a repeating pattern. He looked over at Magissa's fleeing soldiers who suddenly stopped running and then as one, they all turned to face the shape.

Alex tugged at Axis' sleeve; it seemed to be a struggle for Axis to avert his eyes from the scene that was unfolding a short distance away. Alex tugged again, but much harder this time. Axis looked down almost annoyed. "We really need to get out of here. Now!" Alex yelled.

Axis didn't respond, he seemed to be in a stupor as his gaze turned back towards the ever expanding entity. The thrumming sound maintained the same pattern, but seemed to be growing in volume and intensity. Alex tugged again, ripping Axis' sleeve in the process, but still he did not react. He was fixated on the ever changing scene in front of him. Frustrated and scared, Alex looked across at the others, who all had the same vacant expression on their faces as Axis. He looked back at the shape, it was increasing in width! He heard a loud swooshing sound, it sounded like the sails of some huge ship being unfurled. He watched dumbstruck as these 'sails' extended outward and upward to their fullest, blocking out what little light there was on this night. It was at this moment that it dawned on him exactly what they were dealing with.

What they had thought was a second cocoon wasn't a cocoon at all. *It's a dragon!* he thought to himself. His fears were confirmed as a long snake-like neck that had previously been covered by the wings, slowly, and deliberately, extended its way upward as it broke through the mist that partially shrouded the beast. He noted a large horn atop its head and piercing green eyes staring straight at him.

"Dragon!" he roared, looking from Axis to Maven. Neither of them reacted they just continued to stare.

"Dragon?" came a familiar voice. "Not nearly imaginative enough. I am so much more than a mere dragon."

As soon as these words were uttered, another snake-like neck extended upward, showing an identical face to the previous one, complete with a horn atop that could skewer an elephant and the same piercing green eyes that, like its twin, were also boring into Alex.

Still the thrumming pattern continued to emanate from the rear of the beast. He now realised that they were dealing with something that he could scarcely believe. It was a hydra! Alex was frantic; he was trying to alert his companions to the clear and present danger that was a matter of yards away. "Axis! Maven! What is wrong with you? Can you not see what is right in front of you?" No reaction from either of them at all.

The sinister laughter returned.

"They can't hear you, child, they are in a trance. They thought they had defeated me, but I used their overconfidence to lure them in."

At this point, a third face appeared from out of the mist but this one didn't have a snake-like neck or a horn atop its head. But it did have the same piercing green eyes.

"Magissa!" The disgust in Alex's voice was evident.

"So what do you think of your stepmother now?" she said gloatingly.

Alex could scarcely speak. The words wouldn't come. When he was under pressure, he often resorted to humour. "Well arguably, this is a better look for you," he said glibly.

The eyes of the two serpents noticeably narrowed but the eyes on Magissa's face remained as wide and heightened as they were when she was in her human form.

"You are making jokes at this stage in the game? You are either very brave or very stupid." The serpents' eyes remained fixed on Alex as Magissa looked in turn at Maven, Axis and Leomas. A sneer broke across her face; she was obviously pleased with her handiwork.

"Why am I not affected in the same way as they are?" asked Alex.

"This enchantment only works on adults, so annoyingly, you are immune. But no matter, you alone are no threat to me."

With that, Magissa extended to her full height. The hydra was huge. Its torso was at least thirty foot long, with the two necks and heads each extending at least another twenty foot. It then flicked its huge tail; Alex could hear the thrumming sound much more clearly at this point. He focused in on the tail and saw that on either side of it were a group of spines. He noticed that each side seemed to vibrate intermittently. This was surely the source of what was entrancing the men!

"Tell your friends not to go anywhere, Alex; I just need to dismiss my men." The central head sneered at him as the behemoth hydra started to turn around. Alex took the opportunity to once again attempt to rouse Axis from the trance. He shook his arm, tried pinching him and even gave him a swift kick to the shins. Nothing worked. He was aware that Magissa was now addressing her troops.

"You fought well for the most part, but did I not warn you that there would be consequences if you didn't hold your ground?"

Her men did not react at all; they just continued to stare back at her.

"I'll take it from here. Consider yourselves dismissed," she hissed.

Alex saw the left-hand neck recoil and a blue glow started to build at its base. He immediately realised that this wasn't going to end well. He frantically started to search for something, anything that he could use to awaken Axis and Maven. All the time, he had half an eye on Magissa and soon noticed that the blue charge had almost extended the entire length of the left-hand neck. A second later, the neck shot forward followed by an exaggerated spitting sound that was immediately followed by a crisp, cracking sound. Because of his restricted view from behind the hydra, he could not see exactly what had happened, but he knew that whatever it was, it wouldn't have been good. He continued his search for something that would help him to awaken his companions and then he saw it. Approximately twenty foot to his right, there was a shiny black object partially embedded in the ground. Magissa was completely distracted, in the midst of her latest devilry but he was still conscious as to not alert her, so he squatted down and stealthily, made his way over to the protruding object. He was on it in seconds but as he went to grab for it, he was distracted by the scene to his left. He now had a clear view of Magissa's men. Moments ago, they had been frozen in a trance, now they were literally frozen! The blue charge and the spitting sound had been Magissa hitting them all with a blanket of ice.

Magissa addressed her men once again.

"What's this? Are you still here? Well, it is a cold night. Allow me to warm you up," she japed.

Alex knew exactly what was coming next; he grabbed for the black object and ran towards Maven. The right-hand neck had recoiled and a red charge was starting to build at its base. He threw caution to the wind now, as he sprinted to Maven. He removed Maven's scarf and tied it around the Mystic's head, covering his ears. He then held the black object to Maven's ribs for a split second. There was a buzzing noise and Maven convulsed slightly as the Impulse Baton sent its charge into his body. He sprung immediately to life, wielding his staff defensively.

"What the…" he said groggily. It sounded as if he had just woken up. He then looked on stunned at the scene that was unfolding in front of them. Maven then became aware that he had something covering his ears and went to remove it. At the same time, he caught sight of Alex.

"Maven! No!" mouthed Alex.

"Leave it on."

Maven looked confused, but lowered his hands nonetheless. Alex moved in closely so that Maven would be able to hear him.

"You all fell into a trance." He followed Alex's hand as he swept it across all the others who were rooted to the spot. Even Canly, who had morphed back into his human form after his battle with Axis broke off, was standing just to his left and was a member of this captive audience. Then Alex pointed to the hydra. "The noise coming from the tail is what caused it. Are you able to put up some kind of sound barrier? I need to wake the others but they will fall back into the trance unless you can quell the sound from that tail."

Maven nodded. He raised his staff and uttered the word, "Mutum!"

Alex could no longer hear the thrumming sound of Magissa's tail. He gave Maven a thumbs up and Maven removed the scarf. Alex ran towards Axis and held the Impulse Baton to his ribs. Axis' body jerked slightly and he sprung to life, immediately assuming a fighter's stance. He saw Alex, smiled and relaxed his stance, but the smile faded as soon as he looked up to see the massive hydra. The red charge had reached the top of the neck and the head shot forward. Once again the hydra was blocking Alex's view of Magissa's troops but as the sky was illuminated with an orangey-red glow, he knew exactly what had happened.

Even though the thrumming sound could no longer get through, Leomas and his men still seemed to be in a trance. Alex ran towards Leomas, Impulse Baton at the ready. Maven and Axis were on his wavelength. Maven started to use his staff on Leomas' remaining men and Axis located another of the Impulse Batons and started to do likewise. Leomas roared as the Impulse Baton hit his ribs, his trance was now not so deep, so the impact of the Baton hitting him was more potent. Instinctively, he lashed out blindly. Alex didn't have time to move, he closed his eyes, awaiting the inevitable impact. It didn't come. He opened his eyes and looked up to see Axis holding Leomas' arm. He had gotten across just in time to block the potentially fatal impact.

Axis released Leomas' arm. "Good to see you, Leo."

Leomas, who was still a little groggy, shook his head slightly in an attempt to realign everything and looked up to see Axis' face. "You too, my old friend."

He now had his wits about him and was apologising profusely to Alex for so nearly striking him. Alex assured him that all was fine, but was keen to stress that they should all get through the barrier immediately.

The hydra who had been surveying her damage was now starting to turn back to face them. One by one, Leomas' men started to file through the doorway in the barrier.

Axis looked at the still entranced Canly. After what she had just done to her troops, it was obvious to him that Magissa was going to cull anything and everything in her path and as much as he hated Canly, he couldn't leave him to this fate. He looked at Alex and held out his hand for the Impulse Baton, he had lost his when he had come to Alex's defence. Alex just stared back at him, he knew what he wanted it for and was reluctant to give it to him. Axis' look became more imploring. Alex was still uncertain, but reluctantly, he handed it to him.

Axis nodded in thanks and said, "Go with Maven. Get through the doorway. This will only take a moment."

Alex threw him another 'why are you doing this?' look and then ran to join the others.

Axis stood in front of Canly, Impulse Baton poised. He pressed the baton to Canly's ribs. Canly convulsed and roared. As his eyesight started to come back into focus, he saw Axis in front of him, weapon in hand.

His eyes narrowed as he addressed him. "You would try to finish me whilst I was defenceless would you?"

He prepared to resume battle with Axis but then sensed that there was something large moving towards them. He looked on in horror as the huge hydra came fully into view. The lips of the familiar looking central head were moving, but he could not hear what Magissa was saying to him. The left hand head was now looking directly at him and a blue charge had almost made its way to the top of the neck. Canly was no longer entranced, but he was staring, rooted to the spot, as if he still were. The sky was then suddenly illuminated by a blue flash. Axis dived across and drove his shoulder into Canly's mid-section, which sent them both sprawling to the ground. A split second later, they both heard an explosion as whatever had been emitted from the beast's mouth smashed into the barrier just above their heads. Canly was in no doubt that this had been meant for him. He looked disbelievingly at the hydra. He then turned his attention to Axis who had now gotten back to his feet. Canly regained his feet, all the time staring at Axis with a confused look on his face. Axis nodded to Canly and then ran towards his companions.

Canly continued to stare after him for a few more seconds before turning and staring disbelievingly at the massive hydra. Then he morphed into a wolf and tore off to the left, away from the chaos.

Alex, Maven and Leomas turned around to see the hydra drawing ever closer to them. They could see the central head that belonged to Magissa mouthing something that they could not hear as Maven's Mutum spell was still holding up. The right-hand neck had recoiled and the red charge was building. Alex noted that it seemed to be moving up the neck much quicker this time. Perhaps it was because they were now directly in harm's way, or maybe because it was still partially charged from its recent use. Either way, they all needed to get out of there. Leomas and Maven pointed their staffs at the hydra and began firing at it as they backed towards the doorway. Everything that they hit it with seemed to have absolutely no effect. This point was further emphasised as Magissa broke through the Mutum barrier.

"...lutely feeble! You'll have to do better than that!"

Alex could now see the remnants or lack thereof of Magissa's troops – she had totally vaporized them. He was distracted as the discharge from the Fire-head exploded into the barrier just to his left. This brought him well and truly back to the present. Axis re-appeared at this point and was ushering him towards the doorway, using his body to shield Alex. Leomas and Maven had broken away as they tried to distract both of the serpent heads. The Ice-head was charging now and it was undoubtedly building quicker.

Leomas and Maven were through the doorway now and still firing in vain at the hydra.

"Axis!" yelled Maven. "Get Alex through the barrier now!"

Axis looked back to see the hydra right behind him. The left head was cocked, about to spew forth. Just then, a combined shot from Maven and Leomas crashed into the side of Magissa, causing her to be sent off kilter. The left-hand head expelled the ice blast just as the massive creature crashed to the ground. Alex felt Axis pick him up and then heard Axis yell in pain as he launched him through the doorway in the barrier. Alex felt an extreme coldness hit his body as if he had been thrown into an ice bath; this was a huge shock to his system. He found himself struggling to breathe such was the impact of the sudden, sharp reduction in temperature. Despite this, his overwhelming concern was for Axis' wellbeing. He looked back through the doorway but could not see him. Maven and Leomas were preparing to close the doorway.

"N-No! W-wait!" Alex thought he had shouted but in reality, his words came out as sputtered gasps. Each breath he took was like a stiff punch to the stomach, but he managed to suck in enough air to get the next words out more clearly.

"W-we have to wait for Axis!"

Maven looked at him ruefully. "I can't see him, Alex, I think that..."

"No don't say that! He'll make it through, I know he will."

"We can't wait any longer, Alex, we need to close the barrier."

Tears started to fill in Alex's eyes and his vision began to blur as the coldness continued to bite at him. Maven had drawn the door and he and Leomas were moving it into place. At the last possible moment, he saw a large body dive through the opening. The door clicked into place just as a huge orangey-red projectile crashed into it. The door had become one with the barrier just in time and held firm. No one on the Malustera side had seen it, but Axis had been propelled through the doorway by Canly. He stayed there in the shadows just long enough to see the doorway seal. He then morphed back into a wolf and silently, he disappeared into the night.

Alex wiped his eyes and rushed over to where the body was lying face-down on the cold ground. Maven and Leomas were already tending to Axis when he arrived by his side. He crouched down alongside Axis and placed his hand on his shoulder.

"Axis? Are you okay?"

Axis didn't respond, he was lying motionless. Alex looked at both Maven and Leomas for consolation but neither of their looks filled him with confidence.

"Axis?" he yelled again. Still no response.

"What's wrong with him? I can't see any wounds."

He started to make his way around to where Maven and Leomas stood.

"No, Alex. Stay where you are," said Maven. "We will tend to him."

"We need to get you warm," said Leomas. "The temperature fluctuates massively between day and night in Malustera."

Leomas beckoned to one of his men. "Canis, please take Alex with you and get him into a shelter." Canis nodded and motioned for Alex to follow him. Alex did not move; he was still staring at the prone body of Axis.

"Alex, you must go with Canis now. You are not equipped to deal with this temperature for long. We will bring Axis to a shelter, you will be able to see him once he has been stabilised." Alex noticed two more of Leomas' men heading their way with a makeshift stretcher. This seemed to console him somewhat.

"Please look after him." Maven and Leomas both met his gaze and mustered the best smiles that they could.

"He is in good hands, Alex, now go and get warm," said Maven.

He stepped towards Canis but was suddenly aware that they were being watched; he spun round to see the hydra Magissa staring at them all. She had regained her feet and the central head was smirking menacingly at them whilst the serpent heads, with their horns pointing towards the barrier were sweeping their way back and forth, seemingly scanning for some kind of weak spot. Such was their concern for Axis' condition and their comparative safety behind the barrier, they had temporarily forgotten that a huge mythical beast lie on the other side.

Although Magissa's voice was muffled by the barrier, they could still hear what she was saying.

"Oh dear, poor Axis," she said with feigned concern. "Did one of my ice blasts catch the turncoat? Open the barrier and I will melt that for him." She was clearly goading them all and Alex reacted.

The surge of anger that he had experienced earlier when he was in the form of the jaguar seemed to return. He walked as close to the barrier as he could and addressed Magissa. "You evil bitch!" he spat.

The smirk disappeared from her face.

Alex continued, "You will pay for this and for every other atrocity that you have committed."

Magissa got the reaction that she wanted, but wasn't quite expecting the venom that Alex's words carried.

"Now, now, Alex, is that any way to speak to family?"

"You are no family of mine!"

"Oh, but I am and there is nothing that you can do about that," her voice was more callous than usual as she placed particular emphasis on each word. "I am so pleased that your mother is no longer with us to hear you use that kind of language." The smirk returned to her face. She moved to her right to allow the serpent heads to continue to probe the barrier.

"Now be a good boy and go to bed as you have a busy day ahead of you tomorrow, searching for my Firestone."

Canis had now moved alongside and tried to usher him away but Alex stood resolute.

"Do not forget that your *girlfriend* is my guest and I would just be loathed to have to make her stay with me an unpleasant one."

Alex reared up again. "You piece of filth! If you so much as touch a hair on her head…"

"You'll what?" Magissa taunted.

Canis was still trying to restrain him and guide him away. Alex brushed his hands away.

He gritted his teeth and clenched his fists. The anger was building. "I will kill you!"

"Ha-ha-ha-ha!" she cackled. "I believe that someone has found their intestinal fortitude. I actually admire that, to some degree at least. But be thankful that I cannot penetrate the barrier at this present time. Now off to bed and sleep well – if you can."

With that, the serpent heads retracted and the hydra turned around, took a few strides, extended its wings and took flight back towards Arcamedia.

Full of hatred, Alex glared at the hydra that had now almost been swallowed by the darkness. As his anger started to recede, he was once again aware of the extreme cold. Canis placed a hand on his shoulder, Alex turned to look at him, his teeth chattering.

"Come, Alex, we must get you into a shelter now."

He did not put up a fight this time, he allowed himself to be led away from the barrier, glancing in the direction of Maven and Leomas as he passed by, his entire body almost numb from the cold. They had managed to move Axis to the stretcher and had completely covered him in blankets. He was still motionless though. Two of Leomas' men picked up the stretcher and fell into step behind Alex and Canis, closely followed by Leomas and Maven.

****

Varios and his *guests* had been back at the fortress for hours when they heard what sounded like an amplified heartbeat.

Lubb-dub… Lubb-dub. It was distant at first, but quickly grew closer. Lubb-dub… Lubb-dub… Lubb-dub.

It was now so close that Varios and Eliza could feel it pounding in their own chests, mimicking their heartbeats. This caused their entire bodies to shake. If Cordium felt the same sensation, you would never have known, he just sat staring at the fire, oblivious to everything around him.

Lubb-dub… Lubb-dub… Lubb-dub… Lubb-dub!

It suddenly stopped and they felt the floor beneath them shake slightly. A few minutes later, Magissa entered the main chamber of the central tower. She had an accomplished look on her face as she made her way over to them. Eliza looked away, a hundred terrible thoughts entering her mind all at once.

"Hello, my dear. I hope Varios has been treating you well."

Eliza, still concerning herself over what could have happened to the other three Kindred, did not acknowledge her.

"That well?" Magissa sneered.

Still Eliza ignored her.

"Ah, I know. You are concerned about your friends aren't you?"

Eliza spun around and made eye contact.

"Well, I could tell you that they are all dead!"

Eliza gasped as she placed her hands on her cheeks.

"But that would be a lie."

Despite herself, Eliza looked relieved. She glared at Magissa. If looks could kill, their troubles would have been over, right there and then.

"Or I could tell you that they all escaped into Malustera unscathed."

Eliza's glare softened slightly.

"But that too, would be a lie."

Her death-stare returned.

Magissa laughed, she was clearly enjoying herself.

Eliza finally spoke. "What have you done?"

"Ah. It speaks!

"Don't worry; your boyfriend wasn't physically harmed, though I can't say the same for his emotional state."

She paused. A game of verbal chicken ensued. Who would break first?

"What have you done?" Eliza screamed.

"Well, nothing… really. Due to his exertions during the battle, the turncoat was looking a little on the warm side, so I thought that I'd cool him off! He'll be taking a long nap to sleep it off. In fact…he may never wake up." Magissa's shrill laughter filled the chamber.

Eliza was so angry. Tears started to pool in her eyes and roll down her face. A thousand adjectives spun around in her mind, but none formed into anything verbal. All she could think of was of what sort of shape Axis was in and how this must be affecting Alex. She already hated Magissa, but this act had taken her feelings far beyond mere hatred.

"Oh dear! Why so sad?" came Magissa's patronizing reaction.

"Don't tell me that you have feelings for the turncoat too? He doesn't deserve it. There was always going to be a price to pay for the disloyalty that he has shown to me. He would have let you down too, it is engrained in him."

Eliza steeled herself. "What would you know of loyalty? You think your people are loyal to you? They are not, they are just scared. All they need is a reason to rise up against you and fate willing, that day will come soon."

This temporarily wiped the smile of Magissa's face.

Eliza continued, "Axis is the most loyal person I have ever met. It is unconditional. He wouldn't hesitate to lay his life down for his friends."

The smile sidled its way back onto Magissa's face.

"Perhaps I have done him a disservice. As after all, it would seem he has done just that."

She turned around and left the room, her laughter echoing off of the walls as she disappeared down the corridor.

19.

More Time than you Thought

Canis led Alex to the top of a small sand dune, where a handful of Leomas' men were putting the finishing touches to half a dozen structures that looked very much like teepees, complete with smoke emitting from the roofs. He led Alex into the central one and sat him down by the fire. Alex struggled to lift his hands towards the fire, such was the effect that the coldness had had on him. He felt somebody place something across his shoulders and looked up to see Canis wrapping a large fleece around him. He thanked him and turned back to continue his defrosting by the fire. The two men who were carrying Axis appeared in the room and set the stretcher down near the fire. They then turned around as Leomas and Maven entered the tent. The two men saluted Leomas and he led them off to the side of the tent. As Alex looked at the prone body of Axis on the stretcher, he could just about see his nose and part of his right eye. He stared at him much like a nervous parent would look at a newborn sleeping, desperate to see a sign that they were still breathing. He was relieved as he saw the blanket near Axis' chest rise and then fall but still watched for this to happen again, just in case his eyes were playing tricks on him. Maven must have realised this and came and sat alongside him.

"He is still with us, my boy." He thanked Canis as he placed a fleece over his shoulders.

Alex waggled his jaw slightly, trying to instil some life into his numb face.

"What's wrong with him, Maven?"

"He was hit by a blast of ice from that hideous beast. It caught him across the right hand side of his face and chest."

They were both handed a cup with steam exiting in spiralling wisps. It immediately warmed their hands and there was a pleasing smell emanating from the contents within. They both thanked Canis who nodded and left them to their conversation. Alex glanced across to see that Leomas was still in conversation with his two men on the other side of the tent. He was giving them some kind of instructions as he pointed to the door of the tent and then to the floor parallel to where the prone Axis lay.

Maven took a sip from the cup and smacked his lips as the contents passed through. He encouraged Alex to do likewise. Alex blew gently into the cup and took a small sip. It tasted so good! He immediately felt the warmth from the soup. It seemed to heat every part of his body as it travelled down his throat, towards his stomach.

"Good?" said Maven. Alex nodded and took another sip.

Maven continued, "The shock of the cold hitting him stopped his heart, but fortunately we were able to revive him."

Alex looked shocked and slightly relieved all at the same time. "Why is he still unconscious?"

"We think that the ice hitting him where it did has induced some sort of cryostasis."

"Well let's try and wake him," said Alex. He was still numb and struggled to stand up.

"No! That could be fatal! He needs to come out of it naturally," warned Maven.

Alex returned to his seat.

"We need to keep him warm and let the ice melt away of its own accord. If we try to remove it, the parts of him that it is attached to, could also be pulled away."

Maven let this sink in with Alex. After a few minutes he spoke again.

"Alex, you need to prepare yourself for the possibility that he may never wake up and if he does, his physical appearance could have changed dramatically. This ice is unlike anything that I have ever seen before; it is freezing him and burning him all at the same time."

Alex looked sombre as he processed this.

"Axis is the strongest person that I have ever known, he will wake up." He said it in such a way that he was trying to convince himself. "Plus, you have the Derma-Regen. It helped with the bite on his arm; surely it will help with this?" He looked expectantly at Maven.

Maven smiled and nodded. "Positivity is our best ally in this situation." He then drifted into his own thoughts. Deep down, Maven knew that Axis' wounds were likely to be beyond the restorative powers of Derma-Regen, but Alex had enough to deal with at the moment, so he chose not to burden him with this too. He finished off his soup, pulled the fleece tight around him and closed his eyes.

As Alex continued to drink his soup, he made eye contact with Leomas who made his way over. He smiled at Alex. "How's the soup? Have you warmed up?" Alex nodded and smiled.

"We haven't had a chance to talk yet, Alex." He sat down beside him.

"I was part of your father's guard along with Axis. They are both good men, two of the best that I have ever met." He looked at Axis, "If anyone can overcome this, it is him."

Alex smiled wearily, "If you were part of my father's guard, how did you end up here?" Alex asked.

"I was Axis' second-in-command and once he had decided to evacuate you and Eliza, he placed me in charge. Once she had a stranglehold on you father, Magissa demanded undying loyalty from all of the king's guard and army. Many agreed and fell into line; all of us that didn't were banished, along with our families, into Malustera."

Alex looked puzzled. "Magissa didn't recognise you at the border. If you were part of the king's guard, surely she would have?"

Leomas smiled once again, exposing his fangs. "I, along with everyone else who was banished are unrecognisable from the people that we were before. The ravages of life in Malustera have taken a toll on us in many ways, not least in our appearance. My own mother, may she rest in peace, would not even recognise me. Besides, the witch thinks that she is so much better than everyone else; she looks down on all others. Even though I held a high rank in your father's guard, she didn't even know my name whilst I served him."

Alex was hanging on Leomas' every word. He particularly clung to any information that he heard about his father – a man that was a complete unknown to him.

Leomas looked at him; he seemed to be studying him. This made Alex feel somewhat uneasy.

"You are concerned about Eliza?"

Alex nodded.

"She will be fine. She is strong, just like her mother. We will get her back," said Leomas reassuringly.

Alex suddenly looked a little more energised. "You are right. We will. But we are wasting time; we need to find the Firestone. That is the key to rescuing her." He threw the fleece down and got up, and took out the pocket watch.

"What are you doing?" Leomas asked.

"Getting ready to resume the search."

"Now is not the time, Alex, you need to keep warm and rest."

"Time! Time is against us." Alex's raised voice caused Maven to stir. Alex thought about explaining the situation, the Firestone no longer being dormant and the devastation that it could cause, but decided that Leomas wouldn't believe him and he didn't have the time or the inclination to explain either.

"You may have more time than you think. May I take a look at your watch?"

Alex was completely taken aback by this and somewhat reluctantly handed him the watch. Leomas took it and turned it over in his hands. He then started to study the face. If Alex didn't know better, he would have sworn that Leomas had seen the watch before.

After a while Leomas spoke. "Ah, yes. There's the Waterstone. Very good."

"Sorry? What did you say?" Alex had clearly heard what he had said, but was stunned that Leomas would have any knowledge of this.

Leomas smiled. "I see that the Waterstone gem is lit."

"What do you know of this?" asked Alex.

"I was part of your father's inner circle, so I know all about the Origin Stones and the need to house them in the Muleta. I know that once a stone is found, the next in line is awakened," he pointed to the orange stone set in the face of the watch, "and I know of the havoc and destruction that they could wreak if they are left unchecked. And judging by your desperation to resume the hunt, I may know something else that you do not."

Alex was left speechless by this revelation but was also intrigued.

"Now let me see," mumbled Leomas. He clicked the crown once, twice, and then stopped. He had a confused, faraway look on his face, much like an actor who had forgotten their lines.

Alex was suddenly concerned that Leomas had no idea what he was doing and that he was going to somehow undo something within the watch that would render it useless as a tracking device.

"You don't know what you are doing do you? Stop!" yelled Alex.

Maven who had been stirring intermittently had now woken fully and moved in to see what the commotion was. He saw Leomas with the watch along with Alex's concerned face. "Stop, Leomas! That is a precision instrument and should not be tampered with!"

Leomas clicked the crown for a third and a fourth time. He then looked at the watch face and smiled knowingly. "You two worry far too much. Take a look at this."

He held the watch up for them both to see. Both Alex and Maven peered at the watch, they looked a little bewildered.

Maven asked, "What are we supposed to be looking at, Leomas? It looks no different. I only hope that you have not broken it."

"Here," Leomas pointed to the area that surrounded the dial and ran his finger around the circumference.

They both strained their eyes to see what Leomas was referring to; they then looked at each other and shrugged their shoulders. Leomas seemed a little frustrated as he looked at the watch. He stood and walked away from the fire, looked at the watch again and beckoned for the other two to join him. They both obliged.

"Look at the braiding," said Leomas as they approached him.

Once again they peered at the watch. This time they could see a difference, part of the braiding was illuminated. This had been unclear before as the light from the fire had nullified the glow on the watch.

"What does this mean?" asked Maven. He was confused and a little annoyed that someone knew something of the watch that he did not.

"This is essentially a countdown timer."

"A countdown to what?" asked Alex.

"To when the next Origin Stone becomes active," said Leomas.

"The stone will not be dangerously active until the entire circumference has been illuminated. So you see, the clock is against you, but as I said, you have more time than you thought."

This was welcome news to them both. Alex wondered how Leomas could have knowledge of this, but smiled and thanked him, as did Maven. His annoyance that Leomas knew of this and he didn't had faded away.

Leomas smiled and held the watch out for Alex, who took it and immediately studied the face. He noted that the glow had only extended from the nine o'clock position that would house the Firestone gem to just before the ten o'clock position. He was buoyed by this. Considering how long it had been since he had found the Waterstone, if it continued to move at the same rate, they possibly had weeks, months even, to find the Firestone. Leomas looked at him and must have realised what he was thinking.

"It is unlikely that this will continue to move at the same rate. As the power of the stone builds, the timer will start to run faster. But on the plus side, at least we have an indication that doesn't include being burnt alive or the ground collapsing under our feet." He gave a wry smile that neither Alex nor Maven returned. Thinking that his last comment was in bad taste, he then stated, "I also think that I may know where the Firestone is located."

They both looked at him, eagerly awaiting his response.

"But this can wait till morning. I suggest that we all take some rest as we have a long journey ahead of us tomorrow."

Alex wanted to press him for the location, but armed with the new information supplied by the watch, he decided that it could wait till morning. He wandered back over to his seat near the fire and wrapped the fleece around himself. He looked across to see Maven in conversation with Leomas. After a few moments, Leomas left the tent and Maven returned to his seat next to him. He wrapped himself in the fleece and wished Alex goodnight.

As tired as he felt, Alex couldn't sleep. The fire had started to die down and as he stared at the watch, he could quite clearly see the glow now. It was still in the same position, just before the number ten as it had been earlier. He didn't want it to move at all, yet he found himself staring at it constantly, straining to see it move. He was just starting to drift off to sleep when he became aware that the two men who had carried Axis in on the stretcher earlier had returned with another stretcher. There was another body, presumably one of Leomas' injured men. As they set the stretcher down, he could make out the human form of Falmus.

He jumped up. "What the hell is he doing here?"

A startled Maven got to his feet. "Calm down, Alex!"

"Calm down! He tried to kill me!"

Aware of the disturbance, Leomas had re-entered the tent.

"What's all the commotion?" came his gruff voice.

"I'll tell you what," said Alex. He pointed at Falmus. "He tried to kill me and you want to make him a camp mate? Get him out of here. Now!"

"Unfortunately, he was caught in the stampede when we charged for the barrier. He is near death and needs our attention. Besides, I know him, he isn't evil at heart. He has just been corrupted by evil. It wouldn't be right to leave him to the Crassacs," said Leomas.

"I don't think you are hearing me, he tried to ki... The what?"

"The Crassacs," Leomas repeated. "They are nocturnal scavengers and will literally devour anything organic that they encounter."

Alex, who had now calmed down slightly, was intrigued. He had momentarily set aside the fact that his would-be assassin lay not three foot away.

"What exactly are they?"

"We do not exactly know what they are now, but they were people of Malustera once. When we were banished, we realised very quickly that we would not survive if we stayed above ground, such were the temperature fluctuations and the inability to grow food, so we created a subterranean township. The Crassacs are what remains of the people that refused to join us. To survive, they would have had to stay in animal form. Such is the time that has passed, even if they wanted to live amongst us, they would be unable to revert back to their human forms. Their bodies will now be completely animal. What they have evolved into is unclear, but the harshness of Malustera will have changed them irreparably. The humanity that once existed within them will have been completely extinguished in even the strongest willed amongst them," Leomas trailed off, lost in thought.

"You mean you have never seen them?" asked Alex.

"Well no," replied Leomas.

"How do you know they have survived and evolved then?"

"We have seen evidence to suggest their existence, or the existence of something that scarcely leaves a trace of its prey. As you can see, we have evolved and we spend a good deal of our time below ground. Based on our evolution, we can only assume that the effects on them have been far more severe."

Alex was unconvinced. How could anything survive in this cold? He had the feeling that Leomas was telling him a campfire tale in an effort to distract him from Falmus. He glared at Falmus. He didn't want to be anywhere near him but agreed that he didn't deserve to be left out in the cold to die or to be eaten alive by the Crassacs, if they really existed.

He wandered back over to his seat.

"If he wakes up, just make sure you keep him away from me." He looked across at Axis, who was still motionless on the stretcher. He wrapped the fleece around himself, stole one more look at the watch, closed his eyes and drifted off into a restless sleep.

20.

Indistinct Revelations

Alex awoke, initially uncertain as to where he was. He quickly remembered the events of the previous day. A few foot to his right, Maven was still asleep. The fire was now just a few glowing embers that were trying in vain to draw in enough oxygen to bring them back to their former glory.

He looked across to see that Axis was still motionless and in exactly the same position that he had been the night before. Opposite him was the similarly motionless body of Falmus. He too, had not moved from his position.

He removed the fleece, got to his feet and headed over to Axis. As he drew near, he noticed that his face had been uncovered slightly. As he looked down at his guardian, he grimaced. There was a huge amount of ice across the right side of Axis' face. It covered his cheek, part of his eye and ear. As it climbed the side of his face, it disappeared under his hairline. It looked as if some sort of giant leech had attached itself to his face. Despite himself, Alex slowly moved his hand towards the ice. He extended his index finger and gently touched the ice on Axis' cheek. The cold jolted through his entire body, like an electric shock. He felt somebody's hands pull him away. "Don't touch it!" said Maven.

As he started to normalise, he looked at Maven apologetically. "That felt so cold, like it had only just happened. Why is it not melting?"

"Dark magic!" came Maven's response.

"As I said to you last night, this is like nothing that I have ever encountered before. All we can hope is that the heat from the desert will have a positive effect."

Just then, the leathery looking material that was the tent door was flung back and Leomas joined them inside. In the brief moment that the door was open, Alex noticed that it was not yet light outside.

"Ah, you are awake, very good. Prepare to leave. We need to make as much progress as possible before the sun reaches its full potency." Alex looked at Leomas quizzically. "Remember how cold you felt last night?" Alex nodded. "Well that has nothing compared to the intense searing heat that you will be subjected to once the sun is up. We will be forced to take shelter at certain points during the day. We Malusterans are used to it, but we can only withstand the heat intermittently."

Alex picked up his few belongings and along with Maven, they stepped across to the doorway of the tent. He braced himself for the extreme coldness that he expected to step into, but as Maven pulled back the tent door, he was surprised to find that the temperature was relatively balanced.

Leomas appeared alongside them. "This is the only time of day that the temperature is stable."

Alex looked around and noticed that the other tents had all gone, as had the majority of their occupants. Behind them, Canis was packing up the tent that they had just exited. Axis and Falmus had been carried out on their stretchers and were set down as the other men joined Canis in dismantling the tent.

"We need to set off now and eat up as much ground as possible. Unfortunately, as we have injured, we will need to remain in these forms to ensure that we move at the same pace. It would be most unwise for us to separate." Leomas scanned the surrounding area as he said this. Alex shuddered slightly as he recalled Leomas' story of the Crassacs.

He tried to drive this from his mind. "Where are the rest of your men?" he asked.

"They packed up early. I sent them ahead to prepare shelter for us. Believe me, we will need it."

"Where exactly are we headed?" asked Alex.

"Patience, Alex, all will be revealed."

Alex reached into his pocket and pulled out the watch. He went through the now familiar procedure of generating their heading.

"It's pointing northeast."

Leomas nodded knowingly. *Indeed,* he thought to himself.

****

Eliza woke with a start, though she was sure that she had not slept a wink. She sat up in her bed, which was nothing more than a fleece blanket on the hard stone floor. Her thoughts had been consumed by the other members of The Kindred. How were they? Were they in Malustera? What were they going through? Were they all still alive…?

Earlier the previous evening, she had been ushered off to a room at the end of the corridor that led off of the main chamber. The room was completely empty. Varios had shoved her unceremoniously into the room and thrown the fleece at her with more gusto than was required. "Sweet dreams," he drawled and followed that up with his now trademark sneer as he slammed the door behind him. She had heard a series of clicks and realised that she was locked in.

The room was cold and dark. The only light that she had came from a very small window in the top right-hand corner of the room. Upon closer inspection, she realised that it was nothing more than a missing stone from the wall. Such was its height off of the ground, it let in little more than a needle of moonlight. She curled up in the corner, wrapped the fleece around her, pulling it tightly about her neck and thought solely of her companions.

After a while, she lifted herself gingerly off of the ground and stretched. She ached all over. As she was trying to instil life into her aching limbs, she heard voices. Immediately, she ceased her enforced stretching regimen and silently headed over to the door. She could make out Magissa's dulcet tones. She was ordering somebody about.

"Breakfast is in order. Go and get it!"

She then heard a smarmy sounding voice that could only belong to one person.

"How do you think the hunt is going? Do you think that they are on the trail of the Firestone yet?" asked Varios.

"They had better be, or the consequences for our guest will be dire."

Eliza was fully aware that she was being used as bait and knew deep down that even if the others were successful, she would still be subjected to Magissa's wrath. She knew that there was no way that Magissa would hold to her word. Then she heard an unfamiliar voice.

"You must be pleased, Magissa, everything is unfolding just as you have foreseen." Eliza noted a sickeningly obedient tone in the man's voice. She thought to herself, *Another poor soul that she has bent to her will.*

"Indeed I am. It is starting to fall into place, Aldar."

Aldar? Why do I know that name? They were still talking but Eliza wasn't taking it in, she was searching her mind to recall why the name Aldar was so familiar and then it dawned on her, Aldar Molia! The man that replaced her parents at the helm of Kessler. The man who at Magissa's behest had brought ruin upon the city of her birth, her home. She listened more intently now. She heard plates being set down and the clinking of cups, breakfast was obviously being served.

"Now go," she heard Magissa speaking down to one of her servants.

"He truly is a king among kings," said Aldar disparagingly.

It wasn't a servant at all. *Poor Cordium*, she thought. *He is treated as if he is subhuman.*

"This is actually rather good, Magissa. You have found a use at last for the braindead fool," said Aldar.

"Indeed. I certainly don't keep him around for the stimulating conversation."

Aldar laughed much more vigorously than he needed to.

As the laughter died away, Aldar asked, "What of the boy; is he aware of who you are?"

"No, he has no idea that I am…"

Just then there was a scraping noise as a key hit the lock of the door that Eliza was leant up against. She backed away rapidly, a stunned look on her face. Cordium entered the room carrying a tray with some food and a drink. He set it down on the floor alongside her. He didn't even seem to notice that she was there. She didn't react to him either; she still had a look of shock on her face. Before Cordium had entered the room, she had heard the completion of Magissa's sentence.

21.

From the Freezer to the Fire

Alex, Maven, Leomas and company were making quite good progress despite having two injured men on stretchers to carry with them. Fortunately, the early part of their journey had passed without incident. Although they had heard some strange noises in the distance, they hadn't encountered anything, Crassac packs or otherwise. Alex had been on his guard since they'd left camp his head had been on a pivot. On more than one occasion he had been sure that he saw disembodied blood-red eyes staring at them, tracking them. He was starting to think that there was some truth in the tale that Leomas had told him the night before.

He started to feel a little more at ease as the desolate land ahead of them was slowly being bathed in light. But as the temperature was seemingly increasing by the second, he became aware that at this point, the heat was more likely to kill him than any Crassac pack.

It was still before nine o'clock in the morning as they stopped to take on water. Alex and Maven were soaked in sweat; the heat was almost unbearable already.

"It's going to get a lot worse than this," said Leomas as Alex took the water flask over to Axis. He splashed a little around Axis' mouth in order to moisten his lips. He was careful not to get any on the ice that despite the heat, still clung inexplicably to his guardian's face.

"We are still over two hours from camp, so we must press on now." Leomas stretched out his arms and spun around three hundred and sixty degrees. "As you can see, there is no shelter whatsoever. The sun reaches its full radiance at midday. So if we are not at the camp before then, we will all be in serious trouble. Especially you and Maven, neither of you will have any tolerance at all for what is to come."

Good speech, Alex thought to himself with more than a touch of sarcasm. But in reality, it was. Despite the increasing heat, they had definitely upped the pace. This increase only lasted a short time as now Alex and Maven in particular, were really flagging in the mid-morning heat. They had to stop more frequently to take on water.

Earlier that morning, Leomas had given Alex and Maven each a piece of cloth for covering their heads. He now handed them each a large piece of fabric. "Put these on," he said. Alex looked at the makeshift jacket and as he held it up, he noticed that it seemed to be made of the same material as the tent that they had called home the previous night. He also noticed that it had a fur lining.

"Are you mad?" he said. "Are we not hot enough already without putting on a fur coat?"

Leomas looked at him sternly. "We will soon be at the point whereby you cannot let any sunlight hit your skin." He looked at the sweat pouring down Alex and Maven's faces. "You will literally cook in your own juices."

"But the fur?" said Alex. "Do you not have a covering that is more suitable to resisting the heat?"

"This is what we have," said Leomas. "Put them on, you may be pleasantly surprised."

Alex was far from convinced. Reluctantly, he placed his arm into the sleeve, swung it over his shoulders and put his other arm in. As he pulled it into place, he was amazed by the cooling effect that he was experiencing. He was far from comfortable but compared to the intense heat that he had been subjected to so far on this leg of the journey, this was positively heavenly. He looked at Maven, who had a look of surprising comfort on his face.

"You see?" said Leomas.

Alex flashed a conceding smile. "What about you and your men?"

Leomas pointed to the fur that adorned him from head to toe. "We are covered, in more ways than one." He looked at Alex and smiled or at least, it was what Alex decided was a smile. Leomas' fangs splayed out of his mouth menacingly. "Right, we must move on. We have less than an hour to reach the shelters."

The heat continued to intensify as they trudged on. Alex used his sleeve to wipe the sweat from his brow and shook his hand. He could hear hissing sounds alongside him. It sounded as if he had stepped into a pit of vipers. He looked down. The ground where he had deposited his sweat was sizzling. He looked skyward shielding his eyes. The sun looked huge with its waves of heat pulsating down on them. It seemed so much closer than it should be. He decided that the lack of reference points in this desolate place, made it difficult to put either size or distance into context. Besides that, the heat had to be affecting his perception.

After some time, they came to a point where the ground started to rise. Leomas stopped them and pointed towards the horizon. "We have to get over this rise; our shelter should be just over the other side. Take a moment to rest and drink, this is the last time we will be stopping."

Alex drank deeply from his water bottle and then went to check on Axis. *Surely the ice will have started to melt by now?* he thought to himself. Careful to use himself as a shield to keep the sun off of his guardian he removed the cloth that was covering Axis' face and to his dismay, the ice was still as intact as it had been the night before. *How can this be?*

He dabbed the water on Axis' lips, and took one more look at the ice, just in case it had melted and the heat was playing tricks on him. It was still there, glistening back at him, almost defiantly. He covered Axis' face and walked over to check on Maven.

"Hello, my boy, how are you?" There was weariness in Maven's voice that he hadn't heard before.

"I'm okay," he lied. "How are you?"

"Okay, but it's a little on the warm side isn't it? I could really go for some of last night's coldness right about now." He smiled at Alex.

Alex looked at the watch, albeit very briefly. He could feel it heating up rapidly in his hand.

"We are still on the right path. Do you have any idea where Leomas is leading us?"

"None at all I'm afraid. These lands are completely unknown to me. We are in Leomas' hands."

Alex looked over at Leomas who was in conversation with Canis.

"Do you trust him?"

"Well... Yes I do." Alex wasn't exactly reassured by this response.

"How well do you know him, Maven?"

"I knew him in Arcamedia, he was a good man. Magissa is his enemy which is another thing in his favour. Plus, without his help, Axis would not have made it and neither would we." Alex couldn't deny this and did feel a little more at ease.

Maven spoke again, almost to himself. "But in saying that, I do not know what effect this place has had on him."

Concern found its way back into Alex's thoughts but before he could say anything, Leomas called out to them, "Time to move out. We must press on, over the rise and into shelter. Make sure that no part of your skin is exposed to the direct sunlight."

They pressed on. They had been 'fortunate' that up to this point, the gradient of the terrain had been quite kind to them. This was not the case now; it was a steep incline that would have been hard going even without the extreme heat. Progress was slow. Alex and Maven had now both fallen back behind the stretcher carriers. The cooling effect that their jackets had afforded them earlier had all but disappeared. Alex looked up, the sun was no longer directly overhead, it had moved off to the east. His legs felt like jelly and he was starting to feel disorientated, dizzy. He looked over at Maven and saw three of him staring back. He could see Maven's mouths moving but didn't hear the words coming out. He felt like he was spinning, the world was starting to go black. Somewhere in the distance, he heard a roar and then much closer by he heard a deep voice yell, "Don't let him hit the ground!"

The darkness was lifting now. He could feel himself being lifted into the air. He could see light, although it was only a blur. He was then aware that he was being thrown about from left to right, but couldn't do anything to resist it. As the world came back into focus, he could see that he was looking down at the ground. It took him a while to realise that he was upside-down. It took a monumental effort, but he managed to lift himself up slightly and saw that he was over the shoulder of a huge man. His long brown hair was buffeting Alex in the face. He looked back. Not far away, he could see the four men carrying the stretchers with Maven just in front and the rest of Leomas' men just a few foot behind. They were all moving at pace and had concern etched across their faces. He could hear the sizzling noise that he had heard earlier when his sweat hit the ground, but this was far louder.

He looked up; the sun was directly behind them now. How had the sun changed position so dramatically? Was it late in the day? Surely not? He then heard the deep, growling voice of Leomas, "Move! We need to be over the rise before the sun!" It was at this point that he realised that Leomas was carrying him and he was running. He wanted to look forward but could not adjust himself.

Leomas must have realised what he was trying to do. "Stay put, Alex. We are nearly there." He obeyed. The heat was so intense now; it was as if there was no air. Just then, he heard a scream to his right. He tried to arch his neck to see what had happened. The stretcher that was furthest back had hit the ground and the man that was at the rear was screaming and writhing in pain. It took Alex a moment to realise that he was burning. Two of Leomas' men broke stride and headed back down the hill. The first one to arrive there dragged the burning man up the hill a short way. He then took the pack off of his back and started batting his fallen colleague with it. The other man grabbed the two handles at the back of the stretcher, lifted it up and resumed the race to the top of the rise. There was a smell of burning fur and flesh in the air. The injured man, whose back was still smouldering, was now being carried over the shoulder of his saviour. They were running for the rise.

Alex looked back to check on Maven. He wasn't far behind. As he looked back further, his eyes widened as he could clearly see the effects of the sun's heat on the ground. He looked just behind Maven. The sand was starting to solidify and turn translucent. As he looked on, he saw it fracture just behind Maven. How hot must it be for that to be happening to the sand? He needed to warn him.

"Maven!"

Still running, Maven looked up to see Alex bobbing about on Leomas' shoulder.

"You've got to move!"

Maven nodded and without breaking stride, he assumed his fox guise. He ran past the two stretchers. Due to Alex's restricted view, he soon lost sight of him but was relieved that he was now ahead of them. Other than the stretcher bearers, Leomas' men assumed their animal guises, though other than the fact that they were now running on all fours, there wasn't a huge difference. He looked back, the ground was superheating just behind them. "Leomas! You need to run faster!"

Leomas looked back. "Alex. Can you slip down onto my back?"

"I think so, yes."

"Climb around and then put your arms around my neck and hang on tight!"

He grabbed onto Leomas' huge trapezius muscle with his right hand, swung his legs around and then hoisted himself onto his back. He went to reach around Leomas' neck with his left hand and lost his grip. He was going to fall to the ground and be incinerated! He managed to grab onto the pack that Leomas was carrying. The toe of his left foot was dragging the ground and he could feel the heat immediately start to eat through it. He called out and felt the huge hand of Leomas grab his hand and hoist him up, just before he slipped off completely.

"Are you okay?"

"Yes," came Alex's breathless response.

"Hold on! I'm going to morph!" Leomas yelled.

Alex wrapped both arms as tightly as he could around Leomas' neck and closed his eyes. When he opened them again, he was lower to the ground and moving at greater speed. He now had a view of the way ahead. He could see the top of the rise.

One of Leomas' men was just disappearing from view over the top. He looked back, the stretcher carriers were right behind them. He could not see Maven, so he hoped that he had already cleared the rise. As Leomas hit the apex, Alex could see the shelters that he had called home last night, set up under a rocky outcropping. This was the first bit of shade that he had seen all day.

Leomas called out and four men emerged from one of the tents. "Get back there and relieve the others!" They nodded and ran past Leomas.

Alex looked back and saw that they were exchanging places with the men that were carrying the stretchers. They were doing this on the run. It was the most unusual relay race that he had ever witnessed.

The men who had just been relieved, morphed and headed towards the shelters.

Leomas skidded to a halt by the closest tent and told Alex to get inside. He jumped off of the lion and flung himself through the door of the tent. It felt so much cooler in there, he actually felt like he could breathe again. He could hear Leomas outside, directing his men. "Get inside now!" he heard him yell. The tent door was flung open, all Alex could see was a brilliant light, but then the two men carrying Axis ran inside and set the stretcher down. The door opened again, the light was even more intense as was the heat that followed it. Growing from out of the light was a black figure that projected itself into the tent. The door was closed and strapped down by the man who had just entered. Leomas patted his men on the shoulder and made his way over to Alex.

"Well! That was much closer than I would have liked," he said, quite casually under the circumstances.

"Are you okay, Alex?"

"I think so." He was hugely grateful to Leomas and felt guilty for questioning his integrity with Maven earlier.

"You saved my life. Thank you."

Leomas placed his huge hand on Alex's shoulder. "You are welcome. I was extremely loyal to Axis and I know he would want for me to protect you in his stead. After all, you are critical to our cause."

Leomas' knowledge of the situation continued to surprise him. But he didn't dwell on this.

"Where is Maven?" he asked.

"Leomas looked around the tent. "I don't know, I haven't seen him. I'm sure he would have made it into one of the other tents."

"I need to see him. I need to know that he is safe."

"We can't leave this tent for at least two hours, Alex. Nothing can survive out there when the sun is at its peak. Don't worry. I am sure that Maven would have made it."

Alex was far from convinced, he had an ill feeling. First Eliza had been taken from them, then Axis had been attacked and now he was sure that something awful had befallen Maven too.

They sat in silence as they ate and drank.

The time was passing slowly. Alex was amazed at how cool it felt in the battened down tent. Outside, the world was on fire, but had he not experienced the ferocity of the midday sun for himself, he would not have known it, such was the relative comfort that he now found himself in.

Alex was somewhat intrigued by this.

"These tents are incredible. How can they resist the extreme heat and cold? What are they made of?"

"They are made from a mixture of naturally occurring fibres that we blend together. We then cover them in a resin which we extract from a cactus-like plant called a Skatok. These are literally the only plant life that can survive above ground in Malustera, so we know that they can tolerate extremes in temperature. Your jacket is also made in a similar way."

Alex nodded. He was impressed by the ingenuity of the Malusterans being able to create something like this when they obviously had access to so few ingredients.

After a while, Alex spoke again. "As we are stuck here for a while, can you tell me where we are going?"

Leomas nodded. "We are going to an area of Malustera where the landscape is very different. There is no sand on the ground. I believe that it is the dried out bed of a lake or reservoir. The ground has been cracked and reformed over and over again by the sun. I have heard tale of strange phenomena occurring there when the sun sets. My theory is that this is the resting place of the Firestone. Like I said, we will be here for a few hours but as soon as it is safe, we must set off again."

Alex took the watch out of his pocket and flipped it open. He looked at the dial. The glow on the braiding had moved on far more than he had expected. It was now just past the twelve o'clock position. It actually moved another notch whilst he looked at it.

"How does it look?" Alex held out the watch for him. Leomas' eyebrows arched as he looked at it.

"Well, as expected, the strength of the stone is growing quickly, too quickly."

After a while, Alex spoke again.

"I am worried about Eliza."

"I am sure that she is fine. It makes no sense for Magissa to hurt her at this stage, though I do not expect her to stick to her word. We will have to treat her in kind. We cannot afford for her to get the stones. We will need to formulate a plan to stall her and rescue Eliza."

"I think that I can sense her pain," said Alex.

"It is because of your bond that you can sense this. I assume that Axis explained this to you both?" Alex nodded.

"This is further evidence that it is growing in intensity," said Leomas.

Alex considered this a moment. "I think that the pain is emotional rather than physical, but I'm not sure.

"I just want to find the stone and get back to Arcamedia as soon as possible."

"You will. You will. Though I must take you to Interria on the way," said Leomas.

"What is Interria?"

"It is the place that I have called home for the last ten years."

"I just want to get Eliza away from Magissa as soon as possible. Why do we need to go there first?"

"I understand how you feel, Alex, but trust me, there is something very important that you need to see there first. It will put a different perspective on everything."

22.

A Scintillating Idea

Alex was intrigued by Leomas' words and wanted to press him for more information, but his only real concern at the moment was with the other three members of The Kindred. Axis still lay prone on a stretcher. Maven was hopefully safe in a neighbouring tent, though he had serious doubts. As for Eliza, she was in the clutches of the most despicable person that he had ever had the misfortune to meet.

He kept getting thoughts or transmissions in his mind that allowed him to access how she was feeling. It wasn't a clear reception. At this point it was almost like a poorly tuned radio that was searching for a clear signal. Instead, all that came through were fragments. He could sense that she was in pain, but could not determine the type or extent of it. He wondered if she were receiving similar transmissions from him.

He had an idea. He closed his eyes and focused on Eliza. In his mind he wanted to ask her how she was. He wanted to let her know that he was okay and also wanted to give her an update on everything else. Just as he was about to attempt to 'communicate', he felt a large hand on his shoulder. He opened his eyes and saw Leomas looking down at him.

"It is safe to venture outside. The heat will still be searing, but it should be bearable. Let's go and find Maven shall we? Oh, and make sure you put the jacket on."

He would attempt to contact Eliza again later. He jumped to his feet and followed Leomas out of the tent.

****

Eliza sat alone in the cold, dark room. She could still hear the muffled voices of Magissa, Aldar and Varios coming from down the corridor. She had stopped trying to listen to what they were saying, because nothing they said would trump what she had heard earlier that morning. She was still trying to take it in. As shocked as she was, she wondered how on Earth Alex was going to take it. She tried to drive this from her mind by thinking about how her companions were faring. She couldn't explain it, but she was sensing that Alex had been in danger, but was now okay, for the time being at least. How Axis and Maven were was unclear. She had to get out of there, but how? She looked all around, this room was escape proof. She could attempt to morph, but was aware that she couldn't change into anything small enough that would allow her through the small gap some thirty foot above her head. Besides, Magissa would surely have shielding in place to stop anyone from morphing within the confines of the fortress. As she was wracking her brain, desperately trying to formulate an escape plan, she heard approaching footsteps followed by a key hitting the lock.

Instinctively, she ran across to the door and pressed herself up against the wall, just to the right. She had a plan, it was rash, but she thought that the split second it would take for the entrant to realise that she wasn't on her makeshift bed, would allow her to get the jump on them and make a run for it. The hinges whined in protest as the door slowly opened.

****

Leomas unfastened the door to the tent and stepped outside. He held the door open for Alex and beckoned him outside. A blinding light, followed by searing heat hit him as he stepped through the door. He shielded his eyes as he looked skyward. The heat from the sun continued to hit them in waves, but it did seem to him that it was higher in the sky than before. As he tried to make sense of this, he noticed Leomas had started to make his way to the next tent. He followed.

"Canis? Are you in there? It's me, Leomas." They heard the door being unfastened from the inside. Canis appeared.

Leomas placed his hand on the shoulder of Canis. "Good to see you, my friend."

"You too," Canis replied.

Leomas stepped into the tent closely followed by Alex. Alex scanned the room, there were four other men in there and one of them was the stretcher bearer that had been badly burnt. He was lying on his stomach, being tended to by one of the other men. He looked at him and immediately looked away, his injuries appeared to be far worse than he had imagined. He looked on the floor and there was Falmus lying on the stretcher, awake. He glared at him. Falmus didn't seem coherent but he must have felt eyes on him. He looked at Alex, he didn't speak but his eyes seemed to be apologetic. Alex looked away. He saw Leomas checking on the injured man. He watched as Leomas placed a reassuring hand on the man's shoulder, the only place where he hadn't been burnt. "You performed your duties heroically today. We will fix you up."

Alex saw Canis. "Have you seen Maven?" he asked.

"No. Not since we all went over the rise." He must have seen the concern on Alex's face. "I am sure that he would have made it into one of the other shelters in time."

Leomas and Alex both left the tent and proceeded to check the others one by one. No one had seen Maven. Alex feared the worst as they entered the last of the tents. He looked all around; Maven was nowhere to be seen. The realisation had dawned on him that Maven hadn't made it. What an awful way to go. He felt like he was going to be sick.

"Alex! He was here!" Leomas was 'smiling'.

"He left the tent about twenty minutes ago." Alex felt relieved. He ran out of the tent and started to call out Maven's name. He ran back down to the tent that he had been in whilst the solar event was taking place. He flung the door back looking for Maven. He was nowhere to be seen. If he didn't know better, he could have sworn that Maven and his sense of humour were at work. "Maven! Has anyone seen Maven?"

Just then, Maven's head appeared from around the other side of Axis. He looked like an old mongoose peeking up from out of his hole. Alex was so relieved but he was also angry that he had been put through such a range of emotions. When he saw the smile break out on Maven's face, any anger that he had been feeling washed away. "Alex! It is so good to see you, my boy!"

Alex raced over and hugged the old Mystic. "You too! I was worried that you hadn't made it."

Maven looked affronted. "It will take more than the ground melting beneath my feet to take out a wily old fox like me." He smiled and winked at Alex.

Alex returned his smile and then remembered that Maven had been on the ground when he had entered the tent. "What were you doing there?" He pointed on the floor alongside Axis' stretcher. "Hiding from me?"

"Hardly," once again he looked somewhat affronted. "I like a game of hide and seek as much as the next person, but there is a time and a place. I was tending to Axis."

"Is there any improvement at all?" Alex asked.

Maven's mood switched back to serious mode. "I'm afraid not. He is still stable but the Hydra Ice is still as whole as it was when it first attached itself to him." Maven stroked his beard. "If the heat that we experienced on our journey here could not melt it, then I truly don't know what can."

Concern took Alex once again. What could they do to combat Magissa's dark magic? As magically proficient as Maven was, he did not possess the ability to reverse this. Then an idea dawned on him. "Of course! It's so obvious!" he exclaimed.

"What's so obvious?" enquired Maven.

But Alex had disappeared through the door in the tent. Confused and intrigued, Maven followed.

Alex was running from tent to tent. "Leomas! Leomas!"

Leomas appeared from out of one of the tents. "Alex. What is it?"

"We need to set off for the Firestone now!"

"We are making preparations. I need to send my men ahead to set up camp. In a matter of hours, it will be freezing again."

"But you don't understand. We need to go right now."

"What's the rush, Alex?" Leomas looked concerned. "Has the countdown timer moved on significantly? Is the stone activating?"

"No, no, nothing like that," Alex reassured. He took the watch out of his pocket and showed Leomas. As well as showing that their heading was still locked in, the glow around its circumference had gone past the one o'clock position. But they were still not in immediate danger.

"Well, what is it then?" Leomas asked.

Alex was breathless now, a combination of the heat and his excitement to get his words out. "The Firestone is key," he gasped.

"Yes. Yes. We know. As are the other stones."

"No. Don't you see?" said Alex impatiently. "The Firestone is key... key to saving Axis. The power of the stone will be able to melt the Hydra Ice; I'm certain of it."

Leomas looked uncertain but Maven did not. A knowing smile broke out. "Of course! You are a genius, my boy! Come on, Leo, let's move out."

Leomas turned to Canis, "Rally the men. It looks like we are heading out."

23.

Incarceration or Liberation

Eliza was pressed so tightly to the wall that she almost felt at one with the smooth, cold stones. The door stopped just short of her face. She heard footsteps enter the room. There was no time to dally, she peered around from behind the door that was hiding her and saw that someone was making their way towards her bed. They seemed to have not noticed that she wasn't there. She wasn't going to pass up the opportunity that she had been given. She stepped out from behind the door, all the while keeping her eyes on the person whose back was still to her. The figure was collecting her cup and plate. She stepped around the door, heading for the exit. As she moved, the pocket of her jacket got caught on the latch and before she'd realised it, the door had moved. There was an audible creak that at this point may have just as well been her shouting, "Look at me. I'm here!"

She froze, almost certain that she was going to be caught. The figure turned around and looked straight at her. It was Cordium. Though he was staring straight at her, he didn't react. He just turned back around and carried on going about his business. She couldn't believe her luck. Part of her wanted to grab Cordium and take him with her, but the other part knew that he would slow her down.

"Sorry, Cordium," she whispered. "We will come for you, I promise."

She peered left and right. The coast was clear. She could still hear voices coming from her left, so her only option was to head to the right. Nimbly, she made her way down the corridor. She noted that there were a number of closed doors on both sides. After a short time, she came to the end of the corridor; she had the option to go left or right. She quickly made up her mind to go left. There were no longer any doors, just bare walls on either side. She became more cautious, as should she encounter anyone, there was nowhere to hide. The path then started to wind to the right which was worse still because at least before she could have seen somebody coming from a distance, now they would be virtually on top of her before she knew it. She slowed her pace and listened carefully for any indication that she was no longer alone. She heard nothing. As she pressed on, the path continued to bend to the right. This place was a labyrinth.

She was sure that the path was leading her back to where she had started. But then her progress was halted by a closed door. Uncertainty crept in; she was considering retracing her steps and taking the right-hand path, but something in the back of her mind told her to press on through the door. With her left hand, she gently took the handle and she pressed her right hand up against the higher hinge and used her right foot to apply pressure to the lower hinge. She hoped that this unusual technique would stop the hinges from whining as she opened the door. She twisted the handle and the latch came free. She opened the door slowly to a point where it was just wide enough for her to fit through comfortably and to her relief, no sound was emitted from the hinges. As she slipped through, she was greeted by a staircase that seemed to descend into darkness. It was her only path, so with her left hand pressed against the wall for support and guidance, she cautiously made her way down the stairs.

Carefully, she continued her descent. She could feel that they were spiral. As she progressed, her eyes started to grow accustomed to the lack of light. After a while, she reached the foot of the stairs. She could make out the outline of something not far away. It was another door. Somewhere in the distance, there was a high-pitched scream which drew her attention. It wasn't a scream of fear; it was a scream of rage. This was certain to be Magissa's reaction to finding out she had escaped. She hoped that Magissa wouldn't take it out on Cordium but then thought, *What more can she possibly do to him?*

No longer concerned with trying to muffle the door hinges, this time she opened the door just wide enough to peer out. There was a path that climbed to the right but fell to the left. As she followed the fall of the path, she saw that it led to a wall that spanned as far as she could see in either direction. What drew her attention though was a large gate set into the wall and even from her vantage point it was obvious that the gate was ajar. This was her chance. She stepped onto the path trying to look as innocuous as possible. There were a few people milling about, but they all seemed too caught up in their own troubles to really notice her. One or two people looked in her direction to which she reacted by trying to look as downtrodden as they were. This worked, because they soon looked away. *She obviously lives here.*

As she descended down the path, she started to take in her surroundings. Both sides of the pathway were flanked with buildings. At the start of the path, the buildings were large, but as she progressed towards the gate, she became aware that they were gradually starting to reduce in size and quality. One thing that they all shared in common was the fact that they were all in a state of disrepair. It was as if their occupants had lost interest. The gardens were all overgrown, with the exception of the vegetable plots, these were all well maintained. She guessed that this was likely to be the occupants' only source of food.

She was drawing closer to the gate now and as she did she passed a couple who had a look on their faces like death was just around the next corner. She realised that she had a clear run to the gate – to freedom. It was almost a certainty that Magissa, Varios or their guards would be searching for her, so she decided to throw caution to the wind and started to make a run for the gate. She was now sprinting flat out.

When she was approximately ten yards from the gate, she looked back to make sure that she wasn't being followed. All good. As she turned back around she saw Artemas in his human form standing just in front of her. She didn't have time to react. He threw his arms around her middle and picked her up off of the ground.

"No!" she screamed.

Artemas laughed. "You may have gotten the jump on me before when you had weapons, but what are you going to do now, little girl?" He started to carry her back towards the fortress. There was no way that she was going back. She thrashed and kicked, trying to break free. She managed to land a back kick right on Artemas' shin. He was caught off guard and yelled in pain, giving her an opportunity to wriggle free. Artemas was trying to recapture her whilst favouring his shin. She was too quick for him. She dodged his attempted lunges and kicked him firmly between the legs. Artemas went down like he'd been shot. He was on his knees covering the injured area with his hands and yelling obscenities at her.

She didn't stick around to listen. She was once again running for the gate, now almost there. She looked back to make sure that there was a good distance between herself and Artemas, but was shocked to see that he had morphed into a wolf and even though he was running with a discernible limp, he was gaining on her. She needed to slow him down, even if she got to the gate, he would soon run her down. She looked around for something, anything that would aid her in this. There was a small garden just to her left. There was some mesh lying on the ground, presumably to keep pests off of the precious vegetables that were growing there. An idea occurred to her. She needed to time everything correctly, or she would be caught.

She broke left and hurdled a wire fence that bordered the garden. The wolf followed and it leapt for the fence. At the last possible moment, she lifted the top strand. Artemas caught this and went cartwheeling uncontrollably into the garden. He was stunned. Now was her chance. Whilst Artemas was prone on the ground, she started to wrap the mesh around his legs. Once she had done this, she jumped the fence and sprinted for the gate. Behind her, Artemas was desperately trying to regain a vertical base. He was completely tangled in the mesh and kept falling back to the ground. He was growling and snarling, the more he fought, the more he became entangled. As she reached the gate, she turned back to look at him, "Little girl indeed." With that she disappeared through the gate and sprinted for the tree line off to the left.

24.

Ignis Vallis

Alex, Maven, Leomas and company had been walking for some time when they came to an area that looked very much like Leomas had described to Alex. They looked down into a valley, the floor of which looked like a dried out lakebed. It had been so affected by the sun that as they stared at it, the ground seemed to be made up of hundreds and hundreds of large, misshapen hexagons. These were flanked on either side by elaborate looking rock formations, some of which had a polished sheen to them – a by-product of the blistering heat that radiated down on it on a daily basis. Their orientation was such that it almost looked like they had been positioned in this way intentionally. In the distance were two hills that met in the middle at their lowest point. Alex thought that the shape they made looked like the letter M. He looked at the watch. Though the gem that denoted the Firestone was not yet lit, the secondary hands were indicating that they were very much on track.

Leomas pointed, "It is my belief that the Firestone is located somewhere down there. Generally, we do not venture this far into Malustera, but I have heard tale of strange lights around this area at dusk."

"The watch seems to agree with you," said Alex.

Leomas had sent the majority of his men ahead to prepare the shelters. Only Canis and eight others had stayed. They stood watch on the two stretcher-bound men. Axis' condition had not changed and though Falmus was now conscious, he was too injured to walk. Alex, Maven and Leomas ventured down towards the lakebed. It was a deeper valley than it had appeared from above. He looked back from where they had come; he could no longer see those that had stayed above. Eventually they reached the valley floor. Alex looked all around him, he felt like he was in a giant cut out for a swimming pool, with the rock formations adorning both sides, looking like purpose built grottos, all that was missing was the water. He looked at the watch, the secondary hands were unwaveringly pointing directly ahead. He looked at Maven who nodded and gestured towards the oblique hexagons that lay on the ground before them.

"You have the watch, my boy. Have at it."

Alex took a deep breath and cautiously stepped onto the first of these. All was well. As he looked closer, he noticed that there were slight gaps either side of the hexagon that he was standing on. These had been roughly filled in by sand that presumably had blown down from above, creating a makeshift mortar joint. He looked back at his two companions who were now stepping down either side of him. He was glued to the watch as he took his next step. As he landed, the ground seemed to move beneath his leading foot.

"Don't move," said Maven.

Alex averted his eyes from the watch and looked at where his right foot was positioned. It was not completely within the hexagon, part off it had crossed over one of the mortar joints. The ground felt very unstable.

"I am going to support your weight, Alex. When I say now, slowly lift your foot up," said Leomas. Alex nodded. He felt Leomas place his hands around his waist. "Now!" He slowly lifted his foot up, and as he did, he felt the hexagon that he was standing on dislodge. Maven jumped and land centrally on a hexagon several foot ahead. Leomas picked Alex up completely and jumped with him. As they did, the area that Alex had been standing on fell away. Leomas teetered as he landed, one of his huge feet straying dangerously close to the mortar joint that surrounded the hexagon on which he had landed. He regained his balance and carefully set Alex down centrally on the hexagon to his left. Once their hearts had stopped racing, they all looked back at the area that they come from. The part that Alex had been standing on had completely disappeared. All that remained was an orange glow. Maven squinted at this trying to ascertain exactly what it was.

"Stay there," he said, and carefully he made his way back for a closer look.

Alex and Leomas looked on as Maven inspected the area. They saw his eyes widen as he turned to look at them. A few moments later he appeared alongside them, he seemed uncertain of what to say.

"Well?" said Leomas. "What is it?"

"Lava."

Leomas closed his eyes and raised his head skywards.

"Just what we need, more heat," said Alex.

Maven pointed to where he was standing. "These are nothing more than stepping stones but they are very thick. If we step carefully, they should maintain their stability. So let's avoid the cracks shall we?"

Carefully, they each made their way forward, stone by stone. Alex would now only look at the watch once he was safely on the next stone. The sun was starting to set and already the temperature was beginning to drop. Alex moved on a few more steps and looked directly ahead, shielding his eyes. The sun was setting directly between where the two hills met. They looked like a giant gaping mouth, drawing the sun in. They continued on, each of them moving one stone forward and then waiting for the others to make the same move so that they all ended up alongside each other, before Alex started the process again. It was as if they were three playing pieces that could only move one space at a time on this giant, misshapen game board.

Alex looked at the watch again. This time a smile appeared on his face as he saw the orange gem on the watch face glowing back at him. "You were right, Leomas, the gem is lit. We are very close." He looked at Maven and Leomas in turn. They both smiled and encouraged him on. The sun was being drawn deeper into the mouth, so much so that part of it was now obscured from view. Alex looked at the watch face again. The secondary hands were pointing straight ahead; he was on the right path. He stepped to the next stone and waited for Maven and Leomas to appear either side of him. As soon as they joined him, he moved on to the next stone and as he did, part of his foot got caught in a sunken area.

"What's wrong, Alex? Are you okay?" Maven called.

Due to his new-found caution, his trailing foot was still firmly planted on the stone behind, so although he teetered for a moment, he managed to bring his right foot back quite easily.

"I'm fine. There is something different about this stone though." With that, he lowered himself to his knees and ensuring that he didn't touch the cracks around either the stone that he was on, or the one just in front, he carefully pushed the dusting of sand into a heap in the centre of the stone and began to scoop it up and place it on the stone to the immediate right. As he continued to clear the sand, he could make out a shape cut into the stone.

"What do you see?" asked Maven.

"There is a groove cut into the stone." He ran his hand across and all around it. "It appears to be a perfect circle. I think that the Firestone is here." He looked at the watch, the gem was glowing a brilliant orange. The sun had

~ 182 ~

almost been half swallowed. The top of it was now almost level with the two hilltops. Alex started to push his hand into the circle that was cut into the stone.

"Careful, Alex!" warned Leomas as he looked on.

Maven, who had jumped to the stone directly to the left, squatted down and began to study this strange circle. "I don't think pressing on it will do anything, it looks like it houses something."

Leomas who had been looking on in silence, suddenly started to feel uneasy. The temperature had been progressively dropping since they first arrived in the valley, but now he was aware that it was starting to rise again and rapidly. He looked at the sun; its powerful light had seemingly absorbed the two hills as they were no longer visible. Its heat was now trained on the valley that he, Alex and Maven were standing in. He looked across and realised that as the sun continued to set, its heat was being funnelled into the valley. Then it dawned on him that they were in a kiln and a fire had just been lit. The sun's rays were being attracted to the highly polished rock faces that flanked them on either side.

"I think that we should get out of here. Now!"

Maven looked up unaware of what Leomas was seeing. He wiped his brow. "We need a little more time, Leo. We are trying to find the key to solving this puzzle."

"Key!" This seemed to twig something in Alex's mind. "It's a lock. We just need the key." He reached inside his shirt and pulled out the Muleta.

"We really need to go!" Leomas called out again.

"Why? It's not dark yet," Maven retorted.

"It's not the dark that concerns me. Look!"

Maven looked in the direction that Leomas was pointing. The entire horizon now seemed to have been swallowed by the sun. Maven realised that Leomas was right.

"Come on, Alex. We know where this is, we can come back. We need to go now!"

Alex wasn't listening; his mind was firmly fixed on the Firestone. He was holding the Muleta just above the stone and began to lower it in. It clicked into place perfectly.

"Look out!" roared Leomas.

Both Maven and Alex looked to a rock formation to their left. The sun's rays were being absorbed into the lustre of the highly polished rock and you could literally see the heat that it reflected burning into the ground only a matter of feet away from where Maven stood.

Maven was frantic. "Alex, we have to go!"

"No not yet!" cried Alex. "You have to trust me. I can do this!"

Maven looked behind him. The sun was lower now. As it continued to set, its rays were attracted towards the polished face of one of the rock formations deeper in the valley. This caused its reflected heat to be directed even closer to Maven.

"Whatever you're going to do, do it now!" he cried as he jumped back to the stone just behind Alex. He had moved just in the nick of time as the heat was now pinpointed on the stone that he had just vacated. Leomas too had had to move, as the rays were being drawn towards the rock faces on his side and the reflected heat was getting dangerously close to where he had been standing. They didn't want to leave Alex so exposed, but they had little choice.

"Come on, Alex!" roared Leomas.

Alex pressed down on the Muleta, it didn't move. He looked at how it was positioned in the stone; the housing for the Firestone was in the west position. "I wonder?" he said to himself. He tried to turn the Muleta clockwise. To his surprise, it moved almost mechanically into place. It clicked and seemed to sink further into the stone. He heard a cracking noise and recoiled slightly, mainly through the fear that he had destabilised the stone. He then heard what sounded like suction. Dust was being drawn up off of the stone, obscuring his view of the Muleta. He was concerned that the stone was going to collapse and cause the Muleta to be swallowed by the lava that stewed underneath. He reached in trying to remove it, but there was then a whooshing sound that made him recoil. There followed a clicking sound, like something was locking into place. Through the dust, he could make out an orange glow. He waved his hand, trying to clear the haze. He looked down and there, staring back at him was the Muleta complete with a newly acquired Firestone! Alex couldn't believe it. "I've got it! I've got it! It's positioned itself into the Muleta!" He thought back to when he had found the Waterstone and there was a big part of him that was grateful that he didn't have to go through the same process with the Firestone.

"That's great! Now get out of there!" yelled Maven, bringing Alex's mind firmly back to the present.

Alex looked to his left and then to his right. He could see the effects of searing heat either side of him, but strangely, could not feel it. He looked around to see that Maven and Leomas had now retreated some distance; they both had their staffs trained in his general direction.

"Now, Alex! We can't hold this much longer. If we have to move, the shielding will be down." He reached down and tried to pull the Muleta out of the stone, but it wouldn't come loose. He couldn't believe it. He now had the stone, but couldn't remove the Muleta. He could see both Maven and Leomas looking on as the reflected heat was moving closer to them by the second. He grabbed at the Muleta again and tried to turn it back to the position that he had placed it into the stone. It moved! There was an audible click as it released its grip on the stone housing. He picked it up, placed it back around his neck and started to run.

Maven and Leomas saw him coming and lowered their staffs, jumping immediately out of harm's way. Alex heard a noise behind him but didn't look back, he kept on running. Maven was looking in his direction; his eyes were wide with terror.

"Run, Alex! Whatever you do, do not look back. Just run!"

He did as instructed. It was now almost dark but he could feel extreme heat building up behind him. He didn't dare look back, just in case he landed on a mortar joint and destabilised the ground. Maven and Leomas were no longer on the 'game board'; they were waiting for him at the foot of the hill that would lead them back to the others. They were both yelling for him to run. He looked above their heads and could see Canis running down the hill; he was obviously concerned by all of the commotion. He had stopped halfway down. His eyes were wide with terror as he started yelling at the top of his lungs for Alex to run.

He was getting close to them now and as he looked down to make sure that his feet were hitting the stones squarely, he became aware of an orange glow breaking out under the stone to his left. He looked right, the same thing was happening. Curiosity got the best of him, he looked behind and his jaw almost hit the ground as he was greeted by an ocean of lava. He wasn't going to make it!

"Run!" he could hear the others screaming. He was close, but not close enough. He jumped onto the next stone and felt it sink as he landed on it. All around him, the stones were being overrun by the lava. Leomas was as close as he could get to the edge.

"Alex! You are going to have to jump! I will catch you. I promise!" Alex knew that he had no other choice. He pushed down with his legs and propelled himself forwards. He looked at Leomas, arms outstretched. He was never going to reach him. The world seemed to slow down, the frantic situation going on all around him, seemed to have faded away. *So this is how it feels before the end,* he thought to himself, almost resigned to his fate.

The world was falling away. Then he heard Leomas' voice again, "Alex! Grab on!"

He opened his eyes; he was falling towards the lava! But just in front of him was Leomas, staff in hand, encouraging Alex to grab on. He lunged forward with both arms outstretched. He closed his eyes, time seemed to stop. *If this is dying, it doesn't feel so bad.* He then felt himself moving upwards, he opened his eyes to see himself clinging onto the staff and being hoisted up and out of harm's way. Leomas heaved him upwards and flung him part way up the hill that led away from the sea of fire below.

Canis met him and they started to run up the hill, closely followed by Leomas and Maven. They were all completely winded by the time they had made it out of harm's way. Once they had all caught their breath, they stared in awe at the sea of fire below.

Leomas finally broke the silence. "Well I guess that explains the strange lights that I have heard occur at dusk. They call that place Ignis Vallis, which roughly translates to Fire Valley. I never knew why until now."

25.

Enemy Territory

Darkness had now descended and the cold was starting to take hold. Alex was still extremely shaken up by what he had just experienced, but despite this, he was desperate to get to Axis. Maven saw him get up as did Leomas; they both did likewise and joined him alongside Axis' stretcher. Alex looked down to see that his guardian was still in his induced slumber. The ice was still perfectly intact. It looked like a parasite that had attached itself to Axis and seemed to be feeding off him. Alex took the Muleta from around his neck. He didn't know what to do, but knew that he had to try something. The longer that this thing was attached to Axis, the more damage it was doing.

Leomas looked edgy. His eyes were scanning from left to right. "I think that we should get to camp," he said. "It is not wise for us to linger after dark."

"I need to try to get this thing off of Axis first," Alex protested.

Leomas' tone softened, "I understand Alex truly I do. We can be at camp in less than an hour if we hurry." He looked down at Axis. "With respect, I don't think that waiting another hour will matter to him."

"Leomas is right," said Maven. "We must get to camp. I promise that tending to Axis will be our priority once we are there."

Reluctantly, Alex agreed. The stretcher bearers assumed their positions and picked up the two injured men. "We must stay in a tight pack," said Leomas. "To keep warm and I have the distinct feeling that we are not alone."

They set off. It was a clear night; the moon was full which had triggered their heightened eyesight, which in turn, allowed them to clearly see the path that they were taking. It had now become so cold that Alex was almost longing for the oppressive heat from earlier in the day.

They had been travelling for about forty minutes. Every so often, they would hear scuttling noises. Sometimes it came from the left, sometimes from the right. Leomas, who had been on his guard the entire time, reacted to even the slightest sound. He would spin towards the direction of the noise, assuming a protective stance, his glowing orange eyes boring into the darkness, looking for some sign of an impending attack.

None came. They moved on.

"We are close to camp," said Leomas. He pointed ahead. Their path started to curve. "It should be just around the next corner." Alex felt relieved. He felt like a soldier that had been travelling through enemy territory and was almost back at base. Leomas did not share in this relief. He had the feeling that they were being herded by some unseen creatures.

They continued along the path and as it straightened out, they came upon a flat, open area. Leomas was looking up, down, left and right. Even in this light, Alex could see that he was confused.

"Leo. Are you okay?" asked Maven.

Leomas was still searching the surrounding area.

"Leo?"

He looked at Maven, his glowing orange eyes wide with concern. "My men – they should be up there." He pointed towards an elevated area off to their left.

"Are you sure that it is the correct place?" asked Maven.

Leomas looked put out. "Of course I'm sure! I do not take the safety of my people lightly! We discussed it at length. This was the best position; it would have given us a clear line of sight for a good distance in every direction."

"I did not mean to upset you," said Maven. "It would be easy to mistake the location, as every part of this place looks so similar."

Leomas' tone softened slightly. "You are not wrong. Something serious must have happened though to force my men to abandon the plan." He looked off into the distance.

"We can only hope that they have found another site not too far away, as we will not survive if we are exposed to this cold too much longer. Let's press on. Make sure you stay close."

Alex was really starting to feel the effects of the cold. He could barely feel his hands and feet. It was so much colder than the previous night; the lack of cloud cover was certainly contributing to this. He kept knocking into the men as they walked, such was their close proximity to one another. This strange huddle wandering across this desolate place would have looked quite a sight to any onlookers.

There were those who were watching their every move, though they found nothing strange or humorous about what they saw. All they could see was the small amount of body heat being emitted from the group, triggering the only real emotion that they possessed. Hunger.

Some cloud had started to shroud the moon as the group continued across the flat area of land that stretched out in front of them. Alex was in the middle of the huddle, walking between Falmus' and Axis' stretchers. Maven, Leomas, Canis and four of Leomas' other men were all on the outside. Between them, they created a protective circle.

Alex watched Leomas closely. He was definitely on edge. It was strange to see such a huge, powerful man so spooked. As they continued on, they left the flat open area behind them as their path started to climb. Then the path started to narrow, which meant the disbandment of the protective circle. Leomas and Maven led the way, followed by the two stretchers, then Alex, with the remainder of the men bringing up the rear in two banks of two. There was still no sign of anything that even resembled a camp. Leomas stopped suddenly, raising his hand with a closed fist, indicating that those behind should do likewise.

Alex manoeuvred his way between the stretchers. "Why have we stopped?" he asked.

"Shhh! Something is heading this way," whispered Leomas.

Alex, who had been sceptical earlier, could see the dark shape too. He lowered his voice. "What is it? Can you make it out?"

"No. But it could be a Crassac scout. If it is, that means that the main pack won't be far behind."

"What do we do?" asked Alex.

"You and Maven go back there and tell the others to take cover."

"What about you?"

"I need to take this threat out and quietly. If it is a scout, any noise that it makes could alert the main pack."

Despite Alex's earlier reservations, he had become fond of Leomas.

"Be careful," he said.

Leomas turned to face him. "I appreciate your concern, but I'll be fine. Go on now, get back to the others and all of you get down."

They did as instructed and watched Leomas assume a half crouched position as he moved further up the hill. Due to the now restricted moonlight, his eyesight was not as sharp as it had been. He could make out the shadow of something twenty yards up ahead. He couldn't see what it was, but it was on all fours and definitely heading towards him. He thought about morphing, but decided it was too dangerous as this could alert the unknown shape to his presence. Besides, he was more than formidable in this form. He then thought about moving closer, but decided to hold his ground. He would intercept it as it came past. He would break its neck; it would be dead before it knew anything had happened. He crouched low to the ground, poised, ready to grab the creature. He looked on, the shape was moving slowly, uncertainly.

Was this a Crassac scout? he thought to himself. *It would surely be more focused and moving quicker.* He couldn't take any chances; he had to stick to his original plan. The shape was almost upon him now. He grabbed it as it came past, wrapping his huge arms arounds its neck. He started to squeeze.

"No! Leomas! It's me!" came its choked response.

Shocked, Leomas immediately relaxed his grip on its neck, but did not release it completely. He then realised that he was holding onto a rather large coyote. The coyote was now getting its faculties back. Leomas looked closer and frowned. "Lupus? Is that you?"

"Yes," coughed the creature.

All of Leomas' questions came out at once as he released his grip on Lupus. "Are you okay? What happened? Where is everyone else? Why wasn't the camp where we discussed?"

Lupus assumed his human form. Leomas could see that he was injured, but it wasn't as a result of anything he had just done.

"We arrived at the campsite just before dusk. The heat really slowed us down." He paused to catch his breath. "We prepared to make camp, but got the sense that we were being watched. I asked the men to carry on with the preparations whilst I took a look around, but warned them to stay on their guard. I scouted around the entire perimeter, but found nothing. Still something didn't sit right with this place, so I made the decision to move on and find another site." He looked at Leomas apologetically for disobeying his orders.

Leomas realised this and reassured him. "It's okay, Lupus. You know as well as I that we sometimes have to react to a situation according to how we interpret it. What happened after that?"

"We found another site about a mile in that direction." He pointed to where he had just come from. "Pardus and I left the others to unpack the tents whilst we scouted the area. Everything looked good; the ill feeling that I experienced at the previous site had gone. I asked Pardus to go back and set the others on the task of making camp."

"Why didn't you go too?" asked Leomas.

"I was just about to re-join them when I heard a noise. I went to investigate but found nothing, so I made my way back to camp. When I arrived, there was no trace of anyone. Initially, I thought that I had become disorientated and gone to the wrong place, but that's when I found him." Lupus looked sombre.

"Found who?" asked Leomas.

Lupus looked down at the ground. "Pardus," he said.

"What had happened?"

"I don't know. He looked badly injured and as I went to check on him, he was dragged away."

"Dragged away! By what?"

"I don't know."

"What do you mean you don't know? You must have seen something?" demanded Leomas.

"That's just it. I saw nothing at all. I can't explain what happened."

Leomas thought about this a moment and then asked, "How did you get injured?"

Lupus looked at the ground. "I am not proud of this, but when I saw Pardus being dragged away, I ran. I kept looking back expecting whatever took him to be pursuing me and that's when I fell and hit my head." Lupus looked as if he was going to breakdown. "I have failed them and failed you too! Please forgive me."

Leomas offered a consoling hand. "You have not failed anyone. You were not there to assist the others and had you been, whatever befell them would have surely befallen you too." Lupus still didn't look convinced.

"Are you badly injured?" asked Leomas.

Lupus shook his head. "I'm okay. I need to redeem myself, what can I do."

"I'm sure your opportunity for redemption will come but right now we need to get back to the others," said Leomas. He stretched out his hand and helped Lupus to his feet.

They arrived back with the others and explained what happened. "So there isn't a camp. Are any of the tents and provisions still there?" asked Maven.

"No," said Lupus. "Everything is gone. Whatever took the men, took the equipment too."

"We can't stay out in this temperature for too much longer, Leo," said Maven. "What should we do?"

Leomas looked deep in thought as his mind wandered back to his feeling that they were being herded by something of origin unknown.

Finally he spoke. "There is only one thing that we can do," he said. "We have to make for Interria tonight."

Lupus raised his eyebrows.

"How far is it?" asked Maven.

Leomas dodged the question and responded with, "We have actually been on the road to Interria since we left Ignis Vallis."

Maven pressed further. "How far, Leo?"

"Two hours."

Maven was beside himself. "Two hours! We can't last that long!"

Leomas' eyes flashed, "What would you have us do, lie down and die? Or maybe go and serve ourselves up directly to whatever took the rest of my men?"

Maven said nothing.

"No. I thought not," said Leomas. "Interria is our only choice. This is my land, you need to trust me. If we keep our formation tight and stay awake to the danger, we can make it. Now, we move."

26.

Into the Interria

Despite the bitter cold and the men being spooked by the slightest noise, they were making quite good progress. The moon that had been full and bright earlier had now been all but smothered by cloud. This further restricted the range that they could all see. Maven was preparing to place a crystal in the groove atop his staff that would have lit their way, but Leomas stopped him. "We need to stay invisible, Maven. If we are being watched, that will be a beacon to them. As long as we can see the path ahead, we stay as we are." Maven agreed and apologised.

It had now been an hour since they had left for Interria. They had not seen or heard anything strange for some time. Although they were still on their guard, there was a sense that they were no longer being followed, if indeed, they ever had been. The moon was starting to push through the clouds now too. Perhaps things were finally starting to go their way? Freezing but encouraged, they continued on. The next forty minutes passed without incident. They soon came to a break in the path.

Leomas and Maven were in hushed conversation with one another. Alex made his way over to them. They fell silent as soon as they saw him. He looked at Maven, but for some unknown reason, the Mystic would not make eye contact with him. Leomas could see that Alex was curious as to the content of their conversation, so immediately diverted his attention.

"Here, Alex, there is something that I want to show you." He directed Alex over to the left. They were standing on the edge of a cliff that dropped down into the darkness. Leomas pointed northwest. Alex looked down into the valley. The moonlight had once again broken through the cloud and was bathing the valley in a clear, bright light. "You see that huge boulder over there?" Alex's eyes followed the direction of Leomas' finger and he nodded.

"That is the entrance to Interria. We are nearly there." He smiled at Alex, "Warmth, food, safety and comfy beds await us."

They turned left and started to make their way down the path that descended towards Interria. The moon's glow continued to light their way. As good as it was to be able to see more clearly, this injection of light was creating eerie shadows all around them. Alex looked to his left, he was sure that he had just seen the branch of a tree waving in the wind. The strange thing was, there wasn't any wind on this night, not even a light breeze and as he looked closer still, he realised that there weren't any trees on the path either.

They had now completed their descent and were on level ground. The gigantic boulder that signified the entrance to Interria was now clearly in their sights. Perhaps it was the fact that they were so close to their goal or the fact that they no longer had the sense that they were being followed, but Alex noticed a complacency start to set in with the men that were bringing up the rear of the group. They were no longer in formation and seemed unfocused as they talked amongst themselves. He felt that it was only right to alert Leomas to this, so he made his way forward. The company came to a standstill. They were standing in front of a boulder that was at least fourteen foot high and twelve foot wide. Alex wondered how much it weighed as he realised that there weren't nearly enough men there to move it.

Leomas was looking at the huge boulder as Alex appeared alongside him. "We've made it, Alex." He looked pleased with himself.

"Great," said Alex. "But how do we get in? There are not enough of us here to hope to move it."

Leomas smiled. The moonlight made his fangs glisten. "You are correct. You may want to step back slightly."

Alex did as instructed and looked on as Leomas reached over his shoulder and grabbed his staff. It extended to its full length as he held it aloft. He then pointed it in the direction of the boulder and pressed it against its highest point and then proceeded to drag it down its full length, almost as if he were drawing a line right through its middle. He then took a few steps back, nodded to Alex, and folded his arms as he looked at the boulder. A rumbling noise started to build in its general direction and then the ground began to shake. Every one of the company had their attention fixed on this and none of them realised as a huge snake-like appendage slowly drew up behind one of Leomas' men at the rear of the pack.

Slowly, deliberately, a huge spike started to extend out. It looked like a highly polished onyx as the moonlight struck it. It may just have been coincidence, but this seemed to trigger it into action. Propelled by the muscular appendage that it was attached to, it drove into the back of the ignorant victim. His mouth was wide open, like he was about to cry out. But no sound came. The spike had pierced his heart. Such was the force of the impact, it lifted the poor soul clear off of the ground and he was then swallowed by the darkness as the silent attacker withdrew. Due to the noise emanating from up ahead and the furtive nature of the attack, the man just in front was not aware of what had just happened to his comrade. He was equally unaware that another of these silent assassins was now drawing up behind him.

The huge boulder was starting to move. Alex, who was looking on impressed, was expecting the boulder to roll to one side. Instead it broke completely in half and very slowly, began to separate. A faint light was starting to build – an opening was being created. Alex looked back to see the reaction of the others. All of the onlookers had a look of relief on their faces. He noticed another shadow behind the men. He cursed the moon for using his overactive imagination against him. He went to turn back towards the opening. Out of the corner of his eye, he spotted definite movement. He focused his gaze and saw what appeared to be a huge serpent with a large spike extending from it! This wasn't the moon's doing!

"Look out!" he screamed.

Everyone spun around to see what the commotion was, including the man who was most at risk. He seemed confused as he came face to face with a huge spike that floated there menacingly, staring at him, like a cobra hypnotising its prey. He froze, not fully knowing what to do. The man seemed to be under its control, as did everyone else. No one knew how to react. If they charged at it, it would be able to attack before they had time to get there, so everyone just remained rooted to the spot.

Eventually the man seemed to come to his senses. He had to do something. Aware that any sudden movements could be his last, he very slowly reached down by his side and withdrew a knife. He had his weapon and his plan, he now had to strike and suddenly. He dropped to his knees and before the serpent could react, he drove his knife upwards, deep into it. Somewhere close by in the darkness, there was a high-pitched screech as the serpent withdrew. His heart was racing so he remained there on his knees trying to collect himself. His heart rate gradually lessened as relief started to course through his body. He made a move to get up, but as he did, he felt something thud into his chest.

Almost nonchalantly, he opened his jacket and looked down at his chest to see a huge spike breaking through. He looked ahead and the last thing that he saw in this life was a cluster of red, glowing eyes staring back at him.

Leomas and company were slow to react, as they could not quite take in what they were seeing. As they saw their unfortunate comrade being lifted off into the darkness, they drew their weapons and prepared to defend themselves. The moonlight had diminished again and though they had some shards of light above them, the surrounding area was shrouded in total darkness. They waited, primed, ready to defend themselves from the impending attack but nothing came. Then they sensed movement. They all strained their eyes, hoping for a sign of what they were up against. Leomas was the first to make out a red glow moving towards them. It took him another moment to realise that what he was looking at were eyes, but the eyes of what? As his eyes grew accustomed to the darkness he could now make out the vague outlines of faces. As they broke out of the darkness, he realised that he was looking at the face of a lion, and then alongside the lion a cheetah appeared, followed by a coyote. Only their faces could be seen, but judging by their height off of the ground, they were all abnormally large.

Leomas was confused. Was he looking at some of his own? "Announce yourselves. Who are you?" he demanded. No response. Slowly, the lion moved forward, his sand coloured front legs and paws could now be seen. As it drew further into the light, Leomas could see that its back was jet black; this area glinted as the moon's faint light hit it. *Is it wearing some kind of armour?* he thought to himself.

"Stay back!" he warned. "We will defend ourselves."

The lion did not seem to hear, it had moved almost fully into the light. Apart from the face, neck and front legs, the black armour covered the rest of its body. Leomas needed to deter this creature and as he stepped towards it, he morphed into his lion form. The armour clad lion was sizing him up. As huge as Leomas was, this creature was bigger.

Leomas moved in and batted the air with his huge paw just in front of the other lion's face. It did not flinch. *This beast needs a more practical demonstration.* With that, he charged the other lion. Their front paws locked. Leomas was trying to get the creature onto its back. He managed to get a paw free and strike just behind the lion's neck. It did not react at all. Leomas backed away and looked at his front paw; there was a black substance on it. *This is no armour that I have ever seen,* he thought to himself. Again Leomas charged and this time the other lion sidestepped him. As he corrected himself and primed for another attack he was taken by surprise. He was struck in the side by one of the serpent-like creatures. This sent him sprawling backwards. The lion was advancing on him now. The huge beast was now fully exposed in the moonlight. Leomas stared in disbelief. This wasn't a lion at all! Well the head and front legs were, but the rest was – something else entirely. Its torso was feline-esque in shape but was covered in the black substance that he had on his paw. It was like the torso was covered in some kind of exoskeleton, much like you would find on an ant, but much bigger and much stronger. If this wasn't shocking enough, behind the lion was the serpent that had just attacked him. He picked himself up off of the ground and as he looked more closely, he realised that this wasn't a serpent at all. It was a tail, similar to the one that you would find on a scorpion and this was attached to the lion. The armoured lion and the rest of his pack were now advancing on him and his company. It soon became clear that all the other members of the pack had very similar physical traits.

These were undoubtedly the Crassacs!

"Alex! Get through the opening!" Leomas yelled. There was a panic in his voice that Alex had never heard before.

He then turned his attention to his men. "Canis. Get the injured to safety. Raise the alarm inside. I will hold them off."

Alex was glued to the spot. He couldn't believe what he was seeing. He was watching the series of events unfold in slow motion. Leomas was still battling the 'armoured' lion. Maven was trying to keep the Crassac cheetah at bay and Canis, who had just re-emerged from the entranceway, ran past Alex. All in one motion, he morphed, jumped through the air and commenced battle with the Crassac that in some part was a coyote. Alex felt like he was right in the middle of one of his nightmares. He wanted to help, but did not know what to do.

More Crassacs were entering the fray. They moved so silently over the ground, you saw their glowing red eyes long before you heard them. Although more Malusterans were pouring out of the entranceway to join their comrades in battle, the Crassacs were still in the ascendancy and were starting to push them all back.

As Alex looked on stunned, Maven almost backed up into him. "What the… What are you still doing out here, Alex? Get inside!"

Alex snapped out of his nightmarish trance. "Look out!" he yelled. Maven spun round to see the scorpion tail of the cheetah heading right for him. He brought his staff up just in time to deflect the blow that would have been bound for his neck and then expertly spun his staff around and struck the beast squarely across the top of its head. It howled in pain and retreated.

Maven then turned back to Alex. "Now, for your own safety…" He looked at Alex, who was still standing there, stricken. Maven's face fell. Alex was holding his left arm, just beneath the shoulder. His sleeve was stained in crimson. "Oh no! Alex! Are you okay?" came Maven's panicked voice.

The attack that Maven had just deflected had inadvertently hit Alex. The colour was draining from Alex's face and his legs were starting to buckle. Maven lunged in to support Alex's weight just before his legs crumbled completely. He placed his hands under Alex's arms and attempted to drag him away from the battle.

The Crassac cheetah had regrouped and unbeknownst to Maven, it was once again making a beeline for him.

Maven was in a state of shock, he felt totally to blame for what had just happened. He continued to drag Alex away from the melee, all the while apologising over and over again. Alex could hear Maven's apologies, though they became gradually more muted. He was distracted by a tugging sensation around his neck. He was coherent enough to decide that one of Maven's arms must be caught on the chain around his neck. Maven had managed to drag Alex to the area by the huge split boulder that marked the entrance into Interria. As Maven was about to pull Alex over the threshold, he sensed that they were being watched. He turned around to be greeted by the huge cheetah. Though it had bloodlust in its eyes, it did not attack; it just stood there staring, seemingly trying to tempt Maven into making a move. Maven did not know what to do, any sudden movement and he was sure that the cheetah would attack. He looked at Alex, who was fading fast. He needed to tend to Alex. He grabbed his staff and stared at the cheetah. Its eyes narrowed as it started to circle Maven. Maven was just about to rush the beast when he was startled by what felt like a hand on his shoulder. He spun around to see a large man standing alongside him, staring intently at the cheetah.

"You tend to the boy; I'll take it from here."

Maven watched as Lupus passed by and morphed into a large coyote. Maven ran over to Alex and once again began to drag him into Interria. He looked up once they were both safely inside to see Lupus and the cheetah locked in battle.

He laid Alex down on the ground and quickly removed the scarf that he used to cover the particularly raw looking wound around his neck. Alex's need was more important. He quickly pulled the jacket sleeve off of the injured arm. Alex was wearing a light brown jumper under the jacket; half of the left arm was completely reddened. Alex was starting to lose consciousness. Maven shook him and as he did, he could hear the Muleta clinking against the chain near Alex's chest.

"No, Alex. You can't sleep, stay with me." Maven withdrew a pocket knife and cut away the sleeve of both Alex's jumper and undershirt. His entire upper arm was bathed in blood and more was pumping out. Maven removed his water bottle, unscrewed the lid and splashed a small amount of water over the wound which caused Alex to flinch. As the water washed the blood away, Maven got a good look at the wound, albeit a brief one. The wound was approximately four inches long and it was deep. No sooner had the blood been washed away than another pool had been pumped out. He knew that he was going to have to cauterize it. He started to open and close his right hand, much like he had done when he removed the Hindrex from Alex and Eliza. This seemed like a lifetime ago.

As the orange glow began to build around his hand, Maven was distracted and he suddenly stopped what he was doing. He was aware of something moving under Alex's shirt. He grabbed his staff and with the other hand, he slowly opened the garment. He drew his staff back, primed to use it on whatever it was that was trying to break out. He stopped short, his eyes widening. He looked down and was stunned to see the cause of the disturbance was the Muleta. Slowly, he placed his staff down. The Muleta was tugging against the chain that held it in place around Alex's neck. It seemed like it was being drawn to Alex's wound. Although the chain prevented it from getting to the area, Maven noticed that the flow of blood ebbed away every time that the Muleta got close to it. Slowly, carefully, he lifted Alex's head and unclasped the chain. He lowered Alex's head and slowly got to his feet and moved away from Alex. He was holding the chain out at arms-length with the now inanimate Muleta dangling. It looked like he was carrying something highly explosive, such was his consciousness not to actually touch the Muleta itself. He then made his way back over to Alex. As he drew near, the Muleta sprung to life and started to pull once again. It was almost as if it understood and re-sensed the wound. Maven was intrigued. He crouched down alongside the prone Alex and held the Muleta just a few inches above the wound and noticed that the blood flow stopped immediately. Then the blood that was already on the arm started to react strangely.

Inexplicably, it started to break away and form four circles, one centrally above the wound, one parallel to this below and finally, one at each end of the wound. Then a larger fifth circle formed and this one placed itself in the centre of the wound. Maven's brow furrowed. He lifted the chain ever so slightly. The five circles shimmered and started to deform. As he lowered the chain again, the circles reformed.

Just then, Leomas entered the tunnel. He was ordering his people to retreat. He turned around and saw Maven crouched alongside an obviously injured Alex. "Oh no! What happened? Is he okay?" Maven did not answer; he was totally in awe of the Muleta.

Leomas looked concerned. "Maven! What are you doing?"

Still Maven did not answer. The Muleta was pulling harder than ever against the chain now and just as Maven went to pull it away from the wound, the chain snapped and it broke free. The Muleta touched down on Alex's arm with a huge amount of force that caused his entire body to spasm. He then opened his eyes and screamed out in pain. The Muleta seemed to be boring down into his arm. They could clearly hear it breaking into his skin, followed by a tearing sound as it twisted into his flesh. Leomas ran to his aid. He reached out for the Muleta.

"No, Leo stop!" yelled Maven. He jumped up and threw himself between Leomas and Alex. "I think that it is helping him."

Alex screamed again, more loudly this time and started to flail about blindly, desperately trying to locate the source of the pain as the Muleta continued to burrow into his arm.

"It's not helping him, it's hurting him!" Leomas roared.

"No it's not. You didn't see what I saw. Trust me," said Maven.

Leomas looked at Alex writhing in pain and the Muleta, digging deeper into his arm. He couldn't take it anymore; he flung Maven to the ground and lunged for the Muleta.

"No, Leomas!" screamed Maven. From his prone position on the ground, he had gathered his staff and used it to push Leomas' hand away just before he had managed to grab the Muleta.

Leomas grabbed Maven's staff with one hand and reached for the Muleta with his other.

"No! You don't understand!" Maven protested. "You cannot touch the

Muleta. It will scatter the stones that we have collected to the wind and put us back to square one!"

Leomas recoiled slightly, considered this for a moment and said, "I don't care. It's killing him, I have to remove it."

"Please trust me, Leo," Maven implored. "It is healing him, I can feel it. Know that I would take my own life before hurting him."

Leomas stared at Maven, who had an imploring look on his face. He was still unsure.

All of a sudden, the screaming stopped. Alex then got to his feet as if nothing had happened.

"See," said a relieved Maven.

Leomas looked completely bemused by this sudden change. "Alex! Are you okay?"

Alex did not answer.

"Alex?" called Maven.

Still he didn't respond.

Instead, he started to make his way towards the entranceway where Leomas' men were battling to keep the Crassacs at bay. Leomas ran after him. He reached the entranceway first and smashed his staff across the skull of an invader that was getting too close. With that, he drew a straight line across the breadth of the two pieces of boulder. A rumble started to build and the floor began to shake – the doorway was starting to close.

Alex was wending his way through the mass of creatures defending the entranceway. It looked like he was going back outside.

"Alex? Alex?" called Leomas. "What are you doing?" Alex didn't react at all. He was on a mission. All that mattered was that he reached the entranceway.

Leomas ran after him. Once he caught up, he manoeuvred in front of him. Sensing an obstacle in the path, Alex tried to go around him, but Leomas blocked him off.

"Alex. The door is closing; we'll be safe in a few moments." Alex tried once again to go around him. Leomas put a friendly hand on his arm to guide him away.

"Arghh!" screamed Leomas. Intense heat shot into his hand and up his arm, causing him to recoil. Alex continued for the doorway that was now almost closed. He found a gap in the masses and held his hand up just in front of what remained of the entrance; it was almost as if he were about to wave goodbye.

Leomas wasn't sure what was going to happen, but encouraged his people to back away. There was a split second pause and then it seemed like the whole world had been lit up by an intense orange glow. Leomas' men all shielded their eyes as they retreated from the doorway that they had been protecting. All of the Crassacs retreated, some screaming, some howling. The two pieces of boulder suddenly clunked together, becoming one and extinguished both the light and the Crassacs' screams.

Alex turned around as if nothing had happened and then headed deeper into the tunnel. Leomas, who was still favouring his arm, got up and followed him, though he did keep his distance. Alex walked straight past Maven as if he wasn't there.

Maven's face was agog as he tried to take in what Alex had just done.

"Alex?"

Still no reaction.

He walked further until he came upon the still stretcher-bound body of Axis. Alex's face was emotionless as he looked down at him and slowly, methodically, he placed his left hand on the Hydra Ice that was still as perfectly formed as it had been the moment that it had first attached itself to Axis. A warm orange glow started to fill the tunnel. Uncertain of what to do, Maven and Leomas looked on to see Axis' face disappear within the glow. As it diminished, they were astounded to see that there was no longer any Hydra Ice on Axis' face, though its effects had eaten into parts of his face and head. Alex then pulled back the fleece that covered him, opened his shirt and placed his hand on the Hydra Ice that covered his chest. Once again an orange glow filled the tunnel. When it had died away, they heard a huge intake of breath, like someone who had been underwater for far too long. Axis then sat bolt upright on the stretcher. Confusion was written all over his face, as he took in his surroundings and all of the astonished faces looking back at him.

Maven flung his arms in the air. "Axis! My friend. You are back!"

Axis tried to muster a smile, but it hurt too much.

His voice was hoarse, "Where am I, and where is Alex?"

"Just there," Maven pointed. "He saved you." But Alex was nowhere to be seen. Confused, Maven moved in for a closer look. Alex was there but he wasn't vertical, he was in a crumpled heap on the floor.

Leomas ran towards him. He reached down to pick him up, but withdrew slightly; he touched him gently with a finger – no intense heat this time. He reached down and picked him up.

"He's breathing," he called out as he ran down the tunnel with Alex in his arms. He was followed by Maven, a groggy Axis and the rest of the stunned onlookers.

27.

The Aftermath

Alex awoke. He tried to open his eyes but the pain was too intense. He had the worst headache that he had ever experienced in his life. He felt like he had just awoken from a nightmare. He groped around blindly, trying to get an idea of where he was. All he could gauge was that he was in a bed. He lay there in his enforced darkness, wondering how he ended up there and trying to pinpoint the last thing that he remembered.

He became aware that someone had entered the room. "Who's there?" he called out nervously. Once again, he tried to open his eyes. A searing pain shot across his forehead, which caused him to give up on the idea and close them again.

"It's me," came a familiar gruff voice.

"Axis? Is that you? Are you okay?"

"Thanks to you."

"I thought that I… we had lost you."

"Not a chance. He is made of stern stuff, my boy," chimed in another familiar voice.

"Maven?"

"Yes it's me. I too am made of stern stuff," he chuckled.

"I want to see you. But every time I try to open my eyes, my head feels like it is going to explode."

"Here, take a sip of this," said Maven. He guided Alex's hand in the direction of a flask. "It's Leirix. It might help with that headache."

Alex took a sip and as the refreshing fluid hit the back of his mouth, he slowly opened his eyes. Initially, all that he could see was a bluish-orange blur, but at least his head was no longer hurting – well not as much. As his eyesight normalised, he saw some familiar, smiling faces looking back at him. Maven was wearing his best, mischievous grin. Leomas was attempting his friendliest, non-threatening smile – it still needed work.

He then saw Axis. Most of the right side of his face was covered in bandages. As he stared at Axis, a sadness started to build within him.

"Will the wounds heal?" he asked.

"I have Derma-Regen over all of the areas that were affected, so hopefully it will help."

Alex looked around the room.

"Where am I?" he asked.

"You are in Interria," said Leomas.

"What happened to me? How did I end up here?" It was at this point that he realised that his entire left arm was covered in bandages.

Leomas and Maven looked uncertainly at one another.

"What do you remember?" asked Maven.

Alex strained his memory, trying to recall the last clear thing.

"I remember those creatures. They were Crassacs weren't they?"

Maven and Leomas both nodded.

"I'm sorry that I didn't believe you when you told me about them, Leomas."

Leomas raised his hand. "No need to apologise, seeing is believing. I wish that they had been a tall tale. The important thing is that we are safe."

Alex tried to muster a smile, but it was more of a grimace. He then continued to respond to Maven's earlier question. "I remember getting hit by something during the battle and then I woke up here."

Alex was starting to regain his faculties and turned to Axis. "What did you mean when you said thanks to me? How did the Hydra Ice come away?"

All three men looked at one another.

Maven turned back to Alex, his voice was soothing.

"We have much to tell you, Alex, but it can wait until you are feeling a little better."

"Okay," said Alex.

They continued to talk amongst themselves. Alex's headache was no more; the Leirex must have taken full effect now. As he scanned his surroundings, he became aware that there was another person present in the room. They had been lingering in the shadows whilst the others had been talking.

"Who is that?" he asked, pointing to the figure at the back of the room.

No one spoke, as the figure emerged from out of the shadows.

"Hello, Alex," came the woman's soft voice.

His brow furrowed. "Who are you and how do you know my name?" He flinched as he tried to hoist himself into a sitting position in the bed.

The person did not respond, she just smiled and stared at him intently.

She looked somehow familiar to him, yet unfamiliar too. He assumed that she was from Malustera because as with all of the Malusterans that he had met so far, she did resemble an animal just as much as a human. This particular woman bore a resemblance to a lioness, though it wasn't as pronounced in her. There was still something about her that was very familiar.

He continued to stare at her. Then a thought struck. "It's the eyes," he whispered to himself.

He looked around the room and saw his belongings on a small table alongside his bed. He reached for the pocket watch and flipped it open. His eyes darted between the watch and the woman a few times and then it dawned on him.

"Mum…?"

THE END

9 781912 601196